MW00513519

First edition: 2020

ISBN (Print Edition): 978-1-09832-926-6

ISBN (eBook Edition): 978-1-09832-927-3

Inquiries should be directed to ParadisRue8@gmail.com

Inquiries for cover art should be directed to ParadisRue8@gmail.com

Paradis Rue

by

David W. Wallace, PhD

ACKNOWLEDGMENTS

It has taken me over ten years of part time and full time writing and editing for me to bring this novel to you, the reader. I very much appreciate your willingness to share in my dream by reading it.

There are so many people that I must thank for helping me finish this book. First and foremost is my wife and life partner Cheri Fruge' Wallace an accomplished Impressionist style painter and lover of art who peaked my interest in the life and works of the French Impressionist painters at the end of the nineteenth century. As a psychologist, I learned to love the life stories of the Impressionist painters while Cheri taught me about their creations. The study of and appreciation for art that I learned from her has enhanced the quality of my whole life.

I have also been blessed with four amazing friends who reviewed and helped me edit the book. They are all wonderful authors themselves who gave their time and skills in order to make this book more than it could have ever been without them. My cousin, Blake Wallace, who has written and published several novels himself about my hometown of Dallas, Texas and the life and times in which I grew up, was the first to critique Paradis Rue. Thank you "Cuz" for being not only a blood relative but a friend and beacon to my moral self.

Otis Scarbary, another author of novels about people in my new hometown of Macon, Georgia was the next to review my book. His knowledge and generous reviews revealed a bedrock of experience in storytelling that I counted on to revise and edit the book. You're the best, Otis.

The third author that reviewed the book was my friend and professional colleague from my television days, Kristine Jensen. She is detail oriented and creative, a combination that every book writer needs in a reviewer. Kristine is finishing her first book now and I have had the opportunity to review it for her. I can say, without doubt, that her new book will be a great success. Thank you, old friend, for everything you've done for me over the past thirty years.

And, finally every author needs someone like Faye Donaghu. Faye is a professional writer and magazine editor. Her edit at the end of my writing and revision stage was absolutely the "bomb." Faye and her husband, Dennis, are the closest of friends for Cheri and me, and it is wonderful to have people like them in our lives. Thank you, "Fayeness". I count you as a jewel in my crown of lifelong friends and one of the most talented and giving people I've ever known.

My mother, Ruth, and dad, Bill, two sisters, Lisa Dinnin and Teresa Redd, and my brother Rick Wallace gave me a platform of love and self-worth that has fortified me my whole life. I love you all. My daughter-in-law, Dr. Kelly Whiddon, a professor of creative writing at Middle Georgia State University has given me advice and counsel. My two sons, David Wallace II, and Dr. Steven Wallace have been and will always be my pride and joy. Finally, I have benefitted from having met and gathered knowledge, humor, insights and wisdom from my patients, students, relatives and friends from the Army, from my church, and from my many golfing comrades over the years. One cannot write a novel without having experienced passionate emotions in life. God bless all who shared in my life path.

DEDICATION

I dedicate this book to my life partner, best friend and one of the finest people I've ever known, my wife, Cheri Fruge' Wallace. She taught me to love Impressionist art and has modeled love of family, and strength of character, without compromise, since I met her and made her mine. Cheri is a skilled and talented painter and created an original piece of art for the cover of this book. She has also dedicated countless hours helping me edit and rewrite sections of the book. Thank you, Darling, and God bless you, always.

PROLOGUE

This novel takes place in France in the late nineteenth century. It is a work of historical fiction and as is usual in this genre, the story never really happened. There is, however, some historical truth in the book. The Impressionist painters did populate France and Paris at the time and did decide to have their own exhibition. Many of the facts regarding this exhibition are true, and many of the facts about their personalities and life stories are true.

Toulouse Lautrec was depicted in the story as a contemporary of the other painters at the time of the first Impressionist exhibition, but was only a boy still in Albi, France in 1874. He was eventually part of the Paris art and cabaret scene, but it was several years later before he arrived to join the other impressionistic painters. I think he adds a lot to the flavor of Paris and to my story, so he was depicted as an integral part of it.

So, in this, almost fairytale-like story, the historical characters interact with fictitious people who never actually existed. Some of the events, such as the popular cancan and the exciting cabaret scene in Montmartre happened slightly later than the 1870s, but were used to tell a more fanciful story.

I love the French people, culture, and history, but other than having taken French in high school and college, and several trips to France and to museums all over the world to study and admire Impressionist art, I am just a novice in the formality of the language and details of the culture. I mean no disrespect. When I've been in France, I have spoken my broken French, with a heavy Texas accent, and found the people to be accepting, helpful, and even appreciative of my poor efforts to communicate. I hope you more knowledgeable readers will forgive my missteps in language and misinterpretations of culture. I honestly have written a book more from my heart than my head.

The story's principle character is Josay Rue. She is a reflection of the capabilities every young woman has at her disposal. I have tried to make her a role model for perseverance and strength in a hazardous and unfair world. She, through her own strength of character and determination, ultimately manages to grow into a self-actualized human being. I hope you enjoy my story.

CHAPTER I

Josay woke and rubbed her green eyes as her small room filled with the smell of freshly baked baguette bread. Mama always got up early on the dairy farm to begin the day's work of cooking while Papa fed and milked the cows before daylight. Josay loved that wonderful smell, especially on a bright sunlit spring morning.

Josay bounded out of bed and went to the light blue basin to wash her blush-pink morning face with the water she poured from the large pitcher on the rickety table. It was a tiny room with only a few pieces of furniture. There was a bed, a table for the water basin, and a yellow chair that once sat in the kitchen by the back door. She shared a comfortable eight-room farmhouse with her parents and brother David.

Mama had given her the chair when she turned seventeen almost a year ago, and she had painted it herself. The pale yellow paint had been left over from a small sign her father had crafted to advertise his milk and cheese products to people who were on their way to Paris. The road ran adjacent to the farm, and the sign attracted a few hungry travelers, but not that many. Most of their dairy products were bought by people in the nearby village and province.

She carefully combed her satin reddish-blonde hair. Everyone in the family had red hair, but hers was more blonde than red. She and her family were the only people in her village that had red hair of any kind, so she had pondered the possibility that maybe it had been passed down to her from someone who had come to France from the far north a few hundred years ago. Perhaps her ancestors had come to France as invaders. It always delighted her to think of such a romantic, if not dark, thought that her family might be of Viking descent. She had an active imagination and liked to read about such things.

She was an avid reader and her favorite books were about high adventure in all parts of the world. But her life had been anything but adventurous. She was an obedient Christian girl who honored her father and mother, and was well liked by her friends and neighbors in the small farming community. Her family was well respected, and even though they were of lower class in stature, they were considered slightly higher on the social scale because of the quality dairy products that they provided for everyone in the area.

Josay's bright young mind was racing just thinking about today. *This most special and secret day*!, she thought. She could hardly wait for it to unfold. She reveled in the fresh bread smell that gave form to the wonderful and hopeful ideas she contemplated as she brushed her beautiful thick locks.

Josay usually had to do several chores on the farm, like gathering eggs and milking cows. Today was different, however, since her father had hired a temporary man to help build new stalls for the milk cows. The new man had taken over her duties for the day, leaving her time to run a very special errand. She had plans to meet her boyfriend, Donnel.

"Josay," her mother called. "Hurry and get dressed. Are you going to sleep all day? I can't keep your sausage and cheese on the table for you much longer or your brother will eat it."

Josay's brother David was a fast growing teenager of 19 years with a never ending appetite and shoes a half-inch too short for his feet. He was Josay's best friend and constant tormentor. It seemed to her that David was about the only person in the world who could make her laugh while pulling off one surprise prank after another. The pranks were usually on her or their mother. Papa had long since taught David that there were consequences to trying to surprise or play too big a trick on him. Laughter and love ruled the Rue family. Their lives were simple and they were content with that—that is all but one of them.

Josay looked at her starched white dress with the yellow trim hanging in the corner. She had ironed it yesterday and today she hoped she would be beautiful in it. After all, today was going to be the biggest day in her life and she wanted to look her very best. She had taken the dress in about the middle, to show off her small waist, and also lowered the neckline a slight bit. The rounded tops of her breasts would show a peek of cleavage without showing too much.

After breakfast, she agreed to feed the chickens before leaving for her adventure, and once outside, Josay felt the cool wind in her face which caused her cheeks to become a healthy reddish pink. It was invigorating. She whistled a merry jig as she turned and whirled with fresh seed for her subjects.

"Hey Josay, you're supposed to be working. You're not at the Governor's Ball or something" said David.

David briefly joined Josay for a dance around the yard. He was so strong and fully a foot taller than Josay, so she had to step lively to keep up with him. Josay loved David and he her. They had always been close as friends and playmates.

Once a few years ago, some self-important aristocrat had rudely yelled at them as he rode by the farm, "Stupid peasants! You don't even know you're supposed to be unhappy."

In response, David turned, lowered his pants and presented his round freckled back side. Josay fell to her knees laughing and was tempted to follow David's lead, but caught herself just in time.

Their short waltz around the chicken coop ended as Papa called for David to help carry the milk buckets to the wagon so they could be hauled to the early morning market. The milk was fresh and still a little warm having been so recently extracted from the willing cows and then pasteurized for sale.

Josay went in to put on her special dress and was off to begin her big day. She was to meet Donnel Regis just across the field and stream from their small dairy farm on the edge of his family's sizable plot of land. Donnel was the only son of the Count that owned all the fields as far as the eye could see, including the one that her parents used for the dairy.

The Rue family had worked the dairy for the Count's family for three generations. It was a case of one-sided respect. Josay's father respected the Count, but who knew if the Count respected her father. He was just a cog in the Count's business machine. Monsieur Rue was a cog that never seemed to need much attention. The cows made milk. The dairyman brought the milk to market. The Count took his share of the profits. There never seemed to be an issue. Josay's father and family were merely good pieces of farm equipment.

Josay's father was never completely secure, and their allotment of land was as tenuous as the spring rain. Papa was happy to keep his head down. He knew the best strategy was to be taken for granted and ignored. One in Papa's place never wanted to be noticed or to make even a ripple of a wave to attract the Count's attention. Papa's intuition led him to believe that he should never be too much of a problem, nor too successful when it came to the Count. Without knowing it, he was following the advice of the ancient philosopher, Socrates.

Socrates rightly claimed that life was best lived in the "golden mean". He meant that it is better to be average than to be the king or to be the serf. The king has too many problems, most of his own making, and the serf has too many obstacles, not of his own making. It was much better to be in the middle, which is where the Rue family was handily positioned.

Josay couldn't wait to meet Donnel under the large spreading oak tree which was located right beside the small stream. It seemed to her that her slim legs couldn't move fast enough to get there. It was about a kilometer through the fields and woods and she couldn't help but notice the beautiful green of the grass and the wild flowers that were just beginning to bloom. But mostly she thought of Donnel as she walked.

Donnel was tall and slender with dark brown hair and eyes. He was boyishly handsome and the most eligible unmarried young man in the entire area. He was the Count's son. He could have any girl he wanted, but he only had eyes for Josay.

Josay and Donnel had fallen in love almost completely from a distance. They had seen each other on the way to school, each going to their own place of education, which caused them to pass each other going in opposite directions. They usually only gazed at each other, every school day for eight years. Sometimes they even smiled and talked for a few minutes, but there was usually no time for that. It was too dangerous to let others see them together because word could get back to the Count. And that couldn't happen....not yet.

They had been able to see each other in the village, too. On occasion, they had found a way to be partners in games at the county fair and were paired in the country picnic sack race.

They had only been alone together once before today. It was only last week when Donnel expressed his love for Josay in a most direct way. He had asked her to meet him at the tree, and had kissed her on the mouth, a kiss she gloriously reciprocated. The kiss inferred to her that they belonged to each other in a meaningful and lasting way. A kiss like that meant marriage and a life together. It was a life that Josay had only dreamed of and imagined. In her young mind, it would be a glorious life filled with love and happiness.

Today, her mind was very focused on seeing Donnel's handsome face again and of speaking together of their plans for the future. So, when she arrived at the place of rendezvous, she was surprised to find three strange men setting up easels and beginning to paint.

She didn't know it at the time, but they were called "plein-air" painters (outdoor painting in nature). This was a totally new way for artists to paint because historically, painting was all done in studios. One thing that made this possible was that oil paint had recently been put into tubes with screw-on caps that could be transported anywhere. Before, the hues had to be mixed in small bowls in studios. It was a messy process and not conducive to outdoor use.

The three men were about to begin their day of catching the light of the morning sun sparkling on the stream, with the old oak tree in the background.

"Well, hello young lady" the short painter with the full dark beard said brightly. "Just where are you going this fine day?" Josay was surprised and a little startled that a man that she didn't know would presume to talk to her.

"I'm just out for a walk," she said softly.

The two other painters had been talking among themselves as the bearded one continued, "I love your fine starched dress, and the yellow trim is wonderful. You look like spring itself."

"Thank you," Josay responded with eyes lowered.

The other two men tapped the bearded one on the shoulder and before Josay could leave, they all seemed to agree, one with the other, that the tall, older one with the stark white beard would speak for the group.

So, in a soft, almost quiet whispering voice, he said "We would all like to paint you in this setting. My name is Camille Pissarro, this is Paul Gauguin, and lastly our friend Auguste Renoir", he gestured towards the others. "We have come to your area from our studios outside Paris to paint the landscape and the people of your province. We prefer to paint people and nature in their natural setting, in God's own light, instead of in an artist's studio. Believe me, you have nothing to fear from us. You see, here are some examples of the work we have done over the past few days."

Josay was surprised to see these strange vibrantly colored canvases and asked, "Are they finished?" As soon as she spoke she thought she might have insulted these gentlemen and she blushed from embarrassment.

These painters worked in a completely different and unique way that often confused and shocked viewers. They tried to capture "a moment in time", and it often appeared to the unenlightened as blurry and unfinished work.

"That blush!" Renoir exclaimed. "Did you see it?"

All the men agreed immediately and voiced their strong desire to capture this instant color and feeling that the young woman emitted while in this undisturbed natural environment. It was, in essence, the "raison d'etre" for their choosing to follow a new line of painting that departed from the cast of classical realism so popular in France at the time. Josay, the flowers, the stream, freshly colored deep green fields and budding oak trees all seemed to blend into one portrait of nature and beauty.

"Would you sit for us and model? We can't afford much, but we could possibly pay you a very small fee for an hour or so of your time," Gauguin inquired.

"Oh, no. I have an important meet—," she trailed off. Just then she remembered that no one must know she was meeting Donnel. It would be a scandal. It was too early for his father to agree to their courtship and romance. They must have time to develop a plan for convincing him of their love and desire to make a life together.

She could see that Donnel was not yet by the tree, and she was, after all, at least an hour early for their meeting. Before she had completely thought it through, she said, "I have a few minutes if that would help, but not more."

Josay immediately had second thoughts about agreeing to pose for the three Parisians. But the three quickly set up their painting pallets with the appropriate pigments as if the opportunity to catch the picture would suddenly disappear. They were used to painting with amazing speed to capture the elusive light of the moment. Their passion was to paint nature in a blitz of time. Short brushstrokes, and a blaze of color and light, blended to match the vision of the artist.

Renoir directed Josay to bend over at the waist as if washing her face and hands in the stream. He loved the sparkles of light the morning sun was casting off the rippling water and then upon her soft white complexion and strawberry-red cheeks. All around her was the emotion of spring, newness, regeneration and fertility.

Josay did as the three painters asked but kept a keen and constant eye out for Donnel as she splashed water into her face a few times. The cold water woke her up and she felt alive and alert like a fawn coming from under cover to face the world. She was an innocent, and the painters rightly pegged the effect. Josay, the setting and the landscape were one.

"The bird of time has but a little way to fly," remarked Pissarro. He was the old soul of this band of renegade painters and the oldest by far of all the early painting groundbreakers.

"We must capture this moment as we keep our hearts from beating out of our chests."

Pissarro would later come to be known as one of the founding fathers of "Impressionism". He loved nature and painted it with the awe a disciple feels upon entering a place of worship. Pissarro loved the common people as a part of God's creation, but not the center of it. Thus, he painted Josay with her face looking toward the water, with her features obscured by the scenery around her. It was a glimpse of God's handiwork through the eyes of the old Jew.

Renoir noticed Josay as she took the few coins given to her by Gauguin. And as she hurried away, probably never to be seen again, he was sad at the loss of the youth that she owned in his version of the "moment in time." His pastels captured the freshness of newborn puppies, without care or worry, with purity and forgiveness reflected in the eyes, aware of only the beginnings of understanding with all of life yet to be explored.

Renoir was the most deliberate of the three. He had been apprenticed when he was but a young boy as a porcelain painter and had developed his skills from a beginning of painting simple flowers, to painting portraits such as Marie Antionette on the plates and cups. Later he trained at the "Ecole des Beau-Arts" and "Atelier Gleyre." He possessed the skills of the realist Courbet and the passion of Delacroix. So, his version of the scene, and Josay, expressed the human reality of fleeting life, while simultaneously demonstrating the potential for love and hope.

Gauguin was sweating with his heart racing as he painted from his imagination. He saw Josay as an object of true lust and passion in a setting that could be raped as he desired. He painted Josay's breast falling out of a very low-neckline sundress (much lower than reality) as she dipped her hands into the rushing water. And, although Josay's breasts never showed themselves to any of the three, Gauguin could see them in his mind's eye with the focus a hawk keeps on its prey from high above. He was in control, with the prey unable to stop him from owning her completely on his canvas. Stroke after stroke Gauguin painted a visionary masterpiece of desire for her young body and a realized obsession for mastery of her very soul— a forbidden dream that comes true in the mind of a crazed lover.

Almost as quickly as the three painters had met Josay, she was gone. They stayed and finished without Josay ever seeing the completed paintings. She took her money and their brief thanks, and ran away, as if embarrassed by the attention of the masters. Afterwards, each "Impressionist" marveled to himself about his vision of the morning, and the growth of perspective and skill they had obtained from this innocent sacrificial lamb in God's perfect creation.

CHAPTER 2

The three painters walked slowly toward the small village as they talked about the morning outing.

Renoir was saying, "The light made the maiden radiate spring. Did anyone ask her name?"

Pissarro answered, "I think she called herself Josay. She is a local and seemingly, like the other country folk, so very unspoiled. The common people in the countryside speak God's truth to me and it is always my goal in painting to show a glimpse of their human spirit. That girl's beauty is unmatched by anything but the nature that adorns her." [Pissarro was always philosophical about his work and loved the real people of the French countryside.]

Gauguin kept his thoughts to himself. They were more pleasurable to him than the constant haggle over art and technique and the greater meaning of life that usually dominated all the conversations the three men had. His mind was on the delicious body and face he had just possessed in his painting. And, although he already had a wife and several children, his appetite for sexual diversion never seemed to be quenched. He was well known in the brothels and loved to paint nudes. He also, often physically, possessed his models while his paintings were set to dry.

"Shall we stay another night in this place after we eat?" said Renoir.

"I think we should stay, eat, drink and see what other pleasures this town has to offer," responded Gauguin.

As the painters approached the center of the town and heart of the local market, they decided to stop at a colorful tavern and admire the view across the plaza. Pissarro suggested that they set out a few of their recent paintings and offer them for sale.

"Who knows, perhaps someone would pay a few sous for one or two of them," said Pissarro.

He was always in need of money. He had a large family and could never seem to scrape up enough to even feed them regularly. He was known to borrow from the other painters to survive. And, within the past few months of cold and dreary weather, Pissarro had only been able to feed his family a steady diet of potatoes and onions; that is, when he could afford even vegetables. He couldn't remember when he had been able to put meat in his stews. But today, a generous Renoir would foot the bill for his dinner and he would carry at least some of the leftovers home to his hungry family tomorrow.

Right in front of the outside tables, Renoir and Pissarro set out a few of their recent paintings while Gauguin watched.

"Aren't you going to try to sell anything today?" asked Pissarro.

"Not me," responded Gauguin as he took out the painting he had just rendered of Josay.

He loved to relive his inspirations while drinking to excess. Reviewing his paintings was almost as good for him as reality. It gave him an unhealthy thrill. It was like the painting owned the essence of the subject and Gauguin owned the painting.

As Gauguin admired his work, the local tavern owner came up behind him and said, "What a wonderful likeness of Josay you have rendered. How much for this painting? I want it to go over the bar so I can look at it every day."

Gauguin and the other two painters were astonished. Almost never did a customer appear out of the blue to ask to buy a painting, especially in a small and unsophisticated village like this. The establishment they were patronizing was not the kind of place where one would expect to find an avant-garde collector.

Gauguin was taken out of his dream state enough to ask, "How much would you pay? This painting is one of my masterpieces and it would not be cheap," he said to the man. *After all, tomorrow might present me with another model and another fantasy even better than this one*, he thought.

"I will pay 15 sous, dinner, including the wine, and a bed for you and your two friends for the night."

Gauguin was surprised to hear the word "done!" come out of his mouth so quickly and with such ease.

(He was already over the Josay love affair and on to the delight of thinking of one of his other fantasies—bare-busted young Tahitian women laying all around him on the beach in the far off Pacific, tan and willing to give everything to Gauguin only for the asking. An entire harem could be his. He would someday paint them all as willing slaves to his desire.)

"You must be careful with it because the paint is still drying, but it is yours," said Gauguin.

The owner was ecstatic and almost jumped for joy. With a spit on the hand to finalize the bargain, he shook Gauguin's hand and ordered another bottle of vin rouge (red wine) for the table.

Josay waited for hours at the oak tree for Donnel, but he never came. Heartbroken she drifted toward the village as the sun began to set. He had said they were going to plan their escape to blissful adulthood and all the pleasures that it might hold for them. This afternoon was to be a picnic lunch by the water which would most certainly include an episode of romantic affection. Her innocent heart had been excited to the point of bursting over just the idea of Donnel taking her in his arms, talking of their love and maybe going to the next level of what was sure to be a lifetime of commitment. *Where was he?* she asked herself.

Just then, she heard a familiar voice behind her saying, "Where ya going, Sis? Can I come along?"

It was David. Just what she needed to take her out of this mournful mood and change the subject.

"Thought I might go into the village for a walk around and see if they have any new cloth in the store. You are welcome to come along so long as you admit that I can outrun you to the fountain in the center of town."

Off she ran without giving David time to respond. David beat her to the fountain and was sitting on the edge waiting for her, pretending to have been there for hours.

"Where have you been? I've had a fruit pie and a long conversation with three beautiful girls while waiting for you."

"I was delayed by my legion of fine high-born suitors."

They both laughed and began a stroll around the town center.

"There she is," said a street vendor to another person on the street. "I can't believe she has the nerve to show up wearing the same dress."

"I always knew she was no good. Girls like her will do anything to get ahead," one old woman said to a group of others.

"What must her father and mother think, and what will Count Regis do? It's an insult to his high placed moral system, and it can't be tolerated," said another woman.

Josay was confused. "*What were they talking about?*" she thought.

David decided to get more information, so he went to an old family friend at the bakery.

"What is going on? Have we missed something big and important in this backwater village?" he asked.

The big breasted, rotund baker's wife told David about a trio of artists that had come into town earlier in the afternoon.

"They were at the tavern and displayed their recent works for sale. All the paintings used Josay as a model in a landscape by the stream and old oak tree. Two of the three renderings were strange, but appropriate and beautiful. The third was scandalous. It showed Josay with her breasts fully exposed in a more than seductive pose. And, what's worse, Millet, the tavern owner purchased it and placed it over his bar for all to see!"

David quickly ran toward the tavern ahead of Josay and could not believe his eyes. Sure enough, there was Josay in the painting with her breasts exposed, washing in the stream. She wore the same white and yellow dress even now. All the local men were drinking, laughing and staring at the mostly nude picture of his sister. *What had she done? What was he to do? Josay can't see this horrible painting yet. I must warn her. Surely she had a reason for posing like this for men she didn't even know.*

He caught her just before she entered the tavern, and right before she caught sight of Donnel and his father approaching the village center. They dismounted and the Count acknowledged everyone around with a proper, stately nod, and appropriate level of disinterest. Donnel, on the other hand stared directly at Josay. He seemed to penetrate her essence with a kind and loving gaze.

He must have had a very worthy reason for not meeting me at the oak tree, she thought. I can see that he loves me.

Josay intentionally returned his look with a broad yet directed smile. Unfortunately, she failed to notice several men pushing their way up to talk to the Count himself. Something was wrong and she didn't have the advantage of knowing what was coming. Her attention had been solely on Donnel.

The expression on the Count's face turned from passive disinterest to active rage and indignation. The men had told him that one of his tenants had posed for an indiscreet, even scandalous portrait, and that it was now hanging over the bar for all of these peasants to see. Who would have the gall to insult him and his whole village with such immorality?

The Count's son had been trailing along behind him, and was delighted when he noticed something exciting going on in this otherwise boring place. He had not been really happy since his mother had died unexpectedly of influenza several years ago. The death had caused his father to isolate himself and the elderly Count seemed to lose what "joie de vivre" he had once possessed. His zest for life and gaiety was gone. It was now just he and his father in the family, and their relationship had sorely suffered as well.

Josay knew it was undignified for a nice girl to go inside a bar, and completely inappropriate, so she hesitated at the door. But she could hear what sounded like all the air in the tavern being sucked out in an earthquake of a gasp. And for what seemed like an eternity, but was more likely only a second or two, there had been only silence. David hurried to grab her arm, and despite her unwillingness to leave, pulled and dragged her toward home.

Josay had a puzzled look on her face as David said, "Josay, there's a painting of you with your breasts completely exposed hanging over the bar in the tavern."

They both ran from the village toward home.

"I don't know what you mean, David. I posed, but I was fully dressed and it was only for an hour or so. What's going on? There must be a mistake."

"No mistake, Sis. In fact, the painting showed you in the exact dress you're wearing now. I was told that the painter Gauguin said he had sold it to the proprietor of the tavern for wine and lodging."

"But I never took off my clothes!" she again protested with a crying painful moan. "I'll have to think of something to tell Mama and Papa tomorrow. They will believe me. You believe me, don't you David?"

The next morning, Josay was awakened by the sound of dozens of horses and men shouting outside the small house.

"Bring her out! Where is she?" was all Josay was able to hear before two large men grabbed her and took her outside in her night dress to stand alongside her terrified and bewildered father, mother and brother.

One of the men presented himself as the local magistrate and read a large parchment paper that looked to Josay, from a distance, like an elaborately signed and stamped formal decree.

> *"Count Regis, current and rightful owner of the farm now occupied by the Rue family, has withdrawn tenant status of said farm. The Rue family is given 36 hours from now to pack their personal possessions and leave these premises, or suffer under penalty of law, with commitment to an appropriate venue for the crimes of trespassing and theft of property. Additionally, the whore, named Josay Rue, will be banished to a distance of at least ten kilometers from town, with only the clothes on her back, and two days of rations. Anyone under Count Regis' domain, giving aid or comfort to the whore, Josay Rue, from this day forward, will be taken into custody. Swift and severe punishment will be rendered at that time."*

CHAPTER 3

Josay watched the Count's men ride away, leaving her with only a knapsack and basket of food. She felt a cold shiver of loneliness, and the kind of fear experienced when a small child is left alone in an unfamiliar place. She had watched her mother, father and brother as they were restrained from helping her. There were tears and sadness in their eyes as the men took her away. She had barely been given time to tell them goodbye.

What will become of me? Where could I go? Why didn't Donnel help me? Couldn't he have defended me to his father? All of these questions pierced her thoughts and heart at the same time as tears milked down her pale white face. She walked aimlessly along the road that led to Paris. She walked and walked, as if in a fog, for what seemed many hours.

Then, across the fields that were adjacent to the Paris road, Josay saw two men on horseback riding toward her. It was Donnel and David. Her spirits lifted as she thought surely the last 24 hours must have been only a bad dream.

"Hey, Josay," she heard David say.

The sound of his voice was like a church bell chiming on Easter morning, full of joy and happiness.

The horses slowed to a walk and then stopped in front of Josay.

David spoke first, "We're here to help you, Josay, but we bring only a little good news. The Count has relented about Papa and Mama and the dairy. So long as you never come back to the village, he will let them run the tenant farm. I believe it's because Papa is the best dairy-man in the province and he would be hard pressed to find another man as dependable and honest. The Count is letting me stay, as well, so that I can help with the work that must go on, day in and day out."

"I pleaded with father to let them keep the farm and to let you return. But several old ladies told him that you and I had been planning to run away and get married. I don't know how they knew that, but Father became as a mad man, cursing and turning over furniture," said Donnel.

"He has decided to send me away to the military academy in Belgium. He has threatened to punish David and your family if I do not go. He demands that I agree to never see you again."

"This can't be true. Is there no way to explain the truth to him? We must change his mind!" Josay exclaimed with tears in her eyes.

"He is a hard man, and I know him to always actualize his threats. I have only been able to sneak away for this last goodbye while Father is out of town tonight for a meeting with the visiting government agent. He will return late tomorrow and he expects me to be packed and ready to go off to the military school."

"Oh, Donnel, I am sorry that because of me, you will have to leave your home and friends. What can I do to soften his heart?"

"Father has not been his forgiving and gracious self since Mother died two years ago. He seems to want to take out his anger on everyone, including me. He has amassed a great deal of misdirected hatred for everything in the village and even God. He often says, 'How could God let my Cheri die and leave me?' He watches my every move to insure that I do not stray from the path he has chosen for me."

Josay began to sob with large tears streaming down her face.

"He will not easily accept that you and I are in love. We need to give him some time to get used to the idea that we must be together."

"How could this have happened?" said Josay as she began to cry again. "I swear I've done nothing wrong."

Simultaneously, David and Donnel reached out to comfort her, but Donnel got there first and wrapped his arms around her as she sobbed.

"These next few months will be hard, Josay. But I will send help whenever I can," said Donnel.

"We will help as much as we can, too," echoed David, speaking for Josay's small family.

"Here," he continued. "We've brought more clothes, food, and enough money to get you started in Paris, but we can't be away from the village for long or the whole tentative bargain will be in jeopardy. The Count will be watching to see if everyone keeps their end of the agreement. We just can't let him throw Papa and Mama off of the farm. They are too old to start over. You should know that Papa was willing to do anything to save you, which included losing the farm."

"Thank you both for coming, and tell Mama and Papa I am so sorry this has happened and that I love them dearly. I will be fine, so tell them not to worry about me."

"Donnel and I were somehow able to convince Count Regis that throwing Mama and Papa off of their farm would only add misery to an already sad situation. Our sweet parents deeply love you, and hope this scandal will blow over quickly so that you can come back home."

"David, and a few of his friends, plan to sneak into the village tonight and steal that disgraceful picture from over the bar. I'll stay here with you, and tomorrow they will bring the picture here so you can take it to the fellow that painted it. I think his name is Gauguin. You will need to get him to admit that you did not model for him in the scandalous manner appearing on his canvas. We believe that only such an admission will bring the incident back to the truth."

When Donnel finished his explanation of the quickly drafted plan, David hugged and consoled his sister, got on his horse and was away to gather his fellow conspirators to enact the picture theft.

Josay shouted, "Be careful. I love you."

By now the sun was beginning to fade and a sunset of deep crimson and purple was taking shape. Donnel built a fire about a hundred meters from the road in a nest of pine trees and began to make a campsite dinner for the two of them. He was sure that Josay must be hungry and exhausted. He urged her to warm by the fire and let him tend to her. As Josay settled onto the small blanket she pulled Donnel down to her and embraced him as if he was about to leave her forever.

The two kissed softly and then more and more eagerly. They tugged clumsily and fitfully at their clothes until they had rid themselves of those obstacles to their raw emotion and passion. They clung to each other and seemed to melt into one person. Even though neither had made love to anyone before, it seemed to come so naturally as they expressed their deep love for each other. Josay was small in his strong arms, but held him and kissed him eagerly. He responded with the energy and pent-up desire of youth. Josay was so in love with Donnel, she barely felt the pinch of the first insertion as they moved their bodies together in the rhythm as old as time. When it was over, they continued to hold each other as the magic flow of energy ebbed. They were both left breathless as they lay together under the trees. Another kiss, and together they both inhaled a full lung of much needed oxygen. The happiness of the moment was obvious on both of their faces. They couldn't stop smiling, kissing and confessing their undying love for each other.

Finally, they realized that they were really hungry. After a dinner of roast pork and bread, they nestled into the blanket, made love over and over again, and finally fell into a deep sleep in each other's arms.

At first light, Donnel felt deep remorse about leaving Josay and told her that he would forsake all he had to go with her.

In response, Josay said, "We will find each other very soon after this whole mistake is righted. But right now we must not abandon Papa, Mama and David to the Count's wrath."

As Josay was speaking, David rode up with two of his friends and a bag. He jumped off his horse and said, "Here is the painting. You must get away from here as soon as you can. They will miss the picture as soon as they wake up this morning. This horse is for you, so pack up quickly and get moving. I must rush back as fast as possible.

If I am missed from the farm, I will be the obvious suspect for having taken the picture."

Donnel agreed with David and helped Josay pack her bags and the painting on the grey horse. He gave Josay a deep kiss and lifted her onto the mare.

"I will come to Paris for you as soon as you find Gauguin and get him to own his lie. I know we can make everything right soon. Be brave, my darling Josay."

Josay felt her heart sag as her brother and lover rode off down the muddy road back to the only home she had ever known. She was 17 and alone as she turned her grey horse toward Paris.

CHAPTER 4

Along the road to Paris, after an uneventful, but slow paced day's ride, Josay passed a small wagon. A well-dressed woman was in the wagon which was being pulled by what looked like a very old and tired horse. The woman glanced at Josay and nodded as she passed.

Josay had planned to set up a camp well off the road for the night just in case someone from the village had been sent to find her and retrieve the painting she had in the old bag. The thought came to her that perhaps this woman would share her camp. Josay was feeling insecure about spending the night alone in the woods, and the woman looked harmless.

Josay turned her horse around and parked the mare in the path of the woman and the wagon.

"Your horse looks tired and it's getting close to dark. Want to camp together for the night? I have a few provisions I can share," said Josay.

The older woman looked at her as if dumbfounded.

"Why on earth should I want to spend the night with a child that's obviously in trouble and likely on the run for some reason? I do not seek trouble and you look just like a problem waiting to happen."

"Sorry, you're right, of course. There might well be people looking for me and I don't wish to cause you any harm. I'm sorry I asked," said Josay.

"Now wait just a minute," the woman said. "I can't believe you're so honest. Most people would make up some kind of story and try to get me to help them while plotting just how to rob me or worse. Maybe you're cut from a different bolt of cloth. Where are you going, and what's your story?"

Josay took a full, uninterrupted, five or six minutes telling her story as if it were bursting from her heart. She left out nothing and even showed the woman her belongings, money, and of course, the painting by Gauguin. She ended her tale by saying, "I hope to find work in Paris."

The woman just sat there and listened intensely.

"Well, I'll be damned if that's not the most remarkable story I've heard in weeks. Most of the young girls I meet on the road beg for food and lie through their teeth. I honestly believe you. My poor horse is tired and clearly on his last legs, so yes, by all means, let's camp together."

A hundred or so meters off the road, Josay and the woman chose a flat place in an opening near a lively stream.

"I enjoy hearing the water at night so let's put our blankets here," said the woman.

"By the way, I'm Madame Mari Belle La Plume. Have you heard of me by chance?"

Josay was embarrassed to say, "Sorry but I haven't."

"No real reason why a young girl like you from a farm would have heard of me. But actually, I am well known in many parts of Europe for my voice and stage presence. In fact, I'm on my way to Paris to sing at the Lumen Café."

Josay wondered why this 'famous person' might be traveling alone with such meager possessions, but she was naïve and trusting. She kept quiet and continued to listen.

"I appeared in Vienna, Prague and Budapest last year alone." she boasted. "I'm sought by many agents to appear in other capitals, at opera houses, concert venues and the very best nightclubs."

As she talked, she opened a large trunk replete with city stamps of exotic places from top to bottom. From the trunk, she pulled the finest gown Josay had ever seen. She held the dress up and modeled it for Josay as she danced around the fire and hummed a light hearted tune. It was gold with fine lace, exquisite hand sewed beading, and silver bows. The garment seemed to glimmer in the light like diamonds.

"I use this gown only when I appear in sold out concerts," said Madame La Plume.

Josay had never seen anything like this dress. Surely it must cost as much as a full year's wages for the working people she knew.

She asked, "So you are going to sing in Paris?" And before she thought about it, blurted out, "Do you need someone to help you, a sort of maid? I'm very good with hair and I am a quick learner."

"One thing at a time," said Madame La Plume. "Let's eat first and get to know each other."

The two talked for another hour before it was clear that exhaustion was taking over Josay. She had been running on adrenaline for many hours and the weariness came crashing down all at once.

"Go to sleep, my young friend, and we'll talk again in the morning."

As Josay closed her eyes, she was feeling like she might be alright after all. Maybe this was the adventure she had always longed for. It would all be perfect if Donnel and David were with her, she thought, as she drifted into a very sound and much needed sleep.

After ten hours, Josay blinked her eyes as the late morning light flashed through trees above her. She was thirsty and yawned a round and wonderful yawn. It was a little cool but the air smelled fresh and she could hear the sounds of the stream jumping and popping clearly. She leaned over to get a drink of the clear cold water and suddenly had a flashback memory of the terrible day she was painted by the stream at home. Her anxiety was further heightened when she turned around and realized she was alone. The old horse was still loosely tied to a tree, but the wagon, her grey mare, and Madame La Plume were gone. Not only that, but the knapsack of food and her small bag that held her clothes, money and the Gauguin were also missing. A shiver of fear gripped her and the cool fresh breeze she had been enjoying turned to bitter cold. She had been a fool to trust someone she didn't know. She had never been lied to before, but Madame La Plume was a complete stranger, not someone from her small world in the village.

She was in real trouble. She had no idea what to do. She called out, "Madame La Plume, where are you? Please come out."

She knew it was futile. She had been victimized by a seasoned professional. The woman had been so charming and engaging, it was hard for Josay to hate her for what she had done. What's more, she couldn't complain to anyone. She was an outcast and an accused criminal herself.

Josay and the tired old horse took one last long drink and headed back to the road. The horse was too weak to hold a rider so Josay walked along beside it. With each small step on the road, Josay, with only the clothes on her back and a worthless old nag, inched closer to Paris and what would become her new life there.

It was well after noon before Josay and the old horse arrived at the outskirts of Paris. No one had talked to them along the road. She had asked and even begged for help a few times, but assistance and comfort was not offered. She sat by the side of the road, fully exhausted, and allowed the horse to graze in a small patch of green grass. Her spirit had truly reached its lowest point.

An odd looking man approached her. He was short, and seemed to be crippled or deformed in some way. He had on a clean white shirt, a frock coat, bright yellow britches and a bowler hat, and although he walked in a tortured way, he seemed to hold his ugly head and face high, in an aristocratic fashion. Josay, amazingly, was not afraid of him. The emotion she felt was somewhere between pity and disgust.

He spoke to her in high and proper French, "Bonjour, Mademoiselle. Comment allez-vous?"

Josay avoided eye contact and did not respond.

"Oh come now," the man went on. "I'm not going to bite you. In spite of the way I look, I'm a very honorable and righteous fellow. It just appears to me," he went on without missing a beat, "that you could use a friend—any friend. No?"

Josay still kept her head and eyes down. Undeterred, the man introduced himself as Henri Toulouse Lautrec.

"I happen to be on my way to Paris to become an artist."

Henri was the mangled son of Madame and Monsieur Lautrec of Albi, France, who were both of noble blood and first cousins to each other. Lautrec's father was a proud athletic aristocrat, a handsome vagabond known through the south of France for his hunting, fighting, drinking and womanizing. He literally hated that his son was a deformed, stunted, crippled and sickly boy, and abused him verbally at home and in public. He wanted everyone to think that the boy might not be his. But mostly, he ignored his son. His mother loved him, but was more or less unable to help him because she too was under the knuckles of her husband. She was punished for any kindness or motherly love she showed Henri. Therefore, Lautrec focused on his only gift, drawing. He was a natural and wonderful talent and demonstrated extraordinary ability from a very early age. He specialized in pencil drawings of horses and other animals. The small recognition he got from his artwork helped him cope with his otherwise miserable childhood.

When he was about 10 years old, he broke both of his legs and was bedridden for many months. His legs never really healed properly due to a birth defect which ran in his family. The congenital ailment was due to royal inbreeding and a few of his cousins also suffered from the same malady. He had recently been thrown out of his parents' home with not much more than the clothes on his back, like Josay.

What are the odds that I would meet four artists in one week, she thought. She was rightfully shaken and stood up to find herself two or three inches taller than the man. She was more than disgusted at her lack of good luck.

"See here, you. I'm not looking for anything or anyone, especially not an artist. Go away, freak!"

She thought that would do the trick and rid her of this unwanted company. She was wrong.

Lautrec had been insulted, scorned, abused, beaten and betrayed by people much more talented at such things than this young girl.

He simply responded, "Nice talk for a good Christian girl."

Josay was completely surprised by his retort and felt guilty for having heaped her hurt and scorn on this unfortunate.

She quickly said, "I'm sorry. Just leave me alone." And without wanting to, she began to cry.

Lautrec softly put his hand on her shoulder and said in a most sincere and convincing way, "The world is unfair isn't it? We on the bottom tier must hold fast lest we be thrown into the sea of oblivion. Trust me. No one else here cares what might have happened to you, except for me. Please try and look past this deformed body and face and realize that inside is an artistic soul that longs to share friendship and a little hope with someone as lovely and, obviously, as pure as you."

He kept talking as she slowly turned toward him. Happy that he had removed his hand from her shoulder, she stepped back a pace or two.

"I can tell you're in trouble and I can offer you a place to stay and a modeling job in Paris to get you started."(His mother had arranged for him to have a shabby loft flat in the worst part of Montmartre. It was not much, but it had access to a wonderful glow of natural light which she imagined would suit a fledgling artist.)

Lautrec had always been taken with redheaded women and tried to find them to model for him every chance he got. *This girl's hair was more blonde than red, but it was red enough, and the way it reflected the light of the sun was spectacular,* he thought to himself.

Josay pushed him away from her with all of her might, knocking him to his knees. Suggesting that she might model for him was more than she could tolerate.

"I'll never model for one of you perverts again," screamed Josay.

Her pity for this creature was completely replaced with rage at the thought that she had come upon another artist wanting to use her body. As she walked away with her nag in tow, Josay felt strength returning to her through her anger.

Toulouse Lautrec was left sitting on the ground, unable to get to his feet because of his gnarled legs and stubby torso. *What the hell had just happened?* he thought.

It had been the most genuine and selfless proposal he had ever given to anyone. He had honestly felt a kind of brotherly need to help her.

Lautrec sadly thought to himself, *God is merciless.*

Just at dusk, a famished and exhausted Josay and horse arrived in the outside slums of Paris. Everywhere she looked, there were the most revolting, unkempt, unclean and vulgar people she had ever seen.

Surely, this must not be the "City of Lights that I have heard so much about, she thought.

"Out of the way girl!" shouted a burley, hairy man carrying a dead pig over his shoulders.

"Get that damn horse off the road," barked a filthy man and snaggletoothed woman in an ox drawn cart, who proceeded to spit in her direction.

Everywhere Josay looked, there was poverty and despair. Trash and human excrement layered the streets. It smelled awful. Every house, better described as huts or hovels, were smeared with soot and grime. The place was depressing and scary at the same time. Maybe Lautrec was right. He just might have been her best hope for surviving in this place.

As she was about to spontaneously cry again, a slightly overweight middle-aged woman tapped her on the back.

"How much do you want for that thing you call a horse?" asked the woman.

Josay couldn't immediately imagine why this person was pricing Madame La Plume's run-down sway-backed horse.

"I'll give you five francs for the nag."

Josay began to collect her thoughts and realized that she must do something or die. She found herself saying, "Fifteen francs or go away."

"I'll give you eight and not a sou more."

"Twelve and you've got a deal," said Josay.

"Ten, a room and one meal a day for two weeks at our tavern and Inn."

“Where is your tavern? Is it safe?” asked Josay.

The woman looked at her like she was daft and said, “From your looks, you shouldn’t be too particular. But it’s across the street there, and you’ll be eating that nag of yours for breakfast. You could also use a bathtub, soap and water which I will throw in for free.”

The deal was sealed and Josay began her new life in Paris with a room in Le Poulet Tavern and Inn for ten francs and horsemeat stew for two weeks. The free bath was the best part of the deal.

CHAPTER 5

Josay took a quick look at the room she would call home for the next two weeks. It was small. She was glad it was spring because the thin walls were made of wooden planks roughly overlapping one over the other. Unfortunately, some of the planks had gaps which allowed wind and weather to enter. The room was on the second floor and had a small window that overlooked the busy, noisy street below. In the corner, was a single bed without blankets or a pillow, but the sheets looked clean. Actually, the whole room looked clean. There was a square table with a chipped wash basin and a three legged stool. Under the bed was a chamber pot and a small broom.

"Josay, come down at 5 pm for dinner. Everyone that lives and works here eats just before the tavern opens for the night," shouted Madame Foote as she desended the stairs.

Madame Gloria Foote was the ex-wife of the ex-proprietor of this rough establishment. Previously, she had worked in other more fashionable restaurants and cabarets. But she had been betrayed by her husband and was left to pay for the guilt of his many crimes. He was a womanizer and drank to the extreme. Drunkeness made him very mean and nasty. It was his false witness that had caused her to be ostracized out of the legitimate businesses of Paris.

She was a kind woman and very intelligent. And despite the low position in which she found herself, she was able to make ends meet every month by her knowledge of corner cutting and shrewd negotiating. She was also wise in the ways of the world in which she lived, and was not above using a little graft and corruption as needed to survive. She did everything with good humor and a positive attitude. Everyone who knew her, loved her.

The bar in the tavern was long and fronted by fifteen stools with a cracked mirror that ran the length of the back wall. There were a few round tables for guests situated around the main room, each with four mismatched chairs. The basement housed beer, wine and other supplies. In the rear was the kitchen.

The inn part of the establishment housed a collection of misfits and ne'er-do-wells who had been victims of others, or of their own frailties and failures. The Poulet was where you landed when you were at your lowest.

Monsieur Paul, the cook, was the undisputed master of his domain. He barked out orders with a low pitched growl-like voice to his three unremarkable female helpers who doubled as waitresses and bar maids. Monsieur Paul was a talented chef who had fallen low because of problems with his wife. They had lost their baby son shortly after his birth. Her depression over the the loss of the baby had caused her to seek another man and another life. The loss of his wife and son had caused Chef Paul to overindulge in alcohol and become depressed himself. He had been fired from several high level jobs in some of the best restaurants in Paris, and he had ended up at the Poulet. He had been sober for a little while now and was able to make passable food out of almost nothing. The Poulet operated like a precision clock with Madame Foote and her four employees.

When Josay came down to dinner, she was joined by a collection of disheveled, grumpy men. Josay was sure that most of them were drunkards because as soon as a bottle of vin rouge was placed on the table, it was poured and drunk by all. They seemed not to notice or care that Josay didn't get a share. And in only a blink of an eye, the horse stew and crusty bread was gone, allowing Josay only the last scrapings in the bowl. She must get faster and more assertive in the future, she thought, or she might die of thirst and starvation.

"What's your story?" asked the large man closest to Josay as he dribbled food out of the side of his heavily bearded and grizzled face and mouth. "It will be nice to have a pretty young girl to share our table."

Josay guessed that the compliment wasn't given with a polite and honest motive.

"What's your name, Mon Cheri? We're all friends here," continued the man as his fellow tablemates laughed and slapped each other on the back. "I'll bet we'll be *special* friends before the night is over."

"Knock it off, George," said the middle-aged man at the other end of the table. He wore a moth-eaten French cuffed suit. Josay could tell by the way he spoke that he was an educated man who had, in his past, been above such lodgings as the Poulet.

"This young woman needs some time to get into the rut we live and play in."

He paused to swallow a mouthful of bread and then looked at Josay.

"Bon jour, Mademoiselle," he said. "Don't mind George, here. He has no manners at all."

" My name is Josay Rue."

"Well then, welcome to the Poulet, Mademoiselle Rue. I'm Doctor Jacque Muse, at your service. We do not stand on ceremony here. You will learn to fit in very quickly I suspect. I'll bet you will find us more to your liking than the drinking crowd that will be here in the next few hours. They are a rough crew of alcoholics, off-duty prostitutes, pimps, thieves and other vagrants and criminals."

Josay's face showed concern and sadness all at the same time.

"Not to worry, Mon Cheri, a few fallen priests and philosophers also frequent this fine establishment. There is always interesting conversation. This can be the happiest sad bar in Paris. If you choose, you can find many ways to make a profit. Talk can be quite rewarding for a pretty girl like you."

"And, if you don't like to talk, you can always give me a turn under the sheets, or even over the bar," said Big George with a wicked smile.

As he reached across the table to touch her breasts, something came over Josay. It was most probably an undefined rage, fueled by the events of her past few days, that caused her to jump over the table and dive onto the top of Big George. The surprise and force with which she hit him, first with her hands, and then with her elbows caused blood to gush from his nose and mouth. Josay had to be pulled from the top of Big George after she scratched his face and thrusted her knee into his groin.

Everyone was speechless except Josay who said, with a strength she had not known in her life, "Never touch me. I will resist to the death anyone that tries to take me or hurt me. And if I don't get you the first time, you must sleep sometime, and I'll get you then."

Josay sat back down, finished her stew scrapings, wiped her face on her sleeve, and left without saying anything else.

A round of laughter and more back slapping followed her. She could hear them saying, "She's a hellcat and I believe she would cut me or bash my head in for sure. Best keep our hands and thoughts to ourselves," they said as they laughed even harder at Big George having only now recovered his senses.

Josay was alone in her room thinking about all she had seen in just the first few hours at the Poulet. With trembling hands, she bolted her door. She wrote a letter to her mother, which calmed her and brought back the memories of the farm and of the safety of her old life. Much needed sleep thankfully came easily that first night.

The next few days were uneventful as Josay settled into a routine of attending to details. She walked about the neighborhood and found some presentable used clothes to buy with the little money she had left from selling the poor old mare. She met several people and went to church at the small cathedral on the square. She loved the inviting chimes that beckoned services. They reminded her of home and gave her spirit some comfort as she attended the short mass there. But mostly, she was looking for Madame La Plume. Josay knew she was unlikely to get help from the gendarmes, but she reasoned that a woman with such a flair and need for attention should be fairly easy to find. *La Plume will regret the robbery and betrayal she enacted on me,* she swore to herself.

She began to wander further and further into the city of Paris to see how the other parts of Paris looked. She had always heard that Paris was beautiful and clean with manicured gardens and flowers in baskets. She was delighted to find out that all of that was true. The flowers were in baskets but they were also growing wild along the beautiful Seine River that ran through the city. There were sidewalk cafés everywhere and lovely shops selling everything from high fashion clothes to fruits and vegetables. It was alive with activity. She was falling in love with Paris.

While Mademoiselle Josay Rue was getting the lay of the land, she also looked for employment opportunities. Josay didn't have any real skills, other than being literate and somewhat educated. This was a rare trait for a woman of her station in life.

She was also a fast learner. She was observing people as she explored the city. She noticed how they walked, and how they talked and how they interacted with each other. Her recent conflict with Big George, and learning to handle the other scum that landed at the Poulet every evening, built real confidence in her chest.

With the right clothes and the right way of speaking, why couldn't I move up the social latter a bit? she thought. She was adept at mimicking the accents of the upper class citizens of Paris, and believed in her heart that everyone, no matter what the circumstances of their birth, were equal in the eyes of God.

On the anniversary of two whole weeks at the Poulet in Paris, Josay was startled to hear her name spoken from behind her on the street.

"Bonjour, Josay," said Toulouse Lautrec as he walked, or rather waddled up to her. "Pax." (a reference to the Goddess of Peace)

"It took me 30 minutes to get to my feet the last time I saw you."

"It's you again," said Josay. "I seem to be turning up bad pennies everywhere I go. Keep your distance or you'll find yourself in the muck of the road again."

"Honestly, I just want to talk, and perhaps share a petit dejeuner of croissant and tea?"

Josay was hungry and anything other than horse meat stew sounded wonderful.

She shook his hand and said, "I agree to a truce."

They walked a few minutes and settled into a street café.

"I'd rather have coffee," said Josay after they were seated.

"Fine," said Lautrec. "I'd rather have absinthe."

Lautrec started and finished his day by drinking a mixture of red wine and absinthe. He justified his alcoholic behavior because it lessened the very real pain that accompanied his malformed legs and frame.

"Have you heard from home? And, have you found employment? You don't look destitute or famished. In fact, that dress you're wearing, even though it may be last year's fashion, is new, I believe."

"Well, it's new to me," she replied with a slight smile. "I'm fixed for the next week or so, thanks to the good graces of Madame Foote at the Poulet Tavern, but after that, I really don't know what I'm going to do to make a living. I expect my fiancé to come and take me back home very soon. I just need to get by for a few weeks or a month or two. Meanwhile, I need to find two people, Paul Gauguin and Madame Mari Belle La Plume. I have much unfinished business with those two."

"Well, well, well. It seems that I might be some good to you after all. I know exactly where Gauguin and La Plume are at this very minute," Lautrec said with a lilt in his voice.

"Where are they?" Josay asked, eager to learn about their whereabouts and resolve her secret business.

"Let me see," Lautrec verbalized his thoughts. "I think I know a way to make both of us happy. Although I could tell you where they are now, you would be very unlikely to get within three meters of them before the police would arrest you. I'm sure the prison cell they would put you in would be most uncomfortable. I think you are probably up to no good, right?"

Josay said nothing, but turned her head away from this odd, but clever little man.

"There is a way to get to both of them. It seems that I am under contract to design and draw advertising posters for Madame La Plume's upcoming stage production. Gauguin will, I'm sure, be there. He loves watching the girls that dance in the program. He's a letch, you know. If you wore a small disguise, I could take you to the concert as my companion. You could get close and conduct your business without getting arrested. But, I would need something from you in return."

He continued, "Setting up the whole plan might take several weeks and you will need a place to stay, or at least enough money to keep you at the Poulet after your current lease expires. I have a two-room flat. One is the bedroom and the other a small studio where I do my work. I would let you use the bedroom and feed you until your business with La Plume and Gauguin is concluded. For your part of the deal, you must serve as the model for my posters."

"You must be a fool if you think I'll live with you and pose for your posters."

"But, you have never seen my work. I am already rather famous in Montmartre after only two weeks. Have you ever been there? It's one of the liveliest and most amazing places in Paris. There are restaurants, hotels, cabarets, musical theatres, and bars; lots and lots of bars with enough drinks and drunkards to keep the place alive like no other. Most of the artists working in Paris frequent Montmartre and sell their paintings on the square. It's a dream come true for the lost and unwanted souls of the world. I must take you there as my model and have you in the mix of the place before you find your quarry."

Josay had to admit that Lautrec, filled with wine and absinthe was charming and convincing. She still had her reservations.

"How would I know that you weren't going to use me or harm me in some unnatural way?" she found herself saying.

"I'd say you were able to handle me pretty well if our history is to be believed." Lautrec's face became somber as he concluded, "Also, I'm lonely. I have no real friends. We could be partners. You're alone. I'm alone. Together maybe we could protect each other a little."

Josay thought about Lautrec's proposition and added, "Alright, I'll trust you, and for now I'll go along with your proposal. But before I meet La Plume and Gauguin, I want you to educate me. I want to know all about Montmartre, the entertainment, food and art scene, and all the obvious—and not so obvious—traps, pitfalls, and ambushes in which one might get ensnared."

"Ah, that is my specialty," he smiled.

"I also need a few helpful hints about being an aristocratic lady in Paris society. I have spent my entire life in a small village and would benefit from your experience in that area."

"Oui. Oui! You will never be sorry that you've chosen Toulouse Lautrec as a partner and confidant. I will be the envy of every man in Paris." He gave her a large smile and a wink.

Josay didn't know why, but she felt like she was making a right decision. She, unbelievably, concluded their plan with a sincere hug for the ecstatic Lautrec. They agreed to discuss all the details of her stay, and any possible modeling agreements at a later time.

That evening, Josay decided to take her bowl of stew later than usual and sat quietly at the bar eating. The familiar patrons dribbled in and took their nightly seats at the bar and the few tables in the tavern. It was a grizzly scene to be sure. The door opened as she was gazing absently around the room. She noticed a slender, well-dressed boy of about her age enter and lock eyes with her. He looked very out of place at the Poulet.

"What do you want?" the barmaid asked the young man.

"I'm not sure," he responded.

"Not sure? What the hell? Are you lost or something? This is a tavern!" the barmaid said in a volume loud enough to break the dull roar of the place.

As a blush came over his face, the young man said, "I'll have champagne."

"Well, well, we have an aristocrat in our humble establishment. I can't remember if anyone has ever ordered champagne here. You best move along before these working gentlemen decide to give you an unwanted toss into the street."

Josay said quickly, "He's my guest. Leave him the hell alone."

Her language had deteriorated in just the few weeks she had been at the Poulet. She found herself speaking to them in a manner that they would completely understand.

The very large man named George said, "Any friend of Josay's is a friend of mine."

George had decided to be Josay's protector rather than her assailant since the unfortunate mistake he had made on the first night she arrived at the Poulet. He respected her and was very fond of this beautiful slip of a girl who had put him in his place.

At that, everyone went back to their business and the young man moved toward Josay.

"Thank you," said the young man. "I'm looking for Josay Rue."

Somewhat startled, Josay said quietly, "Why?"

"I bring news from her family and her boyfriend, Donnel."

Without really thinking about it or weighing the consequences, Josay blurted out with uncontrollable excitement, "I'm Josay Rue. What news do you bring?"

"Your letters to your family were intercepted by the Count's associates and he has sworn to imprison your brother David on some trumped-up charge and retake the dairy from your parents if you make further efforts to contact any of them again."

"Who are you? Are you here on behalf of the Count to torture me?"

"No," said the young man. "I am a friend of Donnel Regis, a fellow cadet at the Military Academy. He knew I was from Paris and sent me here to warn you to stop all correspondence with your family. He sent this letter for you."

The young man handed Josay a sealed letter and without further discussion, left through the swinging saloon doors of the Poulet as quickly as he had come. Josay took the letter and hurried up the stairs to her room to read it without prying eyes.

She lit a candle since the sun had fully sunk in the west. She then drank a small sip of cognac from the bottle given to her by Dr. Muse earlier in the week. She hoped it would help her face whatever was contained in the letter, and calm her shaking hands.

My Dear Josay,

Father has sent me to the Academy de Artillery in Belgium to become an officer in the Army. This place is hard and demanding. Finding a way to communicate with you further will be virtually impossible for the next six months of my lower classmanship. This is the one and only note I could find time to write or a way to deliver. Ollie, an old friend and middle classman, agreed to smuggle it out to you since he was on his two-week leave between classes and lives in Paris.

My father swears to keep us apart and calls you things I could not write. Know that I love you, and when I can, I will come to Paris for you. I have a friend in Paris, Monsieur Blanc an accountant and bookkeeper who will provide you with a monthly stipend from my holdings to keep you safe. It is not a large amount, but it is all that I could manage without Father finding out. Just go to him and he will know what to do. His address is 55 Rue Semuir.

I send all my love, and as the days pass while we're apart, I remain your faithful,

Donnel Regis

Josay held the short note to her breast and felt relief and hope for her future for the first time since arriving in the city. She spent the rest of the evening thinking about her family and about her dearest Donnel.

CHAPTER 6

Josay had agreed to meet Lautrec to look over his flat. On the way, she stopped at the offices of Blanc and Hover at 55 Rue Semuir. Monsieur Blanc was a Frenchman and Mr. Hover was English. Josay determined this by reading the literature in the office waiting room. It seemed that they specialized in legal and financial transactions between French and English concerns. Josay had worn her most fashionable "used" dress and looked for all the world like a woman of substance. Although she was very young to have business in such an establishment, she took on an air of maturity and confidence as she waited to see Monsieur Blanc.

"You may go in." said the young man in the wire-rimmed glasses without looking up. Josay had no idea just how he knew they were ready for her. The young man at the reception desk just seemed to divine the invitation from the inner office.

"Good morning, Mademoiselle Rue," said the Englishman as he held out his hand for a greeting. "I'm William Hover. Monsieur Blanc could not join us, but be sure I can speak in his behalf about your arrangement."

William Hover spoke perfect French, but with an English accent. He was a clean shaven man of about 28 years and neat to the point of obsession. His clothes were impeccable.

"Please take a seat," he offered politely.

Mr. Hover didn't seem to know or understand Josay's full circumstances because he said, "I understand that you have recently arrived in Paris. How are you enjoying your time here?"

Without waiting for her to respond, he continued, "I find it enchanting and beautiful. Have you tried the Ritz? The chateaubriand is like a dream, and the cherries jubilee is without equal."

Josay nodded. The nod seemed to give an unexpected result to Mr. Hover. He was a man accustomed to being given only a cursory gesture or word from the wealthy patrons he represented. Hover, as an Englishman, often misunderstood nonverbal signs. He was eager to please and fully convinced that Josay was a woman above his station.

"I have the papers. You are to be given the amount of 12 francs per month from the holdings of Monsieur Donnel Regis. I suppose it is some kind of debt repayment or annuity? The paperwork isn't clear," he probed. "This payment is to be given for an unspecified period of time. You may come here to get the money in person or it can be placed in an account in your name at our bank. Have you had time to establish a banking account in Paris?" the eager Hover questioned.

"I have not," said Josay with a very high born accent.

"Well then, let me handle all the particulars and without haste you will be installed in the Bank of Hanover, Paris Branch, with an initial line of credit for shall we say 200 francs?"

Josay responded again without looking at Hover, "I think 500 would be more to my liking."

"Of course, I will make it so. Is there anything else I can do to make your entrance into Paris more comfortable?"

Pressing her luck, Josay said in monotone, "I would like an invitation or two to evening social events so that I might be introduced to the right kind of people."

"Done. I would be most happy to escort you to a small celebration the day after tomorrow at The Ritz. Where should I send the carriage?"

"I will meet you there. I have other business that day and don't wish to be seen arriving with you." said Josay.

"Of course. I will leave your invitation at the door. I do hope to share a glass of champagne with you, and I would love to have the honor of introducing my wife, Elizabeth."

"I look forward to meeting her,"said Josay as she turned and started walking toward the door without saying goodbye. Exhaling deeply but discreetly, she bit her lip to stave off laughter, and departed from the office.

Lautrec cleaned the small bedroom and placed flowers in a blue vase in anticipation of Josay's arrival. He arranged his pallet with appropriate oil colors and placed a new fresh poster paper on the easel in position for painting. As he finished pouring himself an early afternoon wine, he heard a knock on the door.

"Lautrec, is anyone there?" said Josay.

"I'm here," Lautrec said as he opened the door. "Bonjour, Mon Cheri," said Lautrec as he took her hand and bowed to kiss it. "You look marvelous in that dress, a real Lady and much older it seems."

"Thank you," responded Josay as her eyes flashed around the sunlit studio apartment. "I assume this is your studio," she continued. "And this would be my room should I agree to your proposal?" she concluded as she walked through the door to the bedroom hidden by a colorful Persian hanging beaded doorway.

Lautrec had done his best to make the bedroom attractive. There was a brightly colored spread on the bed, a blue vase with two white lilies on a small dressing table and a matching blue chair. The window had no view or curtain and only opened to a brick wall of the building next door. She guessed that the room would be dark on days not as clear as today. In the corner was a coat rack which seemed a crude place to hang clothes in lieu of a dresser. There was an old trunk, however, which would suffice since she didn't own a lot of clothes yet.

She started the conversation about the proposed agreement by saying, "Just exactly what do I have to do to get this room for a few months?"

Lautrec put his hand to his chin as if he had not really considered the question in advance, and said, "I need a model to sit for the advertising posters that I have contracted to do for several businesses and establishments here in Montmartre. You would agree to sit for, shall we say, 4 posters and 2 paintings over a period of 3 months. Each poster would take about 2 days of modeling to draw and color, and the oil paintings would take a few days to a week to render. I believe that totals approximately 8 days for the posters and 2 weeks for the oils which is 22 days of actual modeling work in exchange for 3 months lodging."

"I've had some problems in the past with modeling," she countered. "Let me be clear. No nudity."

"Some of the posters are for nightclub acts, dancers and singers. Others are for circus acts, restaurants and cabarets. I will need to suggest female features, but I agree I will not expose your body directly. For my oil paintings, I will ask you to pose nude for only one of them, but I would not show your facial features and I would choose a pose that is artistic in nature,"replied Lautrec.

Josay thought for a long moment. What he proposed sounded reasonable, but she was very wary of being misused again. Agreeing to this was a large gamble, but she felt that it suited her purposes as well as Lautrec's. She was desperate to move her life forward.

She finally said, "Alright, I will agree to your proposal with one caveat. If I find the nude picture is vulgar or disrespectful, you will give it to me immediately. I may then do as I wish with it. The rules will be strict. I will not be totally disrobed at any time. It must be drawn from the back without my face showing, and only a hint of my bottom will be allowed. I happen to be a respectable person with high moral standards, and no one must know who is in the picture. I will not have my life ruined or stained forever for your gains.

"Done," Lautrec said eagerly.

After all, no one really wanted his oils. He had yet to sell any. His paintings had been refused at the Annual Paris Salon. It was no great loss to him if he couldn't show her whole body or her face. But she was so lovely, he felt a little remorse that he could not capitalize fully.

They sealed the bargain with another handshake, as Josay said, "I must go now, I will contact you next week to arrange my move and set up a modeling schedule. If you need to talk to me between now and then, you can always find me at the Poulet Inn and Tavern."

As Josay walked toward the Poulet she thought to herself, *I have been disgraced, driven from my home, betrayed, and robbed. I have survived all of these insults. Now I have a new job, a bank account, and tomorrow I will attend a party at the Ritz Hotel! I feel strong and determined to put myself in a position to right the wrongs and make things better for myself and the people I love. Nothing will stop me now.*

The next day, Josay busied herself with touching up the only fine dress she owned. She had found it lying on top of a wagon being sold by a street vendor. She was fairly sure that it had been stolen, but she had no way of knowing that for sure, so she bought it. It was a lovely dress and of good quality.

Additionally, she sought ways to enhance her look to appear more elegant and fashionable. A quick trip to the market yielded a fine string of faux pearls and earrings. *I can't tell they are fake, so how can anyone else?* she thought.

She also found a bejeweled hair comb and a bracelet with what looked like rubies. She was sure they weren't rubies but they matched the embroidery on the sleeves of her dress. They were perfect. She found some used long white gloves that just needed to be spot cleaned. Her final purchase was a very fine evening bag that she was certain had been obtained by the vendor through some kind of mischief. The man that sold it to her just appeared before her with the bag and insisted that she see it in a dark alleyway. Most suspicious, it was true, but these few accessories were purchased for just under two francs total.

Josay also needed some makeup and the skill to put it on, having never really worn makeup in her village. One of the women that periodically came into the Poulet after hours would help her, she was sure. Madame Dupree might be engaged in some kind of shady dealings with the men at the Poulet, but she was kind to Josay. Madame Dupree seemed to wear her makeup in the latest Parisian style, so it would be a real asset to learn of her tricks for beauty.

As Josay was leaving the market, she saw a familiar face.

"Hey, you. Yes, you," she repeated as she tugged at the man's arm. "You're Renoir right?"

"I am," he said. "I would recognize that face anywhere, you're the farm girl, Josay. What are you doing in Paris?" he continued in a friendly pleasant way.

"Are you pretending that you don't know why I'm here?" she shot back with a deep-seated hostility.

Renoir was confused and said, "Wait just a minute, young lady, what the hell are you talking about?"

Josay calmed enough to tell Renoir all the details of her expulsion, shame and subsequent recent experiences in Paris.

"Come to mention it, I don't believe I ever saw you or Pissarro after that day they threw me out of town. Is it possible that you didn't know about the Gauguin painting?"

"Of course, I saw the painting, but I assure you, I did not know about the harm it caused you. Pissarro and I went into the village with Gauguin, ate a small meal and left Gauguin flirting with the waitresses.

We came back to Paris that same day without Gauguin, never having seen the uproar that ensnared you. I'm so sorry. I would naturally be willing to set the record straight. You poor child."

His eyes confirmed to Josay that he was truly sympathetic to her plight.

He continued, "Just come around to my studio in the next few days. I'll find Camille and get a notary. We will swear in a deposition that the nudity was in no way of your doing. That Gauguin is a scoundrel and not to be trusted. I still have the painting I did of you and have recently submitted it along with several others to this year's Salon. The Salon is held every year in Paris to exhibit art painted by the most notable artists in France. Having your work selected to be in the Salon could make or break your artistic career. I am doubtful that my painting of you will be accepted by the Salon since it was done in the new style that the critics are calling 'Impressionistic'. The art establishment is very rigid about style and subject matter and our 'impressions' are not within their guidelines. If there is a miracle and they do select it, it would be because of the beauty of the model."

Josay blushed and smiled at the compliment.

"At the Salon, thousands of people would see it, and If someone, by chance, should buy it, I'll give you the proceeds. If it doesn't sell, I'll give the painting to you. It's the least I can do. Besides, I'd like for you to pose for me again sometime."

Everyone wants to paint me. Maybe I should really consider becoming a professional model, she thought as she answered. "You are too kind, Monsieur Renoir. I do not blame you and I will find you in a few days to get the deposition. I am anxious to put this whole terrible event behind me."

They parted after Renoir gave her his address and kissed her hand.

Later that evening, it took Josay over an hour to walk from the Poulet to the Ritz. She was careful to avoid the filth, dirt and muck of the streets, but arriving without any trace of her having walked the entire route was impossible.

She devised a plan that would explain the few patches of mud on her dress by faking an accidental slip as she appeared to climb from one of the fine carriages entering the portico of the Ritz. It was a simple plan and worked like a charm. Every doorman and servant at the Ritz tried to help her and offered to brush or clean the small stains. When they were finished, it looked like she arrived in one of the luxury carriages like all the others.

At the door, she found an invitation as promised by Mr. Hover. She was announced as Josay Rue from Provence. No one seemed to notice her at the announcement, but within seconds, Mr. Hover appeared.

"Mademoiselle Rue, so glad you could join us", he said. "This is my wife Elizabeth."

She was a large woman with a small face and too much makeup. Yet, when she spoke French with her heavy British accent, she seemed to Josay to be feminine and charming.

"My dear, so happy to meet you. I hope we can get to know each other and I look forward to a budding friendship."

Josay believed she meant it.

"And this is Monsieur J.K. Blanc, my partner."

"Enchanted to meet you," he said as he took her hand to kiss it. "I am sorry but business kept me from meeting you in the office. I hope Hover treated you well."

"He was most gracious. This room is wonderful and I love the flowers and music," she responded.

"You certainly make the room more beautiful. This is my client James Sommes. He is also from Provence. Perhaps you know some of the same people," said Blanc.

"Where are you from in Provence? I'm from Marseille, et vous?", said James Sommes.

"Oh, I don't live there anymore. My family moved out of southern France to a place near Barcelona, Spain. I'm afraid I don't know anyone from Marseille, although I did visit it years ago and found it to be one of the most interesting and most beautiful places in the south of France.

"My family has lived there for two centuries," said James. He was a man in his early twenties with light brown hair and dark brown round eyes. Josay could see the kindness in them as he spoke.

"James' family is a member of 'society' in Marseille. His father is Marquise Le Sommes," said Hover.

"Enough. I'm sure Mademoiselle Rue would rather have a glass of wine and a dance than talk of such unimportant matters," said James.

His humble words and manner endeared him instantly to Josay. She took his hand just as a waltz began. Josay had never actually danced in public but she had practiced dancing a waltz in the farmyard, without the music. The music made movement easier and she found her feet responding to the cues and leadership James provided as she covered the whole area of the Ritz ballroom.

What a lovely setting for my first dance, she thought.

Her strawberry blonde hair and beautiful youthful face, body and features did not go unnoticed by the men and women in the room.

"Who is she? She is a vision, and her face lights up the room," could be heard in every corner.

Josay spent the remainder of the night talking to one eager businessman, aristocrat, wealthy lady, or politician after another. She held her own in conversations mostly by keeping her mouth shut and listening hard to whatever people, mostly men, might say.

If some rich businessman said, "Where are you from and how is it that we have never met?" Josay would respond, "How lovely that you would want to know me?, and/or, "I'm sure I would remember if I had met someone as important as you before."

If a woman asked,"Where did you get your dress and bracelet?" Josay would say, "How nice of you to ask. It's a precious thing to me. It was a gift from my dear mother."

Several ladies asked her, "Your hair is so lovely. Who does it for you?" She replied, "I had help from someone who is very talented and clever."

She was a natural at dodging the whole truth. These white lies and lies of omission caused pangs of guilt and tugged at her conscience. But being slightly less than truthful seemed to be of great necessity if she was ever to rise into the ranks of "society" in Paris. She felt that she could not reveal her true self just yet, but there would be time for all of that later. Tonight she would meet lovely people and enjoy the gaiety of the evening.

Before the night was over, James asked to take her home. Josay said, without thinking, "That would be nice." But then realized that she could not have the coach drop her at the Poulet.

So she said, "How stupid of me, I'm planning to stay here, although my baggage hasn't arrived yet."

It seemed an obvious lie as it came from her mouth, but as she observed this evening, everyone, especially young men, seemed to overlook the least believable things from an attractive women.

"Well then, you have time for another drink. Have you ever had pommery?"

Josay nodded in the affirmative, without the slightest knowledge of what James was asking.

The waiter brought several glasses and filled each to the brim.

"To Mademoiselle Josay Rue. Welcome to Paris," said Hover.

Josay poked her tongue into the drink and smiled.

When the others had finished their drinks, Josay said, "I'm very tired. I believe I'll go up to my room and get to bed. I have much business to conduct tomorrow."

Josay hugged the women, allowed the men to kiss her hand and left the group in a flash without saying another word.

She began her long walk back to the Poulet. The whole city was ablaze with romantic light coming from thousands of ornate gas lamps. As she walked down the wide boulevard called the Champs-Elysees, she could see the Arc de Triomphe in the distance. It was brightly lit and so beautiful. She had seen it in a small book about Paris that she had at home and knew that if Napoleon could see it tonight, he would be very pleased. Now she knew why they called Paris, the "City of Lights."

Somehow, Josay made her way back to the Poulet safely that night. She realized that her lies may eventually entangle her, but she felt the whole evening to be a great success. She still missed Donnel and her family, but she was beginning to like Paris.

After only a few weeks she was becoming a fixture at the Poulet, almost a mascot. The drunks knew her, the prostitutes treated her like a sister and the other patrons ignored her for the most part. Madame Foote the owner of Le Poulet, took a special interest in Josay and while their original bargain had long since been completed, she let it be known that she would keep her on if she would wait tables or just talk to the regulars. What she really wanted was a friend in a world where there were none to be found for a woman like Madame Foote.

Josay was very fond of Madame Foote, as well, and considered her a dear friend, but staying at the Poulet was not in her plan. She felt that moving to Lautrec's flat in Montmartre would begin a whole new life for her. It was a growing and exciting area of Paris, and Henri would be able to help her achieve her goal of locating Madame La Plume and Gaugin. She really didn't need Gaugin any longer since Renoir and Pissaro had promised to give her proof that she had been disgraced in error, but she would still like to confront him with what he had done to her and her family. La Plume was another story altogether.

A few days after the evening at the Ritz, Josay got a note from Renoir and found her way to the painter's home. When she arrived, she found not only Renoir and Pissarro present but several other odd looking artists. One after another they introduced themselves as messieurs Monet, Sisley, Cezanne, Degas, and in the corner by himself, a strange looking fellow named Vincent Van Gogh.

"See what I told you. She is a perfect expression of the honesty and purity of God's nature. We could not resist painting her in the countryside," explained Renoir to the very interested group.

As Josay searched around the room, she saw beauty beyond her wildest imagination on the walls. There were landscapes in purple and blue with rosy sunsets. On another wall there were portraits of men, women and children that looked like they had been stolen from the eyes of God, Himself. One in particular of two young girls pinning hats on each other, almost made her cry. The innocence in their faces and the light reflecting off of their hats....so breathtaking! It reminded her of the innocence of her own girlhood. And the colors, everywhere, colors like she had never seen before were more brilliant than even nature's own imaginings.

She noticed that the pictures looked very different up close than they did from further away. The separated short lines of the darker colors beside the lighter ones seemed to run together at a distance to make the most joyous and beautiful effect on the canvas. She was completely in love with this modern way of painting!

"I am very pleased to meet such distinguished artists," Josay said, employing her new found skill of diplomacy. "I feel somewhat at a loss amidst such epic talent."

She could never have known just how true her platitude would become in years to come. She had no real knowledge of any of the painters' works except for the ones she had glimpsed before the three men painted her by the stream and oak tree, and, of course, the beautiful array of pictures on the walls of Monsieur Renoir's house.

"Madame Renoir has made cakes. Shall we invite the notary in to take our deposition while we share a demitasse?" said Renoir.

She entered the room with a large porcelain platter decorated in a Japanese motif and filled with delicious looking miniature cakes. Everyone sat to listen to the disposition as they ate their cakes and drank their small cups of coffee. The room was still and silent as Pissarro and Renoir told their well-rehearsed story of the paintings by the stream, often stopping to acknowledge the moans of disbelief and tragedy the story told. When they had finished, they asked Josay, "Did we leave anything out?"

"No. Not a thing. I appreciate your help and trust that it will be well received. I am hopeful that this will put to rest this awful memory and sad chapter of my life."

Madame Renoir stepped up and said, "I'm sure you would enjoy a little rest and perhaps a quiet time outside."

She took Josay's hand without asking and led her through the small dining room and out the back door.

Once out of doors, Madame Renoir urged Josay to sit next to her, and still holding her hand, said, "What happened to you was terrible. I can't imagine how much you miss your family. Please know that you will be welcome here even if you don't take Auguste's offer to pose for him. We wives and lovers of these art-driven men stick together to make ends meet and to provide for each other and our families."

Josay was relieved to find another kind woman. So far, she had been embraced by Madame Foote, Mrs. Hover, Madame Dupree and now Madame Renoir. It was comforting to know that she had found sympathetic female ears and shoulders upon which to cry should she need them.

"Come back in, Josay," beckoned Renoir. "We have a business proposal for you."

Inside Pissarro took the leadership role and said in his gentle low pitched voice, "We would all love to have you sit for us in Monet's garden."

"Oui. Oui," echoed Monet, "We could all eat, drink, dance and make a party of it by the water lily pond afterwards. My wife is an excellent cook and all our children would, of course, be invited too. Pissarro has tens of children."

Everyone laughed and pointed at an embarrassed Camille Pissarro. "I assure you it would be a fine day and evening."

Josay felt it would be in poor taste to decline and found words tumbling out of her mouth again as she said, "Of course, and I will invite Monsieur Lautrec and a few others if that would be permitted."

Everyone immediately agreed and set the date for a week from the coming Saturday.

"We will start the day out with the morning sun in your face so as to highlight your lovely hair and green eyes. I feel we can be finished by late afternoon and be cleaned up and ready for wine, dinner and an evening of laughter by 7:00, no?

Everyone agreed to the schedule. Josay thanked each one, including Monsieur Van Gogh. He had been particularly animated and polite to her. She hugged and shook hands with all and left, deposition in hand.

On her way back to Le Poulet for her last night, Josay stopped by the office of Blanc and Hover to pick up her monthly allocation. As fate would have it, Monsieur James Sommes was leaving just as Josay arrived.

"Mademoiselle Rue," he greeted her as he bowed to kiss her hand.

Josay was dressed in the infamous sun dress and felt it necessary to say, "Monsieur Sommes, how nice to see you. I have been running errands today and never expected to run into a gentleman. Please excuse the way I look."

Sommes naturally replied, "You are beautiful, and would be breathtaking and appropriate even in trousers."

Josay's face flushed as she thanked him.

Mr. Hover stepped out of his office upon hearing Josay's voice and said, "Bonjour, Mademoiselle Rue. Are you here to collect your stipend?"

"I am," replied Josay.

"Let me go into the office and I will get it for you. It won't take a minute. By the way, your bank account is ready for you with your line of credit attached."

While Josay waited, Monsieur Sommes took the liberty of carrying the conversation in the poorly lit nineteenth century office. "I haven't been able to find your address. When I checked at the Ritz, they told me you hadn't checked in as recently as day before yesterday. That's the exact reason I came here today to Mr. Hover's office. I hoped that he would know how to reach you."

"Oh, I decided not to stay at the Ritz," deflecting the question. "I'm staying with an artist friend of mine. You may have heard of him.

He's quite famous for his posters and advertising art, Monsieur Henri Toulouse Lautrec?

"Yes, I have seen some of his posters around Paris. They are very colorful and whimsical. His work is very distinctive."

"Monsieur Lautrec is going to use me as a model for several of his posters and paintings. I am, of course, flattered that he asked me to do so. You may know his family from the town of Albi. His parents are of royal linage, cousins, I believe."

"No. I am afraid I am unfamiliar with the name."

"Henri is estranged from them right now for a reason that is being kept secret from me. All that I know is that his mother still corresponds with him regularly and holds him dear. Nonetheless, they have encouraged him to come to Paris to explore his artistic talent."

Luckily, without question or concern, James accepted her story about why she had never stayed at the Ritz.

"I'm glad to find you because I wanted to invite you to a party, a week from Saturday at another artist friend's home. His name is Claude Monet. I am told that he has a lovely home and small lake or pond, beside which we will drink wine, eat lots of food, and fun will be the order of the evening. I will send a messenger with the details and address if you are interested in attending."

"Yes. I would love to accompany you to the party."

"Monsieur Auguste Renoir is the artist that is organizing the affair. He has submitted one of his portraits of me to this year's Salon and I feel obligated to go. It might not be as elegant as you have come to expect, but I am looking forward to it. We can meet there and you may bring a few of your friends as well. I am so enjoying meeting and getting to know lots of people here in Paris before I must go home to my fiancé."

Monsieur Sommes said, "You're engaged then?"

"Well almost. We have been close since we were children and everyone expects us to marry someday" she responded.

She felt a twinge of guilt as she told another white lie.

"In that case, I'll act as if you're still open to offers of friendship. I will bring a few of my friends as you have suggested. Are you free for dinner before then?"

"Perhaps, but I can't say just now. I need to find more clothes and other things women must have before being seen in public since my luggage has still not arrived."

The response on the face of it didn't seem to make much sense, Josay thought. But before Monsieur Sommes could reason out the strange statement, and just at the right time, Mr. Hover appeared and handed Josay her money in an envelope.

James Sommes said only, "Very well. I will see you then."

As an afterthought, he tried again by asking if he could escort her somewhere.

"Thank you, but I have a previous engagement," said Josay.

Words any potential male suitor hates to hear and reliably dispatches further attempts to corner a young woman for the moment. He smiled, tipped his hat and left.

Josay said, "Thank you, Mr. Hover." She shook his hand and quickly exited the dark office.

The last evening Josay was to stay at the Poulet, and as she was getting ready to go down for the "food fight" that was dining at the establishment, she heard a pounding on her door.

"Josay, it's David."

Josay quickly opened the door and rushed into her brother's arms.

"David, I have missed you so."

"And I, you, dear sister," David said as he kissed the side of her face and gave her one more strong squeeze.

"What news? Has the Count changed his mind or softened his position? I have a sworn deposition that makes clear my innocence." Josay went on, "I know the situation will all be resolved very soon."

"I'm afraid it might not be so easy. Since the Count learned of your intentions with Donnel, he has decided to expand his prohibition. He seems to care not at all about the painting or your role in its creation now. The deposition is meaningless. He said that should you ever come back to the village, or if he found out that you had seen Donnel, or even corresponded with him, he will throw Mama and Papa off the farm and prosecute them in some way that might lead to prison. I believe that he could do it too, Josay. You know he owns the magistrates and courts in the province. Donnel has been hamstrung at the academy. His cadet overseers have been paid to read his mail, in and out, and there is constant supervision as to his whereabouts. He was able to tell me that he had made the financial agreement with Monsieur Blanc and Mr. Hover before his father became so vigilant."

"I am aware of some of this news because of a note that Donnel was able to smuggle out to me by one of his cadet friends. That's why I have not recently written letters to you, Mama and Papa, or Donnel.

It's very lonely here without communication with the ones I love," cried Josay.

"The money will continue if he can keep his arrangements clandestine. No one will know the nature of his help because It is a blind trust," David continued.

"We must be careful still, and not think of ourselves. Papa and Mama have protested with me that your life is more important than theirs and they have felt great remorse for not having supported you stronger. They love you very much, Josay."

"And now I must leave. It's a long ride back and I must not be missed. I will try to see you or communicate with you if I find a safe opportunity. For now, if you must contact me, use Monsieur Leslie Le Grande, the regional dairy merchant. He is an old and trusted patron of Papa and will carry messages should they be of great importance."

He kissed her again and without giving Josay a chance to respond, he was out the door and gone.

CHAPTER 7

Posing for Lautrec had been much harder work than Josay had imagined. She had to remain still and quiet for extended periods of time. And although Lautrec kept a constant chatter, she was only expected to agree or disagree with "oui" or "non". Very occasionally, she was allowed to add a comment or two. However, the time passed quickly and the outfits she was asked to wear were fun—and sometimes outrageous! For several days, she was dressed as a circus acrobat with ruffled fringed short tights and a headband made of gold lace. Then at the end of the first week, a buxom seamstress arrived to dress her in a bright silver and blue evening gown with exquisite jewelry and peacock feather accessories. Each time she posed, she endured an hour or two of makeup and hair, before what was always a long and difficult posing session. Almost more than the tired muscles and stressed posture, there were the hunger pangs. She was asked to go until early evening without anything to eat except for a small cup of coffee and a bakery roll for breakfast. And yet, she began to admire Lautrec for his work habits. He too went without nourishment, with the exception of the always present cup of wine or some other brew. He worked with a passion and by the end of the first week, and before her engagement with the artists that Saturday, he had completed two posters.

Josay looked at the two finished posters and thought they were vibrant, unique and colorful. They captured her essence while making her someone else. As if by magic, she had become a fine opera singer and a circus performer with flair and glamour.

It had been over a week since Josay had seen or heard from James or any of her friends at the Poulet. Early Saturday morning, Renoir knocked on the door with a lovely simple dress and hat for Josay to wear to the sitting and the subsequent party. He told her that he had been contacted by several of his artist friends and all were going to come to the sitting and the party. In fact, Renoir told Josay that he just might paint her in the morning and early afternoon with the others, and then sketch the entire party separately later that day with everyone in the picture.

Josay asked, "Do you remember that you told me I could invite several of my friends to the party?"

"Of course," responded Auguste. "One of your friends sent over two cases of vin rouge. It is a fine vintage, too. I think his name was James Sommes."

"Oh yes, James is a new friend."

Lautrec appeared in the doorway looking his usual hung over self.

Josay continued, "You know my employer Henri Toulouse Lautrec?"

"Naturally," responded Renoir. "I have admired your posters around town and I have seen your submissions to the Salon. I especially like the painting of the horses in the field. Did you sell any?"

"No, but I make a living with the advertising work. I will certainly come to the party later."

"You are invited to come to the group painting session today as well, if you can get your palette and paint together. Many of the local artists are coming to paint Josay in "plein-air" (out of doors) this morning and afternoon. Then we will all drink, eat and enjoy the evening together," finished Renoir.

Josay came out from behind the changing screen just as the two men shook hands.

Lautrec said, "You look like a vision. I have painted you for days and today you seem to be another person altogether. I will surely want to paint you today with the others."

He grabbed his paint, a blank canvas, and his easel. The three left for Monet's garden, pond and the adjacent lake house.

When Josay arrived with Renoir and Lautrec, several of the artists had already begun to paint the pond and background landscape for the picture they envisioned.

"It's all about the light," said Renoir. "They will only sketch the background but will paint you and the complete scene from what the light dictates."

Josay renewed her casual acquaintance with Van Gogh, Pissarro, Degas, Cezanne and Monet, and then met several other artists including Caillebotte and a woman named Berthe Morisot. All seemed eager to begin this unusual day of painting together.

She decided to ask a question that she feared to ask. "Where is Gauguin?"

"Oh that cad," responded Cezanne. "He has recently left his wife and five children and has gone to Tahiti to paint natives. Everyone who knows him is ashamed of his abandonment of all his responsibilities. He claims to do it for the sake of art, but he's really the most narcissistic man in the artistic community."

Josay followed up with, "Has anyone seen the painting he did of me at the stream? I have heard that a woman named La Plume has the painting."

Josay didn't reveal the details of the robbery on the road to Paris in order to help keep her background and reason for coming to Paris quiet. They all agreed that they had no knowledge of the whereabouts of La Plume or the painting.

There was considerable discussion between the artists about just where and how to place Josay. But they all agreed with Renoir and Pissarro that Josay possessed an innocent essence of spring and youth and they were all excited to begin. Madames Renoir and Monet offered Josay some milk and bread and a cup of tea.

"You look beautiful," said Madame Monet.

"Thank you," Josay replied as she gulped her milk and ate her warm bread. The smell of the bread somehow reminded her of the morning at home when her whole life changed. It was just hours before she had met the three artists by the stream. She wondered if this day would mark another beginning for her life.

Josay settled herself near a large rock and looked at the artists busily setting up and already feverishly brushing on their canvases. Josay didn't really pick the pose.

She was finishing her breakfast and was simply leaning or half sitting on the rock for support when Renoir shouted, "Perfect! The light is and will be on her face for the next several hours. It's the light!"

Josay was instructed not to make another move for the next five hours. The artists worked, talked among themselves and often argued or disagreed, but it was always about color, shading and the light.

"This will be a milestone for our group," said Degas, a small-framed, fashionably dressed man with the accent of an upper- class citizen. "Josay is as fine a model as I have seen, even in the Grand Ballet. She must model for us again."

Lautrec jumped into the discussion and reminded Josay that she owed him at least another two months. This caused all of the painters to turn on Toulouse and protest in unison.

"We can reach a compromise, I'm sure. Perhaps a few francs can get her released from part of her commitment so she might model for you," said Lautrec.

"Now wait just a minute, Henri," said Josay with her anger beginning to rise.

"No one owns me, and if I want to negotiate my modeling time, I'll do it myself. And the money will be paid to me, not to you. Our agreement is for four posters and two paintings as I recall. And if you're not quiet, I'll count today as one of the two paintings I owe you."

This gumption and directness caused everyone to point and laugh at Lautrec and in unison say, "We believe we will deal with Josay directly. She might just be a little too bold for you, Toulouse."

Toulouse firmly agreed and said with a cheerful tone, "Of course, dear lady, I was just testing my limits."

"Enough work for the day. It's time to get ready for the evening," Renoir announced, and everyone slowly stopped painting.

After a very short nap, Josay changed into her casual sundress with a fitted jacket which made it look like a completely different dress, and readied herself for the party. Outside at a distance she could hear music, laughter, and the sounds of carriages and horses coming and going.

"Your friends are here," announced Madame Monet.

As Josay came around the corner she saw James Sommes and several other well-dressed young men and women.

"James, it's so good to see you again," said Josay as she offered her hand.

James took her hand kissed it and made brief introductions. Everyone was smiling and gay and ready to begin an evening sure to be pleasurable and memorable. The entire group rushed out the door and quickly walked to the pavilion next to the small lake where they each got a glass of wine and begin to enjoy the view.

To say the evening was unusual would be an understatement. In the same crowd with James and his well-to-do friends were Pissarro, his wife and his many children, Monet's family, Degas and a few stately ballet dancers, both men and women, a lonely depressed Van Gogh, an already drunk Lautrec, and a group of quite wealthy looking people surrounding Caillebotte.

Although Caillebotte looked like the other painters while painting with them, he was, in fact, a very wealthy aristocrat. He was connected to all the right people. Some of them had come with him, including Mr. William Hover and his wife Elizabeth.

From the Poulet, there was Dr. Jacque Muse, Monsieur Paul, Madame Foote, and of course, Big George.

Madame Foote spoke softly to Josay, "Monsieur Renoir thought we might like to come to this party. We brought some stew," she said as she winked. "And Chef Paul baked a special pudding."

Paul, dressed in a tall white clean chef's hat, touched his lips and kissed them. His depression seemed to be at bay and he had a pleased look on his face. He had been thinking that he was ready for the world again.

Dr. Muse hugged Josay and told her how she had been missed since she moved into her new flat with Lautrec. He looked prosperous and well dressed tonight. He had on a three pieced suit with a watch and gold chain decorating his waistcoat (vest) which was considered a very stylish touch. His frock coat came just to his knees as was the style. And, he sported a black top hat with squared-toed shoes. Josay was impressed but wondered where he got the money for the suit, watch, shoes and hat. *Perhaps, he was working again? she thought. And that would be wonderful because it would mean that he had found a way to give up alcohol. It could mean a brighter future for him.*

George was scrubbed clean and dressed in his best old and worn clothes with a suit coat and a thin bow tie. He smiled, bowed and took Josay's hand and kissed it.

Josay smiled and warmly greeted each one. Somehow they seemed a little like her family even though she had only known them for such a short time. It dawned on her at that moment that she had made much progress since she first set eyes on Madame Foote and the broken-down tavern and inn called Le Poulet.

Caillebotte and James Sommes knew each other as well and soon a small group of wealthy, but friendly people seated themselves near the dance floor and Josay joined them.

"Will you honor me with a dance?" said James.

Josay happily accepted and the night was begun like a shooting star with no boundaries but the heavens.

Renoir was sketching the entire evening but no one seemed to notice. Everyone, rich, poor, upper and lower class seemed to put social stations away as the night extended well into the early morning hours. They were all Parisians and for a time, equal and free. At the end of the evening, Lautrec was in his usual stupor alongside Van Gogh. All the children had long since been put to bed, and the married couples had called it an evening hours ago. And as expected, many of the young people had coupled up, including Josay and James.

Josay liked James very much but in her heart of hearts, still found herself to be in love with Donnel. But when James kissed her after an especially romantic waltz, she did not resist.

"You are wonderful Josay," said James quietly.

Josay came to her senses and resisted her impulses to kiss him again, and perhaps to go even further. She had a very passionate spirit.

She blurted out, "I am almost engaged to my childhood sweetheart. It is true that it is not formalized, but please let's move slowly. I will need time. My head is spinning with the wine, the moon and stars. You are so handsome and charming and I love our friendship, but I must go home now and sort out all of these feelings. I need to get my life in order."

James allowed Josay to leave but only after she said goodbye and promised to meet him again in a few days. They parted with another small but warm kiss.

On the way home, Josay considered future negotiations for modeling with all the painters. She wanted to be in charge of her own time and think for herself for the betterment of her own life.

She had also been imagining another business venture that she would possibly propose to the influential people she had met and who now she considered friends. She knew that her next few moves would be critical and her presentation to them must be reasonable as well as compelling. This idea needed some research on her part but was exciting to her. *If I am successful, it might be possible to make things better for everyone all at once,* she thought.

She enjoyed thinking that her friends from Le Poulet had possibly had one of their most memorable evenings in a long time, and for that she was extremely happy. Josay again felt that she was a different person in Paris. She felt confident, self-assured, and unafraid in unfamiliar places or circumstances. She was equally comfortable with all kinds of people, whether they be rich or poor.

CHAPTER 8

Over the next several months, Josay Rue, daughter of a dairyman, had become the "toast" of Paris.

She had become famous and was invited to many social events. She had made many new friends who were influential and important in the society scene and was accompanied by a number of young gentlemen to parties and the best restaurants in the city. She was most often on the arm of James Sommes, but she was known to accept other men's invitations as long as they agreed that it would not be a romantic date, but an evening as friends only. She was still promised to Donnel and would not think of betraying him in any way.

Josay was also modeling, not only for Lautrec and the other radical painters of the time, but she had quickly become a model for many of the most exclusive fashion houses in Paris. Her time was highly in demand and she was becoming very successful in her career.

Sometimes she would be called to come quickly to model several gowns at a particular fashion establishment, and was unable to comply because she was already engaged on a runway of another fashion house. She was paid well, but sometimes her pay would be the gown or gowns that she was modeling that day. The dresses had always been altered to fit her figure so it all made perfect sense. She was now one of the best dressed women in Paris and was even beginning to start trends in fashion simply by wearing a dress at an exclusive restaurant.

She had been in Paris almost a year, and was now ready to make a big business move. She felt that she needed to take care of herself and her friends with a business of her own. She wanted to open a fashionable dinner club and restaurant in Montmartre. It would have lively entertainment and the walls would be decorated with the paintings of all of her artist friends. The patrons would then be able to buy the paintings if they wished. She would employ some of her friends from the Poulet which would give them a second chance to have better lives. The businessmen would make a profit from the success of the club and all would benefit. Today, she was going to present her proposal for this wonderful venture to her financial advisors and bankers, Monsieur Blanc and Mr. Hover.

As she waited in the lobby of the office, she thought of her parents. Josay had been regularly communicating with them via Monsieur Le Grande, the milk distributor. Every week she had heard about the farm, Mama, Papa and David. With the help of the bit of money Josay was able to send home, David had taken over the management of the dairy and in the past three months even negotiated the use of over a hundred more acres of pasture land. The land was still owned by the Count, but David was making a mark by improving their circumstances. Josay suspected that he was clearly cut out to be a farmer and businessman and that she needn't fret too much about him or her parents. This did not lessen the fact that she sorely missed them.

She had heard nothing directly from Donnel since the note he had sent to the Poulet which was delivered to her by his friend, Ollie. He was becoming a faint memory in the year since she fled her home. It was surprising to her how quickly her deep love for him had begun to dim. She wondered if he was feeling the same.

Why had he not sent any other letters? Surely something was different. Was he still worried about his father's threats? These thoughts plagued her sleep and she had no idea what she could do about Donnel's silence. All she could do is hope he would communicate with her soon.

She found that at the tender age of 19 years, she was able to afford her own place. She had moved out of Lautrec's flat and into her own small but fashionable house that overlooked Montmartre. The house had been repossessed from a client of Mr. Hover's who had fallen on hard times and was evicted. She had no difficulty making the payments Mr. Hover required, and was fortunate that the house had been tastefully furnished by the previous owner.

How could it be that I only had to meet people like Mr. William Hover and James Sommes before their priviledged world opened to me? I will be smart and frugal, and I will make the most of my good luck, she thought to herself as she waited for Mr. Hover and Monsieur J. K. Blanc.

She knew the success of a model was fleeting and could not last forever. She needed security. She called forth all of her inner confidence and grit and smiled pleasantly.

"Mademoiselle Rue, Mr. Hover and Monsieur Blanc will see you now," said the receptionist. Josay thanked him and walked through the open door into what she believed would be the most important meeting of her short life. *Be poised, confident, and self-assured*, she told herself.

"Mademoiselle Rue it is wonderful to see you again," said Monsieur Blanc the older and more senior partner as he kissed her hand. "You seem to have taken Paris by storm. Certainly you have brightened our 'City of Lights' and you look beautiful today—without peer."

Josay said nothing but gave Monsieur Blanc an even wider smile, head nod and curtsy.

Then she turned to look at Mr. Hover and said, "My dear Mr. Hover, it's wonderful to see you and thank you for taking this meeting."

She gave Hover her hand and he gladly took it and offered a lingering kiss to her knuckles. He loved his wife but seeing Josay always made him have butterflies in his stomach.

"Mademoiselle Rue, it is our pleasure to meet with you. I trust your new home is adequate for your needs and I assure you that you have given our institution considerable notoriety since we were fortunate enough to attract you. What is it, only a year ago?"

"You have a good memory, Mr. Hover," Josay responded and went on to say, "I hope we can become more involved with each other in business today."

"How can we help you, Mademoiselle Rue," said Monsieur Blanc.

"Please, both of you, call me Josay," she responded as both men looked pleased and gratified.

"I want to open a cabaret in Montmartre. It would have a stage, seat maybe 150 people and serve the best food and drink in the district. I have met wonderful chefs, entertainers, advertising people, and most of all I have a remarkable woman that understands the restaurant and entertainment business who will help manage it. I think you may have met her at the garden party at Monsieur Monet's, Mr. Hover. Her name is Madame Gloria Foote."

Gloria had fallen on hard times, thanks to her scoundrel of an ex-husband. He had falsely accused her of embezzlement when money he had stolen had been missed. He then took over her position as assistant manager of the successful supper club where they both worked. The owners had not pressed charges, but as a woman, she had little recourse but to leave in disgrace. She deserves another chance to live up to her potential. With a makeover and another chance, she could be a wonderful asset to my new venture. She had the talent and experience already. Besides, I really love her and trust her with my life, thought Josay to herself.

"Most importantly, Mr. Hover could be my business agent and monitor the money so as to protect your interests. I believe Mr. Hover and I would work well together. I haven't discussed it with Mr. Hover and perhaps he couldn't spare the time, but it would be my dream that he be involved in the project."

She looked into Mr. Hover's eyes and displayed her best smile. She had found this to be especially useful lately in both her modeling and in other dealings with Parisians, especially the men.

"I also have a very experienced businessman, Dr. Muse, who will help me manage the establishment and care for your investment. He is a former college professor of economics and a former business owner himself. He was also at the garden party. Do you remember him, Mr. Hover?"

"Yes. I actually do remember meeting Madame Foote and Dr. Muse. They seem very capable."

Blanc started to say something, but before he could get the words out of his mouth, Hover blurted out, "Mademoiselle Rue, I am beyond pleased that you would think of me. But there are many things to consider and discuss. I think we could, at the very least, come up with a plan to get you off to a good start."

Monsieur Blanc said, "Do you have a business plan, and are there other investors?"

"I do, and there are. My investors want to be silent at this time," responded Josay with her new skill of exaggeration.

"They are men of respect and only want to be assured that this venture will be top drawer and properly managed. I can have the facts, figures and other information you may require within a few weeks. If you draw up a list of questions you will need answered, I will make an effort to get those to you as soon as possible. I know we can be happy and successful in this business together. Let us clasp hands as we will long remember the beginning of this enterprise," said Josay with all the efficacy of a seasoned businessman.

She exited the meeting with her loveliest smile again and a small wink for Mr. Hover.

A few days later at Le Poulet, Josay talked over her plan with Madame Foote and Dr. Muse and found that they were more than knowledgeable about every aspect of the cabaret business and were excited about the prospect. Madame knew just where to get the talent they would need in the kitchen, dining area, and even the entertainment portion of the endeavor. Her experience as manager at the elite supper club would be invaluable for the start-up cabaret.

"I think we need not look further for a chef than the modest kitchen here at the Poulet," said Madame Foote. "Chef Paul is a wonderful and experienced chef, especially if he has quality food to work with. He has been much more mentally stable of late. The constant low spirits that were brought on by his wife running away with the Russian diplomat has run its course. He hasn't been drunk in months, and has been talking about looking for another position. You know that his talents are wasted in a place like the Poulet! I will talk to him about this right away."

"What do you think about having Big George as our bouncer and doorman?," asked Josay.

"I think that would be wonderful for him and for you. He is so devoted to you and loves you like a little sister. He would never let any harm come to you if it was at all in his power."

Josay giggled. "He really has changed his tune since that first night here at the Poulet, hasn't he?"

"How exciting, Josay! This could be a new beginning for us all. Thank you for even considering us for your new cabaret."

Josay hugged her and left for home. She had a supper engagement and she must dress for the evening. With corsets, underskirts and overskirts, getting dressed for an evening out could be very time consuming and complicated. She didn't have anyone to dress her and do her hair now that she didn't live at Le Poulet. Madame Dupree had taught her how to do it all herself, but it was a daunting task.

The only thing that worried Josay about Madame Foote was her ex-husband. It was well known that he was completely unscrupulous, and at times, violent. Madame Foote had confided to Josay that he now worked at the Follie Femme, which was located directly across from the location she was considering for her new cabaret. She hoped that it would not be a problem for Madame Foote to be in such close proximity to him on a daily basis. He had already wounded her all the way to her essence, and Josay didn't want him to have a chance to bring her down again.

She had no second thoughts about Dr. Muse. Sure, he had made a bad investment and lost his business, but he was very intelligent and highly educated and was capable of learning from his mistakes. He was already a dear friend and she found him to be caring and honest to a fault.

Josay opened her door to find Renoir standing with Camille Pissarro.

"We bring great news, Josay," said Auguste. "I sold my painting of you by the stream at the Salon to an American named Matthew Stewart. He paid top dollar and expressed interest in acquiring more of my work, and especially another painting of you. As we talked at the Salon, I mentioned that you were looking for investors in your cabaret and he said he might be interested. I think it's really that he just wants to meet you, but it could not hurt to have dinner with him at Maxim's if you're free tonight?"

Monsieur Renoir rushed from one topic to another with the exuberance of a child at play. He said, "Here is your check from the proceeds of the sale in the amount of 40 francs, as promised."

Josay was briefly overwhelmed and hugged Renoir as a child would hug a father. She was happier for him than she was for herself. To have a painting accepted by the Annual Salon in Paris was a big accomplishment. But to have that painting sell for a wonderful price was even better, and she understood the significance of this very good news.

"I am overwhelmed. Of course I'll have dinner, and yes, I'll sit for another painting."

The look on Renoir's face changed a little as he said, "He will want a partial nude. It will be tastefully done, but he insisted on that point. I know how you feel about that but it is, after all, art.

Josay found herself saying, "I trust you."

She partially nodded her head as if to say yes, in a childlike way, but without giving a verbal affirmation. Josay was becoming someone else at that moment. She exposed another trait she did not know she possessed. It was a "sophistication" about art and artists and the role that a model plays in the creation of that art. It seemed that the road to change and success was sometimes highlighted with small deviations and detours. Her reluctance to pose nude was becoming less important than it was only one year ago. She was now a professional model and most models thought nothing of posing in the nude for a tasteful and artistic piece. Her goals now were ones that she did not know existed before. She would be careful, but she trusted her friend Auguste to respect her in every way.

As Renoir and Pissarro departed, Camille called back to Josay, "You have the most beautiful face and heart I have seen in Paris. I know that someday you will remember today as a step toward a future that you cannot anticipate."

Pissaro, at that moment, was thinking of the decision he made all those years ago to leave the West Indies and come to Paris to become a full time artist. It had been a soul altering experience. It had left him and his family destitute at times, hungry at times, scorned as a Jew sometimes, but he was always satisfied that he was engaged in the thing his God demanded of him. He must create art. He felt that choosing art, for art's sake, would also be important in Josay's life, and he was very happy for her.

Josay had banked over 500 francs and had paid off the note for her small house in just a few months of modeling. James Sommes had agreed to pay 3,000 francs for a 10% interest in the business, and James' father, Marquis le Sommes had agreed to invest 2,000 francs for a 5% interest, only after James had browbeaten him over dinner and drinks. She thought Mr. Hover and Monsieur Blanc would loan her maybe 5,000 francs, at a reasonable interest rate, based on the very professional, but somewhat exaggerated business plan she had developed with Dr. Muse's help. She was still over 9,000 francs short of the amount she needed to acquire, build and outfit her cabaret, pay the staff, book and pay her entertainment and who knew what else. The meeting with the American, Mr. Matthew Stewart from Dallas, Texas, took on great significance. She wondered just what she might say to get him to invest.

CHAPTER 9

On her way to the dinner with Renoir and Mr. Stewart at Maxim's, Josay caught sight of a familiar looking woman. She was dressed in a colorful costume with heavy makeup and was surrounded by a group of people who looked as if they were part of a show or circus. As the woman passed a corner gaslight pole, it became apparent that she was looking at Madame La Plume, the villain that had robbed her on the road to Paris on her second night of exile. Josay gasped and stared at her, unable to bring her feet to motion. A sudden and violet temper was rising in her as the woman turned onto the broad thoroughfare, entourage in tow. They were all carrying signs and posters announcing The Great Madame La Plume's premiere tonight at the Montmartre club, "The Follie Femme."

One of the posters was Josay dressed in a circus outfit that she recognized as one of Henri Lautrec's. But then she saw a poster that was a copy of the Gauguin painting that La Plume had stolen from her. It displayed fully exposed breasts and had been altered to show most of the rest of her body. The only thing that was real about the poster was her face. Josay felt faint.

Before Josay could recover her full senses, the crowd and parade had passed by and moved on toward the hill that was Montmartre. She knew she needed to go to her meeting and nothing could be done at the moment. But something inside of her exploded and she found herself running after La Plume.

Just as she was getting closer, someone grabbed her arm and said, “Where are you going so fast?”

It was Lautrec.

“It’s her! The woman that robbed me! And now she is defaming me as well!” Josay said, breathlessly.

Barely able to stop her, the short and deformed and unusually sober Lautrec said, “Now is not the time. She is surrounded by her minions. Besides, I know her, that group, and where to find them. They would have no problem with hurting you. I have had dealings with them before. Come with me, we’ll have a drink and figure out what would be best to do.”

“I can’t right now. I must get to a very important meeting,” Josay said as she caught her breath and regained her control.

“Can I rely on you to help me find them later?”

“Of course, it would be hard **not** to find them I suspect. They seek the attention of everyone. It’s no secret where they will be. Come to my apartment tomorrow and we’ll talk.”

Josay thought that Lautrec might be the only person in Paris that she could trust about La Plume. He already knew her background and had been there from the start along with the Poulet gang. They, and he accepted her for who she was, not the subterfuge she was living while she played at being in Paris society.

“Au revoir, Mon Cheri,” bid Henri Lautrec.

When Josay arrived at Maxim’s for the dinner meeting with Monsieur Renoir and Mr. Stewart, the restaurant was already abuzz with laughter, smoke, song and the occasional scream of delight. It was a place of fine dining with a hint of scandal that the wealthy and social upper crust loved. It was a mixture of who’s who and who cares; a place of pleasure and a haven of forgetfulness, bells and whistles. In this place, the current toast of Paris could be mingling with the captains of industry, the disgraceful politicians, the nobility of many countries, tourists, beautiful men and women, surrounded by delicious wine and food. She loved it here. It was alive.

Josay was welcomed like royalty by the maître d’. “You look radiant.” he said. Josay was getting used to being recognized. The fact that Josay’s cheeks were still rosy from her recent abbreviated chase only enhanced her youthful natural beauty.

“Your guests have been seated at our very best table and await your arrival.”

Four gentlemen, not two as she expected, came to their feet as Josay arrived at the table.

“Please excuse me for being a bit late, I assure you, it could not have been helped.”

Josay was shocked for a second time today as one of the men at the table was Donnel, outfitted in his brass buttoned, red and blue velvet academy uniform.

“Donnel!” she said, as if scared by a ghost.

“I thought you might like to see each other,” said Mr. Hover. “He is here overnight with his regiment on the way to Belgium, I believe.

Monsieur Renoir thought I might be helpful tonight as well , so I came along. I hope you don't mind?"

"Of course," Josay said as she offered her hand and a warm hug to Donnel, Monsieur Renoir, Mr. Hover and Mr. Stewart in turn.

It was an odd feeling for Josay to be sitting at the same table with Donnel. He didn't seem the least bit excited to see her. Instead, his face was stern. He seemed to be angry.

Josay was surprised that she didn't feel the rush of excitement a young lover might feel upon seeing the object of her affection. Perhaps the old adage "absence makes the heart grow fonder" wasn't true after all. She actually barely knew him. Their romance had mostly been in their dreams and fantasies. She had been in his company only a few times in clandestine, or chance meetings in the village. Her cruel banishment had interrupted the natural process of getting to know him before making love to him. The high emotions of that situation had made her more vulnerable to making questionable decisions. The unchangeable reality was that they had made love and pledged to have a lasting future together. She had genuinely missed him and longed for those plans to come true, but as time marched on with no contact or communication, her feelings had slowly waned. She had not realized it until tonight. Tonight, she felt no passion for him as he frowned and ignored her.

Perhaps if I could just talk to him alone for a few minutes, our love could be rekindled, she thought.

They took their seats and the waiter poured bright bubbly champagne.

"A toast to our business venture and, of course, a night of entertainment and enjoyment," said Mr. Hover, having taken the leadership role for the meeting that was by rights Monsieur Renoir's.

"Shall we talk before we eat so we can maximize our time together by saving the most enjoyment as a celebration of business successfully concluded?" said Hover. Mr. Hover always had his business foremost in his mind, even though his hopes for all that the evening might hold were a close second thought. Having seen business dealings go out the window with the stale smell of drunkenness and over indulgence, he knew to talk first, play second.

Renoir started, "Josay and I have discussed creating a place where artists might display their works for sale on a rotating basis in an establishment of entertainment, food and happiness. We would be willing to split the profits of any art sales with Josay to enhance whatever usual revenues might be enjoyed by the cabaret. Josay found out only today artists and their work can bring significant money, especially in an environment supplied with art connoisseurs and well-to-do patrons." Renoir did not say it out loud but thought to himself, *especially when they are tipsy or trying to impress an associate or short term lover.*

"Wonderful idea." said Mr. Matthew Stewart who spoke perfect French, but with a Texas accent.

"Mr. Hover has shared your business plan with me and, of course, I have a few questions. None of them would keep me from wanting to be an investor. I will want to do my 'due diligence,' but unless I find something unforeseen, I want in for the entire 9,000 francs for a 25% ownership."

Josay was astonished, but not more than Donnel and Renoir. Nine thousand francs was not a great deal of money for the multi-millionaire American, but an enormous amount for anyone else at the table.

Matthew Stewart wanted a place in Paris to entertain and impress his friends and business associates. *Being part owner in a cabaret with the ravishing beauty, Josay, couldn't hurt. Hell, I would have paid ten times more to be in a business with her. Plus, I know that Mr. Hover will protect my interests. Win.. win.. win*, he thought.

"Now, business concluded, let's play," Stewart finished, with a full champagne glass in his raised hand.

Donnel stopped the toast by saying, "Don't I have a say in this venture? After all, it's my stipend and reference that has given Josay her start here in Paris."

Josay puzzled at the stern face Donnel rendered as he asked his mood killing question.

"I believe I should have the majority ownership. I would, of course, offer my dear Mademoiselle Rue a 15% ownership and a salary for her role as 'face' the cabaret."

Everyone looked at each other with astonishment, especially Josay as she replied with her now accustomed fortitude, "What are you saying? Of course I have appreciated your help and support over these past months and I am more than willing to give you a small share of the business, but it is my business."

"We'll see about that. Maybe Josay and I could have a small private conversation outside. Please excuse us gentlemen," Donnel said as he pulled Josay to her feet.

As the two departed, the three other men were dumbfounded but continued to celebrate. Since they could do nothing more, they had another drink.

Outside Josay was the first to speak.

"What in the world are you doing, Donnel? I thought you and I were in love and you would be happy for my success. Instead, you have ignored me for months and months and then you show up here with an angry face. What is going on?"

"I don't think a woman in love would be a whore. You belong in the gutter! Ollie told me all about your living with artists, posing nude, and today I even saw your body being paraded around the streets of Paris on a poster. I have seen you in the Paris newspapers pictured in restaurants and cabarets with other men. How could you expect me to continue to love such a disgrace? My father was right about you all along. You are nothing but an opportunistic, social climbing peasant who has made a laughing stock of me, both among my friends at the Academy and in our village! You have obviously been unfaithful and brazen. I hate you!"

"Come with me!" he growled as he grabbed her arm and pulled her into the alley before she could protest, or even respond, to these cruel accusations.

"Since you're a whore, I'll treat you like one." He knocked her against the wall and before she knew it, he had lifted her dress and was beginning to take her."

Josay tried to scream, but Donnel was large and fit. He covered her mouth and overpowered her easily. The rape was over before Josay could even believe this was the same person she had loved.

How could he have changed so much? she thought.

"Now, we'll go back inside and conclude the business. I want 20% and I'll let your family stay on the farm. But I'll expect you to service me any time I come to town from now on and you'll keep your nasty mouth shut."

"Donnel, you have everything wrong. Please let me explain."

He turned away from her and repeated, "Shut up! I don't want to hear any of your excuses. You disgust me."

Josay held back her tears by biting her lip as she straightened her dress and adjusted her hair. All of her life plans had turned in less than an hour. She went from loving him to hating him in an instant.

He is just like his father after all, a self-important arrogant brute. I don't know who this man is but I never want to see him again as long as I live, she thought.

When the two emerged from the street, Donnel said, "We just had a close call. While we spoke, a cart got free from its horse and knocked Josay and me into the alley. Luckily, we were not seriously injured, only a little disheveled."

Having finished his excuse for the look of Josay and her clothes, he went on to say, "We had, however already come to agreement on the business contract before the accident. I will accept a mere 20% ownership as compensation for these months of support. So, if my math is correct, that's 25% for Mr. Stewart, 10% for Mr. Sommes, 5% for Marquis Sommes, and 40 % for Josay. And Josay will be solely responsible for the 500 francs I loaned her initially, now being held by Mr. Hover and Monsieur Blanc.

All the men looked at Josay for acknowledgement.

With more of a whimper than a full throated acceptance, Josay said, "Agreed."

Still stunned and confused, Josay begged to be excused owing to a severe headache from the "accident."

When Donnel insisted on making sure she got home safely, he did not wait for Josay to object but helped her up. All of the gentlemen rose.

Josay mustered a smile and said, "Thank you all very much."

Outside, Josay drew strength from somewhere deep inside and slapped Donnel so hard he fell back into a vegetable stand filled with tomatoes. He lay in the red sludge matching his no longer starched and pressed uniform.

"I agree to your 'business proposal', but if I ever see you again, hear you've done anything to my family, or ever try to rape me or another woman, you will come to know my true dark wrath. Living in the gutter as you have said, I've come to know some very unpleasant fellows who would be most happy to cut you up and feed you to the hogs."

Then as if to highlight her threat, she kicked Donnel in the groin, turned on her heel and walked away, never looking back.

Josay waited until she reached Lautrec's flat before she began to fully realize just what had happened and she began to sob when she saw Toulouse.

"What has happened, my dear friend?" Lautrec asked as he threw open the door and guided Josay to the overstuffed blue chair in the corner.

Without omitting any details, Josay told Henri what had happened with only brief pauses to wipe her eyes and nose.

She finished by concluding, "He was the love of my life and he brutalized me in word and deed. Why? I don't understand. But in the span of only a few hours, I have gone from loving him, to hating him without peer. Can this all be real?"

Lautrec, finally having an opportunity to say something, said, "You need a drink. It has worked for me for years."

Josay did not refuse and the two drank absinthe until they fell asleep together in the large chair.

Renoir knocked on the door but there was no answer. The door was unlocked so he peered in to find his dear Josay asleep on the chair with Toulouse. He had wanted to ask Toulouse an important question before morning, but instead had covered the two of them with a blanket.

CHAPTER 10

Shortly after sunup the next morning, Josay opened her eyes to see a room filled with people busily moving furniture, sweeping, and cleaning. She could smell the wonderful sent of fresh croissants and cheese. As her eyes cleared, more so than her hungover head, she made out Renoir, Pissarro, and another man she could not place. She knew he was an artist she had met before but his name escaped her for the moment.

"Bon Jour," said Auguste, "I think you might remember our colleague Degas?

Josay nodded that she remembered.

"We decided that you needed a temporary office for your new enterprise. Since Toulouse now spends most of his days, and his nights in the taverns, and his flat is in Montmartre, voila', it's now also the office of Mademoiselle Josay Rue."

Degas presented a small sign that he had painted for the front door that read, "Josay Rue and Associates."

Toulouse will sleep either here, or in whatever home is most near when he passes out," said Renoir with a chuckle.

"But I have a house," said Josay

"What successful businessman lives in the office? You will need a private home to get away from work and to have a life of your own. Besides, Henri will actually get better rest and food with this plan. You will be here on a regular basis to make sure he is taking care of himself."

A just waking Lautrec nodded in approval. "That sounds great to me. I love having Josay around. Maybe she can keep me out of trouble," he said with a sleepy smile.

The next surprise was Mr. Matthew Stewart in the doorway.

"I need to get back to Dallas, so I brought my agent Mr. Sonny Bleux. He will help coordinate the procurement of the building site for our enterprise. He can also help with furnishing, decorating, and advertising at no cost to you and our partners. I have already established the necessary accounts at Hover and Blanc's to begin the venture. May I have one of those croissants? By the way, what are you thinking of calling the place?"

Josay shook her tangled red-blonde mess of hair and said, "Yes. I mean, of course, have a croissant. I was thinking of calling it Paradis Rue. It means paradise road in English."

In unison everyone repeated, "Paradis Rue," and began to slap each other on the backs, hug one another and congratulate Josay, Renoir and Stewart. It will be a great success for art and entertainment in Paris. Everyone agreed. Josay smiled, temporarily forgetting her trauma and hurt. She began to help them put a fresh coat of tasteful cream colored paint on the old walls of Lautrec's flat. They installed new curtains, a desk and a freshly beaten rug. Josay was amazed at the transformation.

Mr. Stewart had worked right alongside all the others and when they were finished, he said, "I have started many businesses, but I believe this one will not only be financially successful, but it will be a hell of a lot of fun."

The group had somehow swelled to twelve or fifteen people over the course of the morning and early afternoon. Josay approached one of the artists she did not know and said, I'm Josay Rue, et vous?

The man chuckled and said, I'm Gustave Caillebotte, we met briefly at Monet's house party. I heartily approve of this great venture. I mostly buy the art of these masters but also paint 'une petite.' It will be a joy for me to see them hanging in paradise." Everyone approved, and laughed.

The remainder of the week was spent with a whirlwind of meetings, toasts and planning. Mr. Bleux was really good at his job. He knew everyone. His association with Mr. Stewart, Mr. Hover, and the Sommes family, father and son, afforded him many fringe benefits. Most of the contractors charged less than they would have otherwise, because their involvement was 'almost' a favor to Josay's important partners. Josay learned to compliment, flirt, smile, and use her most agreeable personality at the meetings to enhance Mr. Bleux's straightforward, no nonsense manner. It was a natural and successful partnership. All the vendors, from the architects and local government officials, to the wine and beer merchants seemed to relish their participation in this venture and hoped to be able to come to the cabaret and claim an insider's part of the scene one day.

All the while, Josay continued to model for all the artists, and for several fashion houses. She was becoming almost as recognizable as her wealthy partners. And, although she had never forgotten about Madame La Plume, she had been able to control her anger and stick to business. She decided not to seek her out and cause a conflict just now since everything was going so well. Life and planning went on.

Josay received a letter from her family via Monsieur Le Grande on the morning the construction was to begin on a plot of land directly across from the square. It was a short distance down the hill from the Montmartre Basilica of Sacre'-Coeur. The land had been a stockyard and the entire community was glad to see someone build on the lot to rid the area of the unwanted smell of manure and animal sweat. The square itself had become a place for local artists to sell their works, and vendors of all kinds set up temporary stalls each morning to display everything from textiles to imported curiosities. In short, it was a place filled with life, passion and excitement. People from all social casts came to Montmartre to visit the chapel, shop the square and frequent the many night clubs and bars that were located all around the area.

As Monsieur Le Grande handed Josay the letter, he said in his heavy provencial accent, "I'm afraid this will be the last letter I will be able to deliver from your family. The Count has become very ill and since Donnel is the last living member of the Regis family and the sole heir, he has returned from the Academy to take over management of the family lands and businesses. For some reason, Donnel told me that if I delivered any more messages, he would make sure that my business would be over in his province. Furthermore, he said that he would certainly be watching his investment. You must know he has threatened to throw your family off the farm again and has made it difficult for all of us to trade with them or interact with them in any way. He does not seem to be the same man he was only a year ago when he went off to the Academy."

Josay thanked him for bringing the letter and asked him to wait until she read it. Monsieur Le Grande agreed and walked across the street to have a coffee in a sidewalk café.

My Dearest Josay,

Your brother, father and I hope you are well and happy in your new life. We are proud of you and all you have accomplished on your own. Monsieur Le Grande tells us you are well known, thriving and becoming an important person.

We have seen some of the posters and advertisements with your face and likeness here in the village and of course we wonder about them. Some of them reflect a life that we do not know or understand here in our little place. Your Papa is upset with some of them and I feel a little embarrassed too. David tells us not to worry and that they do not reflect the kind of woman you are or the kind of things you are doing in your life. Nonetheless, they have, for some reason, caused Donnel to impose more sanctions on us on the grounds of family immorality. He wants us to give over the farm and void our contract.

Papa is not well right now. David is handling most of the duties with the livestock and vendors while Papa advises him.

We aren't sure about our future here but we believe that David will help to pull us through. We are making money for the Regis family and that seems to be, at least for now, carrying the day.

Monsieur Le Grande tells us that he can no longer carry our messages but David assures Papa and me that he will find a way to communicate with you.

We don't know when we will see you and worry for you always.

With all our love,

Mama

Josay took only a few moments to dash off a few lines, understanding that Monsieur Le Grande needed to go about his business and was already looking impatient. So she wrote:

Dear Family,

I am well and happy. I have created a moral but different life here in Paris. I miss you all more than I can say but I understand that I cannot, at present, have the comfort of my dear family. Donnel has changed and I know why he has become even more hurtful. I assure you the source of his changed behavior has been the result of his own self-directed evil thinking. He has let lies and gossip color his perceptions and he has acted without seeking or giving an ear to truth.

You do not need to worry about me. In fact, I believe that I will be able to help you more in the not too distant future, from the proceeds of my new business. I know we will soon be reunited and can someday enjoy the comfort of togetherness.

Take care of Papa.

Your loving and devoted daughter and sister,

Josay

Josay gave the letter to Monsieur Le Grande, thanked him and as he was waving goodbye, she spotted Madam LaPlume on the other side of the Square.

Josay decided to approach the woman, but before she could say anything, Madame La Plume said, "I was wondering when we were going to meet. I search for you in the audience at the Follie Femme every night. I have not looked forward to seeing you again because I know I took advantage of you and created an enemy when we could so easily have been friends. We could have helped other, as you pointed out that night on the road. I have no real excuse other than to assure you that I have been abused in my life too, and learned long ago that sometimes one needs to take the advantage, rightly or wrongly, when opportunity presents itself. At any rate, I offer no excuses and fully expect you to hate me and treat me with distain."

Josay was almost speechless. This certainly wasn't what she expected to hear or feel when she finally came face to face with Madame La Plume. She thought she would hate the woman and had dreamed of ways to bring her to ruin and hurt. Instead, she had been, for the moment, totally disarmed.

She found herself saying, "You hurt me deeply and left me, an inexperienced and trusting girl, to potential lifelong harm or even death. But, as it turned out, I found my footing and survived on my own in this world of the 'haves and have nots' of Paris. I am not the weak trusting innocent you met along the road to Paris many months ago. Instead I am a woman of means with friends, partners and a direction for my life. I guess I sort of owe you a 'thank you' for making me stronger, even though you don't deserve anything but scorn and vengeance for your behavior."

"I have been following your rise to prominence, and, of course, I have seen your face all over Paris. You are on track to become quite famous in this city of shooting stars. I know because I have been in your shoes before. You may not guess that I was once the toast of the Seine. But because of an abundance of terrible mistakes, I have lost my footing in my career. I have lost love and the better life that everyone seeks. Is it possible for me to start our relationship over again? I will, of course, pay you for all that I stole and will do whatever you ask to make it up to you."

"I'm not at all ready to completely forgive you, but allow me to think about just how I can extract a fair price for the damage you have caused me. Meet me at my office in three days and we'll talk then."

Madame LaPlume agreed and Josay told her where to meet.

"I will bring that painting I took from you and the few little things I still have. I also apologize deeply for making Gauguin's painting of you into a more revealing advertisement poster for the Follie Femme Club. Gauguin was a frequent customer there where I did my act for several months. Every girl in the place knew to be careful of him. He's a married man but one would never know it by the way he drinks and seeks out women. I remember he was a part of your story that night we spent on the road."

"Yes, he's a part of the story and I would very much like to have the painting back. As for Gauguin, I'll deal with him myself," said Josay as she turned and walked away without a goodbye.

Her mind was turning with repressed hate and anger for Gauguin. As she moved away from Madame La Plume, it was beginning to overflow and explode. She suddenly reversed her direction to scream and let go of her negative emotion toward Madame La Plume, but La Plume had already disappeared into mass of people in the street. After staring at the crowd of unknown faces a few minutes more, Josay was glad that she had not totally vented her anger. She decided it was much better to save it for Gauguin.

CHAPTER II

Josay felt the early morning chill of a brisk wind coming through the cracked window in Renoir's parlor. She was standing semi-nude in front of a fireplace posing for Renoir, Lautrec, Degas and Monet. It had taken them weeks to get her to agree to pose, but now as she stood there with a towel covering her as if she were just getting out of the tub, she felt quite natural and safe. The session had been planned by the artists after much discussion and argument. Most wanted her to pose out of doors, but Josay would not allow that to happen again. And, although she was becoming much less modest with her modeling and fashion, something felt wrong to be without her clothes in nature. It was likely, she thought, because of that first painting she posed for with Renoir, Pissarro and Gauguin.

Josay had an important meeting with Madame La Plume tomorrow as well as a later meeting with all the owners to discuss progress on the construction of the Paradis Rue. The two messieurs Sommes, Mr. Hover and Donnel Regis had agreed to the meeting and Mr. Bleux was representing Mr. Stewart. So, as she posed, her mind raced with questions and strategies for both encounters. Josay could hear the artists quietly discussing the light, colors and shades of colors as they worked to create their paintings.

One discussion, however, was not about the current efforts but about the official Paris Salon's refusal to accept their paintings. If one happened to be accepted, it was put in an area with no lighting, or in a corner where it would not be seen. Each one considered the guidelines for submission of the art to be narrow, rigid and a means to suppress creativity and the advancement of artistic style and emotion.

Josay wasn't knowledgeable enough to follow all the technical talk but she did hear the raw emotion with which each artist expressed his opinion.

At last the time for posing was finished and Josay retired with the women around her to dress. The conversations among the women centered on the great hope that Josay's café cabaret would be a success and prompt the sales of many paintings. But there was one unexpected train of discussion.

Madame Pissarro said, "All of us here wish you the greatest success in your new business. But we feel somewhat apart from the joy of your enterprise because we know that we will be excluded from the nightclub. Our lives are not as exciting as yours and while it seems right for you to open such a place, average ladies like us will not be able to afford the clothes or the accessories necessary to look presentable. Even our best dresses would be considered as trash. We might be mistaken to be whores."

Josay had never thought of this kind of discrimination but what they were saying was certainly true. Either you were a high born aristocrat and able to come to a cabaret with your husband in all the right clothes and with all the luxurious accessories money could afford you, or you were a business woman of the night, peddling your body.

"I will find a way to have you all in my club. You are my friends and just like your husbands, you have helped make my life in Paris possible. I assure you that my establishment will be reputable and while I can't possibly keep certain types of people out of the club, I will ensure that anyone that comes to my place will be safe and respected, whatever they choose to wear."

All the women seemed to trust Josay and before she knew it the entire attitude of the women around her changed from duty to anticipation. Perhaps this place would offer some solace from their mundane lives of cooking, cleaning and taking care of children. As they helped Josay dress, they all seemed happier than Josay could remember.

When Josay returned to the room filled with canvases and paintings, she was overwhelmed with the colors of the oils, and the magic and creativity of each artist's effort. Every painting was different with a wide variety of brush strokes, shades of paint and interplay between light and shadow. All of the painters were looking at their colleague's work and offering critiques and advice. It was a metaphoric ocean of Josay images. In some paintings, the dreamy water was calm like turquoise glass, and in others it seemed to break as if a blue and white wave was crashing on the shore. They were all different and Josay imagined that they expressed the soul of their creator.

Josay said, "I am overwhelmed with your work. Surely these paintings need to be seen and admired by everyone."

"We agree," said Renoir. "But the established way to get your work recognized and reviewed is to have them displayed and judged at the Annual Paris Salon. Unfortunately, the rules and criteria for subject matter and style almost completely excludes our work from being accepted for entry. Last year when I entered the painting I did of you by the stream, it was marginally accepted on a technicality and actually sold. So what did they do? They changed the rules to keep that kind of effort from slipping through the cracks. We want to paint real people in natural places, not Greek gods and goddesses in Roman temples."

Everyone loudly agreed.

"But what are we to do?" asked Degas. "I am known for painting the opera and ballet, and I come from a classical and aristocratic artistic education. But I have grown to believe that my work , in many ways, is fenced-in by the Salon's backward thinking. Many of us believe we should have our own salon that would not limit any artist's subject matter or style. Our group has recently been labeled 'Impressionists', in part because of a critic's article that was meant to be negative. The art critic said that Monet's painting 'Impression, Soleil Levant' (Impression, Rising Sun) gave the impression of nature in an instant of time, but the painting itself seemed blurry and unfinished. It is actually a beautiful rendering. But since then, all of us have been labeled as part of this so called 'Impressionist' movement. Let us embrace this and stage our own salon."

"Oui," said Pissarro. "But how could we ever afford to stage such an exhibition? Most of us barely keep potatoes on the table for our families."

"Very true, Camille," continued Degas. "There must be a way. We just need to find resources. We must sell paintings and achieve some measure of success. Perhaps we could dedicate the revenues we hope to make from displaying our work in the Pardis Rue for the purpose of supporting a salon of our own."

Josay was the first to speak and said, "I will certainly donate my portion of the proceeds to your salon. And perhaps, I could influence a few wealthy men in the fashion and finance industries to invest in such a worthwhile project. Paris is all about life and beauty and there are many lovers of the arts who may also be risk takers. Perhaps it is time for them to take a risk for the sake of these beautiful works of art."

"Here. Here! Beautifully said, Josay," replied Renoir as he clapped his hands together with excitment.

Lautrec was popping the top of a bottle of wine as the entire group of artists, wives, and children in the room exclaimed a cheer for Josay's declaration.

"We drink to Josay, our future salon, and all of the arts and artists of Paris who long for freedom of expression," said Degas.

The rest of the day and evening was spent in celebrating, eating and drinking.

The next morning, Josay once again had a headache and thought to herself, *I wish I could exercise better judgement the night before important meetings.* At least she was in her own home and was able to bathe and prepare. But before it was time for her to leave for the meeting at Lautrec's, her headache had subsided. She looked and felt wonderful again.

She wore a bright blue dress that hugged her corseted torso and accentuated her small waist and youthful breasts. Her waist was small already and a restrictive corset was not something she preferred to wear, but this was the latest style of the day. The front of the dress was flat and sleek against her body all the way to the floor. The back, however, was bustled with billows of fabric and overskirts to make the derriere look full and fluffy. Her hair was twisted into a complicated but exquisite arrangement on top of her head. A small, flower-adorned hat angled downward toward her forehead. She wore white gloves and carried a parasol and small purse on her wrist. She was the picture of beauty and feminine style. She wanted to look her very best today.

"Bonjour, Madmoiselle Rue," Josay heard the voice of Madame La Plume saying just outside her door. "I am here on time, I hope."

Josay fully opened the door and was slightly shocked to see Madame La Plume in garish evening attire.

"Please come in," said Josay as she opened the door giving La Plume a full up and down look.

"I brought your belongings and the rolled up painting that I took from you on the road that regrettable night. And I have enough money to pay you for the other things I took, including the horse and wagon. I know it will not make up completely for my terrible behavior, but I was in an awful place at the time, without friends, family or resources. It was the only way I could see to save myself. It was unforgivable and I would not blame you if you threw me out and called the authorities to take me away. It is often said that you become like the people you surround yourself with. In show business, there are some mean and self-serving creatures. I was used and abused for many years and when you found me on the road that night I was trying to make my escape from a hurtful relationship and a profession of utter degradation. I was a good singer and performer but my manager, who was also my lover, made me provide sexual favors for wealthy customers. I was a show business prostitute in the truest sense of the word. So, when I was able to steal my show clothes and that old half dead horse, I made my getaway. I had been on the run for over a week, without money, food or plans when I met you."

La Plume began to cry real tears.

"Stop, please," said Josay. "Sit down," she continued as she felt her compassion overtake her. Josay could not help but hug the crying La Plume as she directed her onto the sofa.

Josay kept her arm around La Plume and said, "I have dreamed of the time when I would have the advantage over you and would be able to exact the revenge that you certainly deserve. What you did to me put me in danger of death. You left me with nothing but a dying old horse. Now as I see what I believe to be your honest and contrite explanation, your motives become more clear. I am not saying that I completely forgive you, but I do understand how hopeless a woman can feel in our society. I have been there too, thanks to you and others."

The two women, one middle aged with the lines of a hard life on her still attractive face, and the other a flawless beauty in the prime of her youth, sat on the couch for a few minutes before La Plume spoke again.

"I think there might be a way I can repay you in the future. I know you might have trouble trusting me, but I do know show business. I have seen most of the dirty tricks and I can assure you I know most of the people who can be trusted and those who would take advantage and steal from you without remorse. You are building a café cabaret, no? I could help you manage it, and keep you safe from the traps that you are too young and inexperienced to know about. I could also perform as needed to fill in or serve as an on-stage moderator. I would do this to make up for what I did to you for only room and board. I am, of course, available since my own entry into the show business of Paris was a flop. I'm sure you might think I'm doing this for myself again to take advantage of you. Truly believe me that, this time, I'm not just thinking of myself. I want to help you almost as much as anything I have ever wanted to do in my life. I want forgiveness, and a friend."

Josay was taken by surprise. This meeting was leading to an outcome she could never have expected. It was true that she was a novice when it came to managing and evaluating show people and cabaret acts. She had planned on leaning on Madame Foote's experience in that department but La Plume seemed to know the "dirty dealing" side of things that Madame Foote may not know so much about. Therefore, after only a moment, Josay found herself saying, "You sound sincere with what you are saying. I think everyone deserves a second chance in life. So, I think I would like having you as a friend and employee. I will watch you closely at first, but I think we could become successful together."

La Plume hugged Josay and said, "I promise you will never regret this decision. I will work to make your dream come true and along the way I can regain my vision of being a good person again."

Josay asked where La Plume was staying and La Plume said she had a week to week room just a short distance from Josay's house.

"Bring your things here and you can share my house. I will agree to give you a place to stay and food for your work until I am able to evaluate your worth to the project. In fact, I will take you to a meeting with my business partners this very day and introduce you as my show manager. I believe this second chance may be able to transform your life, and you can't have too many friends. Shall we shake on it as men do?"

"No," said La Plume. "We will embrace as women do."

The deal was concluded. Josay now had two of the kind of show business insiders her café would certainly need, Madame La Plume and Madame Foote.

After La Plume brought her trunk and a few carpet bags to Josay's house. It was fast approaching the time for the two of them to go to the Lautrec office for the meeting with Josay's business partners. Josay felt uneasy as she thought of seeing Donnel again. Just how could she be around him and work with him? She knew she must summon all her strength to face him for the sake of David and her family.

La Plume had quickly put on a more appropriate female businesslike attire, and together, they walked the short distance by way of the Montmartre square to Josay's office in Lautrec's flat.

As the two approached the makeshift office, Josay saw her brother David waiting just outside. She ran to meet him and they clung to each other in a deep and loving embrace.

"David," said Josay. "How I've missed you, Mama and Papa. Are they well?"

"Yes they are well but I came bearing bad news. Count Regis has died and left his property to Donnel. The Count had debts that must be repaid. And now that he has passed, his creditors are asking for repayment before the property can fully be established in Donnel's name. Donnel does not have the money that he needs to pay the debts. He wants to sell off property and the first thing he intends to sell is the dairy. He is asking for 1,500 francs and all we have is 500. We don't know what to do. He acts like he would rather boot us off the farm than offer us terms or give us more time to get the money. He has changed."

“That ruthless man. It seems impossible that he could have changed into such a monster in only a year and a half. How could I ever have thought I loved him? We need a plan.”

Madame La Plume having overheard the conversation said, “I have known many men like your Donnel. Perhaps I can make a suggestion?”

Josay quickly introduced David to Madame La Plume and responded, “By all means, please do.”

“Does he own any part of your cabaret project?”

“Yes. He owns 20 percent of it,” said Josay.

“Maybe we can get him to sell ten percent to me. I will offer to pay him 1,500 francs for the dairy if he gives me 10% of your cabaret. He would still own 10% of the cabaret and I would own the dairy outright. I will then sign the dairy over to you for the 500 francs that you have already. We would be in the cabaret business together because I would keep 10 % of the business. I can raise the 1,000 francs if you don't look too closely at the bargains I make with prospective vendors and suppliers for the cabaret. It will still be a win-win situation for everyone concerned. No one will be robbed, but I would need a month to put all the pieces in place. It is the least I can do to repay you for your forgiveness and kindness.

“Let's try to catch him before he goes inside and I will do the talking and negotiations. The entire plan relies on just how much he needs the money. I've dealt with his kind before and I think I can make it seem that I'm selling you out and deceiving you. That will surely sweeten the pot from his point of view.”

Everyone agreed just as they saw Donnel riding up on a white stud.

"What's this?" asked Donnel, "A group of low bred characters, I can assure you."

David struggled to attack him but Josay held him back and said, "I understand you are trying to take the dairy. I warned you not to try that ever again, but maybe we can do each other a good turn and all can be worked out for the best. This is my club manager Madame La Plume who has a business proposition for you before our board meeting."

Everyone stepped back and La Plume confidently faced Donnel directly and without fear. "It might be a good idea for the two of us to talk without Josay and David."

Josay tugged David's arm and they went across the avenue to wait for the outcome of the stand-up meeting between La Plume and Donnel Regis. The meeting was over in less than five minutes and Josay could see animation and some harsh facial expressions on both sides. But to her amazement, Donnel motioned for her and David to come back and announced that they had an agreement that made La Plume the new owner of the Rue Dairy and a part owner in the Paradis Rue, effective in one month's time. The details of the agreement were to be held in confidence until the final paperwork and payment details were completed.

They did acknowledge that they were going to ask Mr. Hover to draw up the legal documents with all the stipulations and requirements, and pending the final payment of 1,500 francs, after the board meeting. Without another word, Donnel and La Plume walked straight into the office leaving David and Josay standing in the street.

"Give my love to Papa and Mama and I will send a letter to you as soon as I am able to talk to Madame La Plume. If the Count is dead, I hope this means that I can safely resume contact with you, Mama and Papa. That is the only good thing I can say about this turn of events."

Josay thought to herself, *Have I been fooled by La Plume again. Was I a fool to so easily trust a woman that had so fully and hatefully betrayed me before? She now has a secret deal with my enemy and it involves my family's lives. I have no recourse but to trust her for the time being."*

She entered the office to see her partners all seated around the table. Josay felt a chill go up her spine as she sat in the same room with Donnel Regis.

The meeting was orderly and expedient. Mr. Bleux reported on the progress of land acquisition, architectural considerations, budgets and personnel. There were few questions and other than the introduction of Madame La Plume, there were no surprises.

At the end of the meeting, Renoir asked the board for their endorsement of the hastily proposed salon suggested at the meeting last evening. He went on to ask that the salon be scheduled as near in time to the opening of Paradis Rue as possible so as to capture and link the two events in marketing and excitement. The money needed for the salon would be borrowed and paid back when the paintings began to sell at the new cabaret. It would be a small amount, due to the fact that a photographer friend of one of the painters was willing to donate an office space that he was not using for a time. No one objected, but the full endorsement was tabled until the next month's meeting. Time would be given for Renoir and his colleagues to devise specific ideas for the marriage of the café and the salon of the rebellious impressionistic painters.

After the meeting, Monsieur James Sommes and Mr. Hover took Josay and Madame La Plume out for dinner and a festive evening. Thankfully, Donnel declined to go with them and Josay was able to breathe a good deep breath for the first time since she saw him.

They all enjoyed the evening and James insisted in taking the ladies home to Josay's house. He really wanted to talk to Josay about her attachment, or rather unattachment to Donnel Regis. The right moment did not present itself and he thought better of discussing it in front of Madame La Plume. He was very fond of Josay and had been since the very first time they were introduced. He and Josay had spent a lot of time together in the past year and a half and he was eager to take their relationship to a more serious level as soon as possible. She seemed to be fond of him but he felt it time to find out just how fond of him she was. But, unfortunately that discussion must wait.

CHAPTER 12

Josay had always known that Mr. Stewart had feelings for her and wasn't investing in her cabaret simply because he found it to be a potentially lucrative venture. She had encouraged the flirtation, not only because she wanted him to help with the project, but because she felt a strong attraction to him. She had kept him at arm's length so far because of her commitment to Donnel, but that was no longer an issue. When Mr. Stewart came to town this week, Josay decided to finally accept one of his many invitations to go out for dinner. She suggested they go to Montmartre to see and dine at "The Follie Femme" with Madame La Plume.

She justified the acceptance by telling him that she needed to introduce Madame La Plume, her newest business partner. He had been unavailable and absent from the last board meeting and hadn't met her as yet. She had also told him that she wanted to preview a few acts that Madame La Plume thought might be good enough for the opening of Paradis Rue. But she knew the real reason was to see Matthew and to test her new feelings for him in an exciting atmosphere.

Mr. Stewart was right on time and Josay and La Plume had almost finished getting dressed to go out. The truth of the matter was that Josay was ready, but she knew it was better to make a man wait a few minutes. La Plume greeted Mr. Stewart and introduced herself to him while Josay made final touches to her makeup that weren't really needed. La Plume was adept at charming men herself and although she was already thirty five, with makeup, she sometimes looked younger than that. She was more than able to hold her own with men in any conversation. When Josay finally joined them, she entered a room already bubbling with laughter and charm. Josay greeted Mr. Stewart with a small curtsy and offered her hand which Matthew promptly took and kissed.

"I see you two are already acquainted," she said. "Shall we go? I'm excited to see The Follie Femme and to preview the acts for our new cabaret. I have also been eager to spend the evening catching up with you, Matthew," she finished, with her most inviting tone and manner.

He was a very physically fit man of 33 years and was just under 6 feet tall. He had light brown hair with sun-bleached blonde highlights and aquamarine blue eyes. His face had a healthy tan and his cheeks often turned pink when he laughed or became excited about something.

Matthew looked amazing to Josay. He wore the latest men's fashion in eveningware and the narrow blue tie he wore around his neck, complimented his eyes. His top hat and white gloves finished the look which made Josay's heart flutter. She had to make herself look away so as not to stare at him. He was the most beautiful man she had ever seen in her young life.

Outside, the three were welcomed by the footman to climb into a most fashionable and elegant coach. It was the finest transportation

Josay believed she had ever seen. When inside the cab, Matthew seated himself on Josay's side and used his cane to signal the driver to get underway to the cabaret.

When the three arrived and entered Follie Femme, Josay had never seen such an exotic place.

The décor was garish red and black with gold touches. But with low lighting, it was rather elegantly appealing when paired with the velvet and satin curtains and furniture. The music filled the air and the sweet smells of perfume and aromas of fine dining mixed to create a heavenly olfactory experience. Sights and sounds blended together to carry Josay away into an expectation of sensory pleasure. She was determined to fully experience this place and to allow herself to have full enjoyment of the vogue Paris nightclub scene—especially since it would be with Mr. Matthew Stuart from America!

He had a manly strength with unwavering confidence, without being unkind or overbearing. This was his most attractive feature to Josay. He made her feel safe and comfortable when in his presence. He had a jovial and witty way of speaking, and his Texas accented French was very endearing.

When they stepped inside the club where La Plume had recently been employed, they could hear a vibrant musical revue taking place on the stage.

All were greeted by a familiar doorman. "Bonsoir, Mademoiselle Rue, and welcome to Follie Femme," said a decked out Big George. He looked wonderful in his evening attire.

"Good evening to you, George," she said with a slightly puzzled look.

After they had checked their coats and hats, Madame Foote, who was obviously acting in a managerial position here, said, "Good evening, Mademoiselle Rue."

She showed them to the best table in the cabaret.

"It's lovely to see you tonight, Madame Foote."

They hugged and she whispered in Josay's ear, "May I talk to you privately in the powder room in a few minutes?"

Josay smiled and nodded almost imperceptibly, but sat down at the table with Mr. Stewart and Madame La Plume.

As they took their seats, they spotted the elder Monsieur Sommes who was asked to join them. Marquis Le Sommes, was with a beautiful dark haired woman he introduced as Madame Sussee Bonne, an old friend of his departed wife and a business associate.

"Where have you been hiding this beauty?" said Matthew of the still very attractive woman.

"Far away from you to be sure," he responded and everyone laughed as Mr. Stewart kissed her hand and expressed his joy of meeting her.

"Are you from Paris?" asked Josay.

"No. I'm from Normandy. I met Monsieur Sommes because he and my husband did business together. We have vineyards and apple orchards. I understand that very soon we will be doing business with you at the Paradis Rue. I am so excited. You will all come to my estate someday, of course."

Josay immediately liked her and gave her a sincere embrace.

Josay spoke without thinking of any ramifications, “My family has a farm and dairy.”

“Of course. Where is your farm?’

“It’s much nearer Paris than Provence. We will have to share a coffee and talk about farming someday.”

Before the meal was served, Josay excused herself to go to the powder room. She really wanted to know why Madame Foote and her other friends from the Poulet were here tonight.

Madame Foote joined her in the powder room and spoke quietly and excitedly. “I incredibly found someone to buy that dump of a Poulet which will cover my outstanding debts. You may remember Dominque the bar maid and part-time bartender? She recently married a man of means who was willing to buy it. Most of the same people still live there, including me, but I will be glad when I can afford to move out.

“I was able to negotiate a job for me here as the food and beverage manager. Then I hired Chef Paul as a sous chef in the kitchen, and Big George as the bouncer and doorman. Then I recommended Dr. Muse as a bookkeeper. I thought the four of us could get more experience for our future at the Paradis Rue, and the money will help us to live until it opens.”

“That was an excellent idea, but I thought that your scoundrel of an ex-husband worked here!”

“He was beaten and thrown out on the street two weeks ago, and told to leave town forever or face dire consequences from the owner here.”

Josay smiled happily, “Good riddance to smelly garbage.”

She dashed back to the table before a very fine meal of escargot and sea bass was expertly served, there were several champagne toasts and the atmosphere could not have been more joyful.

The house lights dimmed and the stage lights came up indicating that the show was about to begin. First there was a dog act from Russia, then a juggler from Egypt, and a fat tenor from Italy. And finally, as the orchestra began to play a melody of the new and popular rage in Paris, out came the chorus of show girls to dance the "cancan." It was magical, sexy, rousing and unbelievably festive. Everyone clapped to the time of the music and the women didn't seem to mind a few breasts that came loose from there tethering or the flash of silk underwear and striped hosiery. It was Paris in a nut shell and Josay would certainly have girls dancing the cancan at the Paradis Rue.

Mr. Stewart, like all of the other men, was naturally mesmerized and enchanted by the beautiful scantily clad women on stage. But, more than that, he was under the spell of the music, wine, and the gaiety of the entire experience. It was all part of the beauty of Paris—"The City of Lights"—which could transcend all problems and worries. It made Matthew ever more attracted to the apple-cheeked, strawberry blonde beauty that was Josay.

He put his arm around her and her body began to tingle all over. She looked up at him, and he kissed her in a passion driven force that took Josay's breath away. Whether it was the mood of the music, the bubbles of the champagne or the piercing blue eyes of Matthew Stewart, she fell headlong in love at that very moment.

After the show, La Plume introduced the owner of the cabaret, Monsieur Phillipe Voight, who had come over to their table to greet them.

He spoke over the laughter and mirth in the room, "I hope you are having a wonderful evening. Very nice to see you again, Madame La Plume. I hope you don't blame me for your recent misfortune. You understand, of course, that the reason you were asked to leave was just a business decision."

"Of course, and I have landed on my feet with these lovely people who are soon to be your competition."

"Paris is big enough for lots of cabarets, and Montmartre is just the place to cluster them together," he said to Josay. "I welcome you to the neighborhood," he continued, as he winked at La Plume.

After meeting the acts La Plume wanted Josay and Matthew to see, and as they were leaving, a drunken Toulouse approached them.

"Mon petite Josay and Monsieur Stewart, will you join me and my companion, Mademoiselle Dupree, for a drink?"

Josay recognized the prostitute from Le Poulet who had been her friend. They had not seen each other for over a year.

"I must decline," said Matthew. "The hour is late and I must get these lovely ladies home."

"Oh, I insist," said Lautrec as he lost his footing and fell into Josay, grabbing her dress to stabilize himself. The dress ripped from the top which exposed a portion of her left breast as he fell anyway and hit the floor.

"Henri, I think you have gone too far this evening. Time to go home," said Josay.

Josay covered her breast with her hand as Lautrec was saying, "My apologies, but please let me make up for it by buying a bottle with my last franc."

Before Mr. Stewart could punch him, Josay came to Henri's rescue by saying, "It's alright, Matthew, Henri is an old friend who has overindulged in celebration tonight."

Big George lifted Lautrec up, put him over his shoulder and out the back door. Josay was hoping that Madame Dupree would take care of him until he slept off his drunkenness.

These episodes were getting more and more common, she thought to herself with dismay.

Outside the Cabaret, La Plume lingered and told Josay, "I'm going to go back and talk to a few of the best girls to see if I can count on them to come to the Paradis Rue when the time is right. I'll see you tomorrow."

La Plume disappeared back into the café. Inside the Follie Femme, La Plume motioned for Phillipe Voight, the ruthless owner of the cabaret to come to the office door on the side of the building. Inside, La Plume took a seat in an overstuffed leather chair and took a cigar from the humidor and lit it. As a slow puff on the cigar yielded a circle in the air, in walked Phillipe who had a large scar on his otherwise handsome face.

"La Plume, I told you never to come back here," said Voight.

"I think you'll be happy I did," said La Plume. Fate has smiled on me yet again and I have wonderful news for you that will get me back in your good graces."

La Plume and Voight had been lovers while she had worked for him at the cabaret, and despite trying not to, she had fallen in love with him. He was a ruthless brute, but he was smart and even more devious than she. She was desperate to get his attention and affection again.

La Plume went on to tell Voight about her bargain with Donnel Regis and how she might be a part owner of the Paradis Rue and owner of a dairy farm. All she needed from him was a few francs, 1,000 to be exact, her old job back and a little help with the plan. She promised him that if all went well they could be in total control of the Paradis Rue.

"Alright La Plume, how do I know that you can make something like that happen. You lie through your teeth as well as you breathe."

"It's as easy as eating a French pastry! Josay Rue may seem to be a business savvy celebrity model, the hoity-toity 'toast of Paris'. But I know she is a naïve little farm girl. I am privy to all of her secrets and I manipulate her like clay. And I am living in her house and can keep my eye on her every move."

As always, Voight was interested in lining his pockets and asked for more details that La Plume quickly delivered. After an hour or so, they hatched a fool proof plan to acquire the Paradis Rue. They shook on it, and the handshake led to more intimate relations that lasted the entire night.

The love making meant a lot more to her than it did him. He was tired of her. He had his pick of many younger and more attractive girls. But he decided that he could force himself to tolerate her until this business was completed.

Mari was satisfied that pulling off this plan together would be the glue that would solidify her relationship with Phillipe. She would do anything to be near him and this would be her ticket to love and a future. She was sure of it. She was so close to having everything she ever wanted.

Josay and Matthew got out of the beautiful coach at the Ritz and with a kiss for an invitation, the mildly buzzed couple went straight upstairs to Matthew's candlelit suite. As the door closed, Matthew gently turned Josay's face toward him and kissed her full lips very softly. His kiss made her whole body tingle again. She looked into his beautiful eyes and kissed him back with the fervor and passion of a young girl in love.

He was very aroused by this amazing girl. She was not only beautiful beyond compare, but she was so smart and kind. He noticed that everyone at the nightclub seemed to know her and love her and she returned their love in a sincere and generous way. She had never even been to that club before. *Does she know everyone in Paris? he thought.* But most of all, she made him feel young and alive and he loved that feeling, and he loved her.

He carried her to his bed. They were soon completely naked in the soft glow of the candlelight. He began to run his fingers lightly up and down her body while kissing her all over. Her whole being ached for him. Soon the bed covers were pulled back and the two were enmeshed in each other's arms.

Then their bodies finally became as one as he whispered, "I love you, Josay. I love you. I never want to be without you again as long as I live."

It was so much more romantic and sensual than the only love making she had ever known. Josay remembered the loss of her virginity with Donnel and the hateful rape she experienced with the same man. Matthew was a careful and slow paced lover. He was experienced and used all of his skills to pleasure her. Josay never realized that intercourse could be so satisfying and fabulous. After several hours of making love, the two fell into a deep sleep, enfolded in each other's arms. Only the bright sunshine awoke them in the morning after a full night of what one could only call, "heavenly."

Matthew asked Josay to meet him in a few days when he returned to Paris from a necessary business meeting in Normandy. Of course, Josay agreed dreamily, as they parted. Josay kissed him deeply and felt a joy and comfort in her soul that she had never known before. She did not want him to go. She wanted him to never leave her presence again, ever. She was madly in love with him, but she knew that he must go take care of his business.

"Goodbye my dearest Josay, I will be back as soon as I can. I truly wish I didn't have to go because I can't get enough of you."

He turned and left her in the room to dress for the new day.

CHAPTER 13

Mr. Stewart never came back to Paris from his Normandy business meeting. His agent Mr. Bleux hand carried a letter from Matthew that explained that he must return to the USA for the most urgent reasons that he did not explain. He did, however, express his great love, and expectations for a happy reunion in the next few months. Josay was saddened by this, but thought she could certainly use her time well in his absence with meetings, modeling, and working toward the opening of the Paradis Rue.

Among her whirlwind of meetings and work, Josay happily reunited with her artist friends to get their salon in motion. The league of rebellious painters and artists embraced the name 'Impressionists' and began to use the term themselves. Monet, Renoir, Pissarro, Cezanne, Sisley and Degas had taken leadership roles, but all the painters and sculptors joined in the planning sessions that usually morphed into festive celebrations of food and drink. These occasions sometimes involved even wives and children. Josay was always glad to be included in those meetings and celebrations. It was her sincere desire to help them in any way that she could, and that meant she must get her cabaret up and running to feature their art. She was eager to do just that.

Mr. Bleux took Josay, Madame La Plume and Madame Foote aside and told them that he had heard of a new building ordinance being developed. He suspected that it was coming from someone in the Paris underworld who had some measure of influence at city hall. Officials were known to take bribes on occasion and this might be just that. Furthermore, he thought it might be detrimental to their plans to get the Paradis Rue finished on time. Although he had a good handle on such people in the manufacturing business, he felt completely out of his element in the bar, restaurant and entertainment industry. He had no clue who was trying to sabotage their project.

Madame La Plume was quick to take over the conversation by telling everyone about her experiences with this kind of blackmail at the Follie Femme.

"I lost my job when I stood up to what I thought were idle threats from the back street villains of Montmartre. They are well united and have their grips on the politicians who make most of their money through graft and corruption. We need to tread lightly, but I know just how to handle these underhanded scoundrels."

"We are so fortunate to have you to help us wade through this swamp. I suggest that you investigate these people and advise us at our next board meeting in one week's time," said Bluex.

Mr. Bluex asked Josay if she could get Dr. Jacque Muse to help him with the office work. He reminded them that he worked first for

Mr. Stewart and the volume of time he was spending on the Paradis Rue project was putting him off course.

"He is working part-time for the Follie Femme right now, but you are right. He would be a great help with the bookkeeping, and could be your liaison with our financial firm of Hover and Blanc," replied Josay.

La Plume found this to be a perfect solution. Dr. Muse was getting in the way at the Follie Femme. If he found out what she and Phillipe were doing to foil Josay's business, he would warn her and ruin their plans. She needed him to go elsewhere without creating a scene.

La Plume spoke pleasantly, "I will ask our friend Mr. Voight at the Follie Femme to release him from his duties and loan him full time for the next few months to the Paradis Rue project. I will also insist that Mr. Voight keep him on salary as a small contribution to the effort."

La Plume couldn't stop the slightly evil smile, with her left eyebrow cocked, that crept onto her face. Luckily for her, no one noticed it.

Renoir asked, "Would Dr. Muse be able to help us with the Impressionist Exhibition as well? As artists we aren't good with numbers and contracts. I see these two ventures as twins from the same lovely mother."

Josay looked to Mr. Bluex who said, "I think that will be an excellent idea. Dr. Muse can have a small desk in my office to meet with associates and handle inquiries for both businesses."

Just as the group began to leave, Madame La Plume pulled Josay to the side. "Sometimes these things turn into dirty business. I want you to keep yourself far away from any possible accusations of corruption. I am very capable of swimming with these sharks and whales. I know what they want and where they are vulnerable. The less you know about what I'm doing, the better. I will take Dr. Muse under my wing, as well, to keep you at a distance from any suspicion of wrong doing. You just keep modeling and using your influence as the 'face' of the business until all of this storm has past."

Josay hugged her and responded, "I don't know what I would do without you."

Then La Plume said, "I want to move our office out of Lautrec's flat. It does not often present the best environment for any of us. I will thank him for his loyalty and the use of his home, but it's time to move on. In the future, we will call Mr. Bluex's office, our office, and Dr. Muse's desk, our business center. I know Mr. Stewart will agree."

"I'm sure he will and perhaps we could muster up a table and a few chairs in the alcove where I planned to put Dr. Muse. Now that I have Dr. Muse to help, I can provide some secretarial, filing and clerical help as well," finished Mr. Bleux.

"Before we all depart, Monsieur Lautrec has invited everyone to a new club in Paris called 'The Beaumont', which is near the Arc de Triomphe on the Champs-Elysees. He is doing advertising posters for them and said that if I would agree to be sketched tonight, the club would allow for eight or ten of us to have a lite dinner, a few drinks and we could all stay to see the show."

Madame La Plume, Madame Foote, and a few of the artists were quick to express their interest in attending. Mr. Bluex excused himself because he had a previous engagement and promised to inform Mr. Stewart and the other board members of the office and personnel decisions.

"Tonight then," said Josay as the group departed.

Madame La Plume went straight to Mr. Voight's office at the Follie Femme.

"Our plan is working. They took the bait. Using your influence to get those ordinances put into place has worked. Josay and the others are like fish that are hooked on a tight fishing line. Even Mr. Bluex took the bait. I was also able to get rid of that pesky Dr. Muse. We need to get Monsieur Donnel Regis wrapped up as well. His jealousy and hate for the Rue family can be easily turned against him. I'm sure we can get all of his ownership in the Paradis Rue, and the dairy farm without much effort."

"What's next?" asked Monsieur Voight.

"We need for one of your minions to post a 'work stoppage' notice at the Paradis site. It will allow me the leverage, and I need to pull this off. I can't believe she is so naive and the artists and other businessmen are so trusting. This could be one of our easiest and most profitable cons."

Josay had never seen anything like this, the largest night club in Paris proper. It was three times the size of the Follie Femme and probably twice the size of the planned square footage of the Paradis Rue. The group was seated in the front row of tables, but off to one side so that Lautrec could sketch Josay and also approach any woman he fancied to pose for him during the evening. He was a well-known figure now and within minutes the table was surrounded by show folk, prostitutes, and other café regulars from every social station. Everyone liked Toulouse and were eager to engage with him. He was charming and fun and always the life of the party. But tonight he was in his work mode and went right to work sketching Josay.

Josay was wearing a bright emerald dress with gold trimmings and a shiny gold comb in her hair studded with green glass stones. The green accentuated her green eyes, and with her reddish blonde hair, it was a striking combination. Josay was easily the most beautiful woman in the room. Everyone knew her from her posters all over town and she was treated like a celebrity. So much, in fact, that the owner of the cabaret came over to her table and brought a fine bottle of champagne, on the house, to make a toast and to be seen with her.

"Your beauty in these lights enhances the entire room, my dear," gushed the Beaumont manager. "You are welcome to come here anytime you like."

"Thank you, Monsieur. It is my pleasure to be here."

Also, we offer our sincere thanks to you for agreeing to model for our newest poster display. It will highlight the popular rage of cancan dancing and our great guest singer from the United States, Miss Dorothy Adolphus. Please enjoy the dinner and show and if I can do anything to make your evening better please do not hesitate to call on me directly." he said as he clicked his heals and bent over to kiss Josay's hand.

The show began. Josay and all the nightclub patrons were taken to the highest mountaintop of emotion immediately when the cancan chorus girls came out and danced to the wildly exciting music of the expert orchestra. The skill and beauty of the dancers and quality of the musicians far exceeded anything Josay had ever seen or heard. It was far better than the show at Follie Femme which Josay had loved. The cancan girls surprised everyone when they came back on stage in response to a thunderous ovation for a bare breasted encore. The initial gasp from the audience turned into an uproar of approval especially from the men, but also cheers of delight from the women. It was sexy, thrilling and artistic at the same time. Josay was carried away. She would have to work very hard to compete with this kind of entertainment.

The headliner of the evening was a tall beautiful brunette wearing a sparkling red gown and a diamond tiara. Miss Dorothy Adolphus sang in a way that Josay had never heard. Her voice was crystal clear, strong and true, even when reaching the highest notes possible. It carried Josay's mood from the peak of happiness to a depth of emotion that brought tears to her eyes. The audience was completely enraptured with every new ballad. When she exited the stage for the final time, after several encores, Josay was very sad that her act was over. Miss Adolphus was a real star with talent that thrilled and lit the room and everyone in it. *I would love to have her sing at the Paradis Rue*, thought Josay.

When Miss Adolphus had finished, La Plume excused herself, ostensibly to talk to the dancers and artists back stage. Her real mission was to slip away from Josay in order to spread her poison among the cancan girls and especially Miss Adolphus. She told them all in turn that Josay's new café was going to be tied up in litigation and that there were ownership and management issues with this very inexperienced venture. She swore them all to secrecy. La Plume was a silver-tongued devil, and had the knack for becoming everyone's trusted friend in an instant, as she had so aptly demonstrated with Josay herself. When she talked to the manager, she was sure to tell him to be on the lookout for the Paradis Rue to try to steal his best help and entertainers.

In only half of one hour, she had sewn seeds of resentment, mistrust and distain so deep that it would surely cripple the Paradis Rue project among the show business people for months to come. Josay would need a miracle to get her club off to a good start. Asking everyone to keep the secret from Josay was the final insult. It showed just how adept La Plume was at sabotage.

Josay was still a celebrity in Paris and she could be used until she became a problem. La Plume convinced them all that she would stay close to watch Josay as the silent representative of the Follie Femme, the Beaumont and the other good establishments of Paris.

When the night was over, Toulouse showed everyone his drawing of Josay as a celebrity watching Miss Adolphus. All who saw it thought it was wonderful, including Josay. The drawing became a poster, and in less than a week Josay's face was all over Paris advertising the Beaumont and Miss Adolphus. It made her even more famous.

CHAPTER 14

Josay was in such demand with her modeling, she had no time for the complicated issues with permits and regulations for the cabaret. She was relieved it was being handled by Madame La Plume. Josay carried on making money and earning an increasing amount of fame and celebrity in Paris.

Josay was also quite involved with her artist friends and their salon planning. They had secured the venue which was to be at 35 Boulevard des Capucines. It was set to open on April 15th and would run for one month. The paperwork for their small loan from Blanc and Hover was signed, and the project was set into motion. Josay's picture at the stream by Renoir was to be the logo for the exhibit and Lautrec set about producing posters and other forms of pamphlets and flyers to be used to get the word out about the event. Everyone was extremely excited and, as always, Lautrec had a party at his flat where everyone toasted each other, especially Josay.

Over the next few days, Josay was beginning to feel comfortable in her role as entrepreneur and model when she received a note from Mr. Bleux that she needed to come to his office as soon as possible. As

Josay entered the outer office she saw that the little desk in the corner where the Paradis Rue had been conducting its business had been pushed into a corner. There were piles of paper work in the trash and on top of the little desk. When Josay walked into the room she saw a grim faced Bleux and Madame La Plume.

"I'm very sorry to tell you that Mr. Stewart is withdrawing from the Paradis Rue project," said Mr Bleux after taking Josay's hand to greet her. Mr. Bleux was always quick to the point and although he usually conducted business without emotion, Josay read sadness in his voice.

"But why? Is it the legal difficulties and problems?"

"I'm afraid not, Josay. I am embarrassed to tell you that Mr. Stewart is a married man with two children. His wife has discovered that you and he were engaged in a romantic as well as a business relationship. She has forced him to liquidate most of his businesses in France and sever all dealing with the Paradis Rue. He will not be coming back, and he has told me to deliver this letter to you personally. I regret that I, too, must leave your enterprise as the principle business manager. Mr. Stewart has authorized me to surrender all of his interests in the Paradis Rue to you, and to take a few weeks of my time to help you get apprised of the progress, as well as the difficult position your business is in currently."

Josay blinked back tears of shock, mingled with a form of deep grief as she took the letter that Mr. Bleux handed her.

As Josay made an effort to speak, Madame La Plume said, "I, too, am sorry to bring you ill tidings on the government issues. You might as well get all the bad news at once. It seems that now that you have Mr Stewart's portion of the business, it is clear that you cannot, by ordinance, be the principle owner of this kind of business. Current law forbids any woman under the age of 30 years to own a cabaret. I have contacted the messieurs Sommes and neither one of them want to continue with the project as principle owner or managers. It looks as if you will need to find another partner willing to accept primary ownership of the business in your stead."

Josay's head was spinning and she couldn't seem to understand just what was being said at the moment.

She finally responded, "Both messieurs Sommes want out of the business too? But we're friends and I'm sure that if I talked to them they would want to continue."

"I just came from a meeting with them and they are in a difficult position as well due to the revelations of your affaire with Mr. Stewart coming into full light. The older Monsieur Sommes has had some difficulty at home with his lady friend, and I think the younger Monsieur James Sommes is especially hurt to know of your relationship with Mr. Stewart. At any rate, both of them want out of the project and have asked me to help Mr. Bleux find a suitable business solution to the entire mess."

Josay was stunned. In the course of five minutes, she had lost what she felt sure would be the love of her life, and the business project of her dreams. Wide eyed and with the backbone she had developed in the past year and a half, she gathered herself up enough to say, "I see. Well, I guess Madame La Plume and I will need to find a new path for the Paradis Rue and I will need to make a few adjustments to my personal life. Mr. Bleux, will you please excuse me so that I might think about all that has been said."

"Of course. Please feel free to use my office," said Mr. Bleux as he bowed and left the room.

Before he had fully left the room, Madame La Plume had Josay in a sympathetic embrace and offered her a handkerchief. Josay's face showed overwhelming grief with open sobs breaking through all of her best defenses.

"There, there," said La Plume. "We will get through this and come up with a solution that solves the business problem. But I fear the loss of Mr. Stewart will be the more difficult disappointment to navigate."

Madame La Plume was an expert in knowing just what to say while hiding the fact that inside she was jumping for joy at just how well this con was going. She never could have guessed that the gift of Mr. Stewart's home life problems would work out so well. She knew the letter she had sent telling Mrs. Stewart about Matthew's affaire would eventually turn the tide toward her ambitions.

"Let's get out of here for now and I will see you home to read your letter and get some rest."

A shaken Josay agreed and again drew from her inner strength to exit the office after saying au revoir to Mr. Bleux. She went home with La Plume without talking.

At home, Josay retreated into her room where she opened the sealed letter from Matthew Stewart.

My Dear Josay,

I have no words that could excuse myself for the hurtful way I have ended our affaire. I can assure you that I felt a real love for you that will remain in my heart forever. However, I cannot leave my wife and the family I cherish. It is not that I do not love my wife; in fact I love her very much. It's that when I met you, I realized that a person can love more than one person at the same time. Allowing myself to fall in love with you was neither practical nor fair. It was certainly the most unfair to you.

I will not contact you again. I assure you it will be more difficult for me than for you. I have not been able to put you out of my mind and I believe I will never be able to do so. It will be a burden I will carry with sadness the rest of my life. But, I must say goodbye forever.

Mr. Bleux will let you know that I have given you all my shares of the Paradis Rue business and I've asked him to help you maneuver through these next few turbulent weeks of transfers of ownership. It is the very least I can do.

In conclusion, I don't think my heart could stand to hear another word from you. I'm sure I would drop everything and make a mess of the lives of everyone concerned by coming back to you. Just know, that for a brief period in time, I loved you with all my essence.

Matthew

Josay felt a brief stab in her soul and then a rush of compassion mixed with anger. Meeting Matthew was good and bad luck, but she would survive. She would always survive. She marked this date as one of the worst days of her life, and she had experienced some really bad days since her eviction from her village. She was again completely on her own.

CHAPTER 15

A week later, Josay felt sick. She threw up several times. She found it necessary to cancel a meeting to discuss a new way forward for the business. She didn't even feel like seeing Renoir and Pissarro and begged them to come back at a later time. She wrote a letter to David explaining her difficult position with the business and asked La Plume to post it for her.

After a restless night of constantly waking up trying to plot her next best move, Josay finally got out of bed just before the sunrise. She decided to invite her old Poulet and artist friends over for a late lunch to talk things over. After a quick bath, she felt renewed and finished getting dressed.

She noticed that Madame La Plume had either left very early before she awoke or never came home last night. The last time she had seen La Plume was when she left the house to post her letter to David. She thought it curious, but nothing more.

Madame La Plume had, indeed, not come home after she left Josay's little house. She, instead, hurried to the Follie Femme to discuss her next moves with Phillipe Voight. Along the way, she carefully opened and read the letter Josay had written to her brother David before posting it. The letter detailed the business problems she was soon to confront and asked David's advice. She did not seem to know if she should try to fight city hall or let the entire business go away.

She also suggested that she had been sick every morning for several days and was beginning to think that she might be pregnant. She shared that the baby's father was her former business partner, Mr. Matthew Stewart, and that a marriage to him would be impossible due to the fact that she had just been told he was already married and had two children back in America. She expressed regret that she had trusted this man and that she had been cruelly betrayed and abandoned by him. She asked him to keep the news of the possible pregnancy to himself for the time being.

She expressed her anxiety about the future of her parents and the dairy farm, and the dire need to somehow get ownership from Donnel Regis. Madame La Plume's plan could not work without the extra 1,000 francs that she had not been able to raise yet.

La Plume carefully resealed the letter and partially smudged the address such that it might take time to get to David or might even be undeliverable. La Plume felt a sense of pride at her cleverness and ability to overwhelm the stupid trusting people of the world. She felt no remorse for deceit, fraud or stealing. She was of the opinion that anyone not smart enough to protect themselves, got what they deserved. She knew that she had gotten hurt and betrayed over and over in her life, so why shouldn't she do it to others before they could do it to her. Her utmost vow was that she would never allow herself to be vulnerable again.

By the time La Plume arrived at the Follie Femme, she found Voight in the back room where he conducted business, and most often slept. He was sprawled out between two partially clad women and all three of them were asleep. It looked like he and the girls had indulged in lots of late night reverie. She couldn't help but feel a pang of jealousy. But she knew that Voight was just using them to amuse himself.

Sure, they are very young and pretty to look at but are only babies with not a clever thought in their stupid heads, she reasoned to herself. *They are no match for me to be sure.*

Empty bottles of liquor and wine were strewn everywhere. La Plume knew that this was not unusual for him. He would wake up with a hangover but it never clouded his judgement or kept him from his business duties. La Plume woke them and told the girls to leave.

"Why are you here?" said Voight. "And what makes you think I was through with those two? Are you that jealous?"

"I have news, important news that will require us to revise our plans for the Paradis Rue," replied La Plume.

"What is it then?" he said as he poured water into the basin and splashed his face. "I have a lot to do today."

La Plume detailed the recent revelations about Monsieur Stewart, the messieurs Sommes, and the new news of Josay's potential pregnancy. She did so, like a sergeant reporting to a commanding officer, without emotion, clear and concise. La Plume was an excellent strategist and she knew that it was unwise to omit or color information when she presented it to a proven professional criminal like Voight. She had seen him hurt and even kill underlings for dishonesty or self-interest in reporting. He always wanted accurate information, good or bad and the teller would have to face the consequences knowing that his or her fate would certainly be bad if there was a lie or incorrect dispatch. Never try to cheat a cheater, especially a proven psychopath like Voight.

Voight gave La Plume his undivided attention, and only stopped her occasionally for a clarification on some detail or other as she completed her report. Mr. Voight sat pensively and looked at La Plume for a full minute before he said, "It seems that we might just be able to turn a good profit on this one. What would you say might be the next step?" finished Voight in his straight to the point style of business.

"I think the next step is to get control of the assets of the Paradis Rue while the shareholders are leaving the project. Why don't we ask Donnel Regis down to the Follie Femme for dinner and a little gambling? He certainly needs money and I think we can get his share of the business and the dairy with a little effort and some bad luck at the roulette table. I doubt that he is an experienced gambler and I know he's a hateful man with easily shaped motives." said La Plume.

"We certainly know how to turn that screw," replied Voight. "You invite him down and even send a carriage for him and I'll put the pieces in place at the cabaret. What about the other owners and Josay herself?"

"I'm thinking that if we play our cards correctly, we can get hold of all the shares of the Paradis Rue. We can use the dairy farm as leverage with David and Josay Rue. But you will need to get our friends in city hall to press for an ownership decision from the partners. Josay believes that she can't own the business because of her young age, and none of the other investors want it right now. It appears that we can cash in all our chips and get our prize if we act in an organized fashion to complete our plan. It will take a little time and we must work closely together to make it happen," said La Plume with a sly smile.

"First we get Donnel Regis. Then we will get Josay to trade her share of the business, which amounts to most of the shares, for the dairy?" clarified Voight.

"Yes, and one other thing," said La Plume. We will need to fire all of the Josay Rue associates before they get wind of the scheme.

"I don't know who you are referring to. What do you mean her associates?"

"Let's see. There is Madame Foote, Chef Paul, Dr. Muse and that big goon named George that watches the door," she said.

"I suggest that we fire them before we make our move on Donnel. Otherwise, one or more of them, especially Dr. Muse or Madame Foote, may be able to piece the plot together and upset our lovely apple cart. If they get wind of the swindle, it will all be over."

"We have a plan then," said Phillipe. "Good girl. It's early, but let's have a toast and you can spend the day and night here with me, Mon Cheri."

La Plume smiled. She had accomplished what she was really after.

The next day, Josay met Renoir, Lautrec, Pissarro, Monet and several of the other artists to discuss the up-coming Impressionist Exhibition. The elaborate signs and posters by Lautrec and Renoir that were posted all over the city had already created a buzz in the art scene.

The date was set, the location had been procured, and everything was falling into place.

"For the venture to be a success, we will need to have a few thousand visiting patrons. Those visitors will need to buy food and drink. Madame Foote and Dr. Muse have been successful in negotiating with several vendors. These venders will pay us a small percentage of their gross sales for the opportunity to sell their offerings at our exhibit. It will be advantageous for the vendors and all of us," said Renoir.

"Additionally, Dr. Muse has been able to get a lower permit price from the city by agreeing to have a free day for the children of Paris on the final Sunday of the exhibit. Some of us will offer to paint with the children in a kind of 'workshop.' This concession will save us a great deal of money in fees and permits and will promote goodwill from their parents and Parisians in general."

"What have we missed, mon amis?"

"Since we are allowing any artist to submit their work without passing judgement or issuing a formal permit, how are we to decide how many works each artist will be able to show?" asked Pissarro. "And, some places will be more desirable than others owing to light, proximity to entrances and exits, food venues, and so forth, than others. How will we decide on logistical questions?"

Dr. Muse raised his hand to speak.

Renoir said, "You are among friends and you can speak anytime you like without permission, my dear Dr. Muse."

All agreed and chuckled at his formality.

"I suggest that a small committee be tasked with collecting these types of concerns and posting a bulletin board upon which any and all may respond. I would be willing to chair this committee, as I have had some experience in these matters.

Anyone who wants to sit with me on this committee is welcome," said Dr. Muse.

Lautrec said, "I can stay sober long enough to attend a meeting or two of this kind."

Everyone laughed heartily.

"I too would like to be on this committee," said Josay. "And, I recommend that Mrs. Elizabeth Hover be on the committee as well. She knows the society scene and knows a lot of influencial people. I count her as a good personal friend of mine and a true patron of the arts. I think she would love being involved in this endeavor with us."

In quick order Renoir, Berthe Morisot and Gustave Caillebotte also volunteered. The first committee of the exhibition of the 'Impressionists' was formed.

Everyone agreed and began to eat and drink as they submitted their concerns and suggestions to Dr. Muse. The committee planned a meeting to consider the issues and submit their recommendations a week hence, since time was of the essence. April 15th was approaching fast.

As the group was about to depart, Renoir thanked everyone for coming and raised his glass saying, "Here's to our exhibition. May the world come to know the essence of our artistic light through Impressionism."

CHAPTER 16

One week later, the little committee composed of Dr. Muse, Josay, Renoir, Lautrec, Morisot, and Caillebotte met at the home of Mrs. Elizabeth Hover, the English wife of Josay's financial advisor and friend, William Hover. They would attempt to respond to the many questions of logistics surrounding the Impressionist Exhibition.

Mr. Bleux had asked for a short meeting before the committee arrived between Josay, Mr. Hover and himself. The three of them were secluded in Mr. Hover's library. Josay was very apprehensive about what news she might hear since Mr. Bleux had already informed everyone concerned, that he was leaving the project because of the complications caused by his employer, Matthew Stewart.

Mr. Bleux was the first to speak. "Unfortunately, I am the bearer of ill tidings. The city building permits have been put on hold due to the ownership issues, and we are about out of money to continue to build the cabaret unless we can quickly bring these technical issues to resolution. All of the materials have been bought and are piled up around the building site. But with the work stoppage order, the carpenters and tradesmen who have been contracted to do the work are standing around doing nothing. We are bleeding money because of this.

"Mr. Stewart has advised me to turn over his shares of the project to Josay, but unless the construction is completed, I fear that none of the shares will be worth a franc. The messieurs Sommes have also offered to sell their shares to Josay for a fraction of the money they have invested, but again, their shares will be worthless without a completed project. Naturally, everyone is unwilling to invest further in the project. I have not been able to reach Monsieur Regis about his shares and I fear that he will also be unwilling to provide additional resources for the project. His holdings are small and don't make much difference in the decisions we need to make today anyway."

Mr. Hover finished their meeting by saying, "Josay, I'm afraid that as a representative of Blanc and Hover, I cannot authorize any further investment beyond the rather small amount that currently remains in your account. I am truly sorry, but we fear that the project might just be dead with all the unfortunate problems with construction and regulatory issues."

Josay felt like crying but she stopped herself. The deep and powerful strength inside her took over again, and she said, "It is, after all, just a business and we will find solutions together or dispatch the business. I am currently in negotiations with friends that might just lead to a quick solution."

She was thinking of La Plume. Like a fish who is completely unaware of just how deeply the hook had been set, she went on to say that she thought La Plume would have concrete plans for a resolution of the problems in only a few days. A deep sigh of relief was expressed by the two men because they were both very fond of Josay and wished her well.

That same night Donnel Regis was greeted at the door to the Follie Femme by Madame Mari Belle La Plume.

"Welcome to our club Monsieur Regis. I think we can combine business with pleasure tonight."

"Yes, I believe we can," said Monsieur Voight. "I'm Philippe Voight owner and manager of this establishment."

As he extended his hand to shake with Donnel, two showgirls approached and took Donnel by the arms, one on each side.

"These ladies have been instructed to make sure you enjoy your evening and if they aren't to your liking, just let me know. We have many options in this club. After you have had dinner and a little time to settle in, we can discuss business."

La Plume led Donnel and the two girls to their table in the center front row where the small party settled in for dinner and drinks.

"It will be a couple of hours before the first show," said La Plume. "Would you like to try your hand at roulette after dinner? We would be happy to give you, shall we say, 100 francs to play with, compliments of the house."

Donnel nodded his head while the two women poured more wine and entertained him at the table. Everyone was gay and full of alcoholic spirits. Donnel soon began to take liberties with the women which they encouraged rather than resisted.

"Can we play roulette, I'm very lucky?" said the blonde.

"I'm lucky too!" said the brunette as both girls helped a more than willing Donnel out of his chair and across the room to the lavender colored door adjacent to the main room.

Madame La Plume followed the little threesome across the room, through the lavender door, and into the gaming parlor.

As they approached the roulette table, La Plume said, "One hundred chips on the house for Monsieur Regis, and a bottle of champagne."

The roulette man stacked four piles of red chips in front of Donnel and he began to play. Money so easily acquired in the hands of a man with not much luck, soon disappeared. Especially since the table could easily be rigged to insure the lack of luck. Several more ladies and a hand-picked group of on-lookers soon joined the party. The women were taking tips from Donnel as he mostly lost, but occasionally won. La Plume was an expert at making cheating seem normal and holding out the carrot at a never achievable but approachable distance from the pursuer.

As the evening wore on, and as the one hundred francs disappeared, a drunk Donnel asked for, and received, credit for more and more chips. The table was now crowded with showgirls, prostitutes, and other patrons of the club that helped create an ever more magical climate of merriment and well-being. In the two hours before the floor show was to begin, Donnel owed the cabaret over fifteen thousand francs. Mr. Voight interrupted the fun and escorted Donnel back to his table to see the cancan show at his front row table.

Voight had changed the chip color from red to blue and then to black chips. Donnel had never noticed this or even realized that each color chip had a difference in value. He was blissfully unaware of the huge debt he had already incurred, and with his two original escorts, he happily sat down to enjoy the show.

Josay asked Lautrec and Renoir to meet her for dinner at the old Poulet.

"I'm afraid I will soon lose my dream of owning the Paradis Rue and I won't be able to complete my original bargain with you and your artist friends to hang and sell art on the walls of the club," Josay said. "But, maybe we can find a smaller but more achievable plan after all. Pending final resolution of the Paradis Rue project, I suggest that we try to obtain the very restaurant we're sitting in and transform it from a hovel to a pearl by our own efforts and sweat equity. Madame Foote, Dr. Muse and Chef Paul have left the Follie Femme's employ, and are willing to help us restore and then run this establishment. In turn, I will negotiate with the remaining shareholders of the Paradis Rue for the acquisition of this place in turn for my shares of the Rue project. I think we could time our opening to coincide with the Impressionist Exhibition and direct interested art patrons to the renovated Poulet for a sort of 'meet and greet' party with the artists. Patrons could see much more art in a more relaxed environment. I think if we plan it correctly, we can get ownership of the Poulet for a song and make it a meeting place for artists and patrons from around the world after the Impressionist Exhibition is opened.

Renoir was the first to respond and beat Lautrec to the punch by saying, "I'm sure you have all of our support. You have the heart of an artist and the love of our community. Let us put our hands together to seal this plan and keep it to ourselves until the Paradis Rue deal is resolved."

Josay added as she gazed around the shabby room, "The Paradis Rue is still the best option for us and it's not completely dead. It is our first and best option. But the small restaurant and tavern is a backup plan. Our only enemy with this plan would be the time factor. It would take a while to make the place presentable enough to even consider it."

"We have other business to discuss," said Lautrec.

"With the opening of the Impressionist Exhibition coming in a fast approaching time frame, we are about to come to a shortfall of funds. We need to compensate the workmen who are now trying to complete the logistics of the venue for the show. A few temporary walls will have to be erected in order to hang more paintings. We have about 200 paintings, at this point in time, from 51 different contributors. The response has been larger than we really expected, happily.

If we are going to have night time viewers, we must have lighting. That means we must purchase gas lamps and they must be installed. Dr. Muse believes that in the next few months we will need about 500 francs above and beyond what we have borrowed from Blanc and Hover to open the doors. Business is not my forte, but we must find a new source of funding or all will have been for nothing," said Lautrec with a less than happy look on his face.

"Let me work on that," said Josay. "I have just over 300 francs still in my account at Hover's bank. I will withdraw enough of that to temporarily satiate the wolves coming after the salon. Madame La Plume is working to resolve the problems I am having with the cabaret. I am still modeling for the fashion houses to make more money, and you are all still painting and so are our other artists. We may have to consider a bit of a larger fee for entering a painting in the exhibit. If everyone works together we can make enough money to meet our goals and live happily ever after. The three raised their glasses and laughed out loud."

Donnel was now fully inebriated and after the floor show was over, his girls, under the direction of Madame La Plume, ushered him back through the lavender door to the casino.

"Monsieur Regis, perhaps roulette isn't your game. Why don't you try pharaoh? It is a game that requires the kind of acute thinking and decision making of a man like you," said the brunette.

The girls took Donnel to an already prepared place at the table and the dealer asked Donnel how many chips he wanted.

"How about 10,000 francs," said Donnel and the girls squealed with delight. Mr. Voight watched his victim from across the room and smiled the knowing smile of a con man that has captured his mark.

In less than ten minutes, Donnel was out of chips and Mr. Voight came to the table to escort Donnel to the office in the back of the building.

"Monsieur Regis, I hope you have had an entertaining evening," said Voight. "Madame La Plume is a wonderful hostess and knows how to meet the needs of a gentleman."

"Oui, oui," responded Donnel while slurring his words. "And I'd like to get back to those girls. I'm not through with them if you know what I mean?"

"I believe I do," said Voight. "And Madame La Plume will have them waiting for you in one of our suites as soon as we finish our business. First there is a small issue of the 25,300 francs you owe from your gambling."

Just as he finished saying 25,300 francs, two large muscular men appeared from behind the curtain in the office. "Perhaps you could just tell me how you want to cover your debts and we can talk about the Paradis Rue business."

"I fear I don't have even half that amount of money," responded Donnel with a giggle. "Can you give me a little credit? I'm sure I can win all of it back on the roulette table. I just had a little bad luck. I feel the good luck coming back into my veins."

"I feel like I'm partially to blame for your problem by giving you the first hundred francs. Gambling can sometimes be addictive. You did, however, ask for credit on all of the rest of the money, all on your own. I granted you the credit based on the fact that I assumed you to be an honorable and high placed gentleman. Now you tell me you don't have the money. What am I to do? I would not enjoy having to treat you, Sir, like a common welcher and have my boys break a few of your bones."

Donnel sobered up a bit and suddenly realized the scope of his predicament.

"Ah, wait Monsieur Voight. Maybe there is a way we could reach a favorable agreement," said La Plume. "Right now Donnel has a small ownership in the troubled Paradis Rue project. The project bogged down with legal and funding problems as well as new personal problems between Josay Rue and the other shareholders. It seems that Mr. Matthew Stewart has backed out of the business along with both of the messieurs Sommes. They have all given their shares to Josay Rue. She can't own the business for technical reasons. Do you see where I am going with all of this, Monsieur Voight?"

"Yes, Madame La Plume. You and I could step up and save the project if we could acquire a few shares."

Madame La Plume took over, saying, "I would guess that his position in the business would be worth maybe six or seven thousand francs? And, I understand that he might be willing to let go of some of his family holdings, like the Rue dairy and adjacent pasture lands. The farm and pasture lands might add another 12,000 francs. That would be, let's see, 20,000 francs. It would be a good start toward settling the bill he owes.

"I should think that you might give a gentleman like Mr. Regis a few months to settle the remainder?"

She addressed Donnel directly, "I believe that neither the Paradis Rue project nor the dairy are of great value to you without capital. What we propose seems a fair bargain for you and a way for us to negotiate with Mademoiselle Rue to move the Paradis business forward."

"You planned this, you SLUT!" screamed Donnel as he grabbed La Plume.

The two large men were quickly on Donnel to pull him off of La Plume. One of them slapped him across the face causing him to fall backwards onto the couch.

"Are you accusing us of dishonesty?" asked Mr. Voight. "Because if you are, we can certainly just call the nearest police officer. You can explain just how we made you run up your debt, and how you are refusing to settle it. Perhaps debtor's prison would be more to your liking?"

"No. No. That won't be necessary."

The big men let Donnel come to his feet and he straightened his coat and pants.

"I never really wanted to be involved in that Paradis Rue project and the dairy and adjacent lands are not important to me. I want to leave this room without debt."

"I don't see how that is possible unless you have some other asset to add to the solution," said a stern Voight. He never let a fish off the hook until he had safely eaten all but the bones.

"I have a large house and several rental properties in my village. I never wanted to be a squire and oversee a bunch of lazy peasants. Maybe you could mortgage my house, its furnishings and the rental properties for the remaining part of the debt. Give me three years to repay you. I do wish to regain my family's house. Would that be acceptable?"

"Let's see, I get your shares of the Paradis Rue project, the dairy and adjacent pastureland and the mortgage on your house and rental properties. If you don't finish paying off the entire debt in three years, I own your house and furnishings and all of the rest of your properties. And you get a clean slate with me and can walk out of here with all of your bones intact. Is that right?"

"Oui," responded a humbled Donnel Regis.

"Apologize to Madame La Plume. Then we have a deal."

“Of course. My deepest apologies, Madame.”

“I will have all the paperwork ready for your signature tomorrow morning. In the meantime, please consider yourself once again a guest of the Follie Femme and with the exception of gambling credit, enjoy all aspects of the establishment for the remainder of the night.”

Voight gave a nod to his goons and the two girls reappeared. We insist that you stay with us until all of our business is completed.”

CHAPTER 17

Josay was very sick the next morning and was coming to the inevitable realization that she was definitely pregnant with Matthew Stewart's child. She was feeling emotional and vulnerable when Madame Gloria Foote knocked on her door. As she saw her friend, Josay began to cry.

"Whatever could be the problem?" asked Madame Foote. I am sure that together we can come up with a solution to all of these business problems.

"It's not that," Josay said, as she began to sob even more. "I'm pregnant with a married man's child."

She didn't name Matthew Stewart but Madame Foote could easily guess from the clues Josay had supplied.

"He has told me that he will never be coming back to me and he doesn't even know I'm having a baby. He told me he loved me and wanted to be with me always. I was convinced that this was true, and that he would be the husband of my dreams. I am so naïve and foolish.

I have loved only two men in my life and both have turned out to be liars and have abandoned me."

Gloria Foote was shaken to her core to hear that her dear Josay had been taken advantage of in this cruel way. She knew how that kind of betrayal could feel from her own life experience.

Gloria put her arms around Josay, "We will find a way. You have earned true friends who will see you through these business and personal problems. I will never abandon you and neither will your many other true friends."

Madame Foote loved Josay like the daughter she never had. She pulled Josay to her and gave comfort as Josay cried a full ten minutes on her shoulder.

When she had gotten part of the despair and hurt out of her heart and mind, the tough independent Josay returned to say, "I will work this problem out and my baby and I will be happy."

At the same time, Henri Loutrec sat in a corner of the Poulet with Van Gogh drinking wine left over in jugs from the night before.

"You are truly not much fun, Vincent," said Lautrec. "I think that you and I must be the lowest kind of people in the world. We are certainly not well loved, are we?"

"You are right, Lautrec," said Van Gogh "But I believe we are two of the most honest painters in the world. We show the world as it is. Although, I wish I had an ounce of hope for a more beautiful and loving place."

There was always some kind of surface ugliness in every work of art produced by Lautrec, and also present in most of the paintings of Van Gogh. With Lautrec, it might be a slightly crossed eye, or a too tight pair of pants on his models. With Van Gogh, it was oddly colored shades of paint that changed reality into his tortured world view. The overall impression that was left to any viewer of their collective art offerings was amazement. It was an introduction to the strange world of beauty that was born from such inner tortured souls.

"I think we should get drunk, Vincent. But first we should start a rumor about La Plume. I believe she is dishonest. But no matter how earnestly I approach Josay with the truth, she will not hear that La Plume is anything but a savior for the business and even for her personal problems."

"What kind of rumor?" asked Van Gogh.

"Let's say she is trying to swindle Josay out of her interest in the Paradis Rue. Actually, I think she just might be doing that, although I have no real proof. I think I saw Donnel Regis at the Follie last night with La Plume, and I know for a fact that Donnel Regis is a villain. Let's paint them together at the Follie Femme in deeply unflattering portraits and hang the paintings here at the Poulet for all to see."

Van Gogh was confused from too much wine and forgot where the conversation started but agreed to paint whatever Lautrec was talking about. It seems that Van Gogh had also had a healthy cup of mind dulling absinthe before Lautrec had arrived.

The two gathered their paints and easels and went across the room into an open, but shaded, window to create paintings in muted sunlight.

Later that evening, Josay went to meet with La Plume at the Follie Femme. Josay had been wondering where Madame La Plume had been keeping herself. She had not been sleeping at Josay's house, even though her possessions were still there. It was a little troubling. Josay was hoping that her friend Mari had been working to resolve her business problems before all was lost, but there had been no word on this for a while.

After an early dinner, and pleasantries, La Plume sprang the trap.

"I think I have a solution to all of our problems. You see, my friend Monsieur Voight has acquired all of Donnel Regis's shares in the Paradis Rue, and your family farm with all of the pasture lands adjacent to the dairy."

"But how.......?" Josay began to speak.

"Please, just let me finish. I know the nature of the legalities and unfair ordinances surrounding construction and ownership of the Paradis Rue have made it impossible for the project to move forward with you at the helm since you are female and under 30 years old. I am also aware that your other original shareholders no longer want to be a part of the project for one reason or another. Mr. Voight has offered to save you from disaster. He is willing to give you the deed to your family farm and the pasture lands that surround it in return for all of your shares in the Paradis Rue. He will also pay you a stipend to be the 'face' of the establishment so long as you continue to participate in advertisements and endorsements. It is a good bargain! I know you have some of your heart embedded in the place, but this would help create a way for you and your family to grow and be secure. Life has been hard for you from the day I first met you on the road to Paris. You look tired, mon ami."

Madame La Plume told a good story. By the time she was finished Josay's head was spinning.

"I was under the impression that Monsieur Voight, and you, were going to help me get past the questionable legal obstacles that have been thrown in the way of the completion of the Paradis Rue. I know that my situation has changed as far as the other owners of the project, but I didn't think I would have to give up the entire investment to you and your friend. I was thinking that I could transfer most of the shares of the Paradis Rue to my brother, David, who can legally own a cabaret," she said.

"What about the deal we made that you were going to purchase our farm and land from Donnel for 1,500 francs and you would then sell it to me for 500 francs. You said that you would make some sort of deals with all of the venders and come up with the 1,000 francs that we didn't have already for the farm, and then, it would be mine. You were to get 10 percent of the Paradis Rue. This new deal is not what we agreed to at all. The Paradis Rue is far more valuable, in monetary terms, than the dairy farm, so I don't think it to be a great 'bargain' for me. But it seems that you leave me little alternative in the matter. Mari, you know that my family is the most important thing to me, and I have to secure their future. You have left me no alternative but to sign away my dream business to you and Voight."

Josay reluctantly signed the papers and agreed to the outlined terms of Mr. Voight's offer. She had been trusting La Plume to look out for her interests, but this certainly was not the outcome she had expected or wanted. Josay realized that La Plume had robbed her again.

Her own trusting nature had let La Plume be in a position to find out just how to take advantage of her deep love for her family and farm. It was the dairy or the Paradis Rue. Of course, she had to think of her dear family first.

By midnight, Lautrec and Van Gogh had finished their paintings and had hung them on the tavern wall of the Poulet. Van Gogh's painting showed La Plume with Donnel counting their money in a dark room of the Follie Femme. Both characters were painted with candle light illuminating glowing red cheeks and orange skin with eerie shadowy and sinister eyes. The money was falling off a warped table and onto a floor littered with ham bones, dirty cups and dishes. A small sign hung on the wall showing a haggard bare-breasted cancan dancer and read, "The wage of sin is death."

Lautrec's painting showed a deformed and wrinkled La Plume embracing a big-nosed Donnel in his torn military uniform as they sat at a dimly lit table in the corner of the Follie Femme. The bright colors of Lautrec's painting oddly clashed with the dark background of the room. It was evident that these were two immoral people reaping the consequences of a poorly lived life.

When the paintings were hung, everyone in the room applauded. It seemed that everyone in the underworld of Paris knew of the lying and cheating of La Plume and the unscrupulous brutality of Voight. But no one in the underworld was brave enough to warn Josay or anyone close to Josay. Lautrec had not been told either, but after seeing La Plume and Regis together at the Follie Femme, he intuitively guessed that something was not right.

All the business dealings were concluded. When Josay went to get the deed to her property at the office of Mr. Voight inside the Follie Femme, Voight said in a matter of fact way, "You are now the owner of your family farm and surroundings. It's now time for you to begin to fulfill your agreement to model for posters and advertisements."

"Of course, Monsieur Voight," replied Josay with defeat in her voice.

"I am now the owner of the Paradis Rue property and the construction will soon be renewed. I expect the place to open in the middle of April. I want to do an advertising blitz with you at its center and I'm agreeable to having the grand opening coincide with the Impressionist Exhibition on April 15th as planned. That is, so long as the exhibition doesn't get in my way. You see I have my own plans for the opening of Paradis Rue. I have employed several artists to produce my posters and flyers. You will find they are quite different than yours."

As he was finishing his sentence, three artists that Josay had never seen before, entered the room.

"Now, just take off your clothes and sit over on that bar with your legs crossed," said Mr. Voight.

"What? No!" said Josay as she looked toward La Plume.

"I'm sorry my dear, but I agree with Mr. Voight. We need to use your many assets to sell the place," said La Plume as she took Josay's arm and looked her in the face. "You would be wise to do as he says. He's not as kind as I am. Willingly or unwillingly, you will submit. You have been paid and you are now owned."

La Plume ripped the top of Josay's dress to reveal her breasts. Before she knew it, she was stripped naked and standing in a room filled with lecherous thugs and laughing whores. Mr. Voight fondled her breasts and grabbed her around her shoulders. He forced a kiss and put his foul smelling tongue into her mouth.

"My, my. I think we will have an excellent business relationship. In fact, I think we should start right now. Two large goons held Josay's arms as Voight dropped his pants, turned and forced his swollen penis inside Josay as she screamed. Everyone in the room, especially La Plume, laughed and joked.

When the assault was finished, Josay was made to sit for the painting. The prostitutes put deep red lipstick on her lips and bright red rouge on her cheeks. She looked just like a sad-faced clown. She was in shock and the makeup hid the paleness of her face as she struggled to keep from fainting.

Somehow she found the inner strength to endure the humiliation and horror long enough to finish her sitting, gather her portfolio of legal documents, wrap herself in a smock, and exit the room to the light of a purple and red setting sun.

She hailed a carriage and went to her little house. She was still in shock and felt nauseous, but found a note from Madame Foote asking her to meet at the Poulet as soon as she could. Josay needed to see her friend. She sobbed silently in the privacy of the carriage. *I blame myself for trusting that horrible excuse for a human being, Mari Belle La Plume! she thought.*

When Josay got to the Poulet, she found her friends eating, drinking and talking about the two new paintings Lautrec and Van Gogh had done. Madame Foote saw immediately that Josay had been hurt and came to her with a hug and ushered her from the room before the other patrons could see her swollen red eyes and smeared makeup. She took Josay up to the old room that had been her first residence in Paris almost two years ago. (Although Madame Foote no longer owned Le Poulet, her former barmaid and friend did, so this kind gesture was not questioned.) Madame Foote helped Josay clean herself with a clean basin of water and a clean towel. She helped her into bed and felt her heart breaking for Josay.

When Josay told her all that had happened, Madame Foote swore that together they would get justice for this horrible crime that was obviously very well planned ahead of time. Gloria reasoned that Voight had sacked her two days ago, and had also fired Chef Paul, Dr. Muse and George because he wanted them out of the way. La Plume must have told Voight that they were all friends of Josay. He didn't want any of them at the Follie Femme while any of this was taking place. Now everything was making more sense to her.

Dr. Muse was downstairs having a coffee and glass of brandy. Madame went down to get him to verify and file all the legal papers. The papers were in order and Josay was the owner of the family farm and two hundred acres of pasture land for a total of almost three hundred acres.

"At least Voight and La Plume signed over Josay's farm. I just wonder how they got it from Donnel Regis," said Madame Foote to Dr. Muse.

"I don't know yet. How is she? She looked very wounded when she arrived."

"Yes, she was wounded in the most cruel way. She needs rest and time to recover."

She went back upstairs to comfort Josay, and took her a small sip of brandy to help her sleep.

"Thank you for the brandy. I will go home tomorrow and tell Mama, Papa and David about the farm," she told her friend.

At least her family would be secure, she thought as she settled into her old bed and fell into an uneasy sleep.

At the same time, Donnel was riding back to his home after his great disgrace and degradation. *All of this has happened because of that bitch Josay, he thought.* He no longer owned the farm or adjacent pastures and had little or no control of his ancestral land and property. *I will go back to the military life and leave this place forever, he concluded to himself. But I will leave them with something to remember me by.*

Donnel stopped by the pub just outside town and paid twenty men to gather at midnight to put a torch to the Rue dairy.

"Kill as many cows as you can and burn the buildings and the fields. And if the people burn to death, that's alright with me as well."

They were instructed to wear masks and never to speak, shout or yell during the attack, and never mention the event to anyone upon completion.

Just as the bell struck three in the church tower of the village a short kilometer away, twenty men rode out to destroy the Rue family farm. They approached without shouting or calling out as they were instructed, and before David woke from the sleep of an early rising dairyman, the barn and fields were ablaze. Fortunately, David was almost awake and the sounds outside caused him to go to the window soon enough to see three men coming to set the house on fire. He got to his shotgun and fired at the charging men. It was enough to frighten them to a speedy retreat. Papa, Mama and several of the farmhands immediately jumped into action to save the house. The barn was already too far gone. By the end of the attack, a large percentage of the cows survived along with the little white eight-roomed home. Most of the outbuildings were burned beyond repair, including the one that held the bottles and processors for the milk.

It wasn't a total loss, but a significant one for the Rue family. They mourned the loss of the barn and other property, but more importantly they were deeply saddened by the horrible cruelty and slaughter of the innocent and gentle cows. The badly burned ones would have to be put down to prevent more suffering.

At least none of the people on the farm were hurt and for that they were very thankful. But they were all trying to come to grips with why this attack was perpetrated on them. There was only one person who hated them enough to do this thing, but it wasn't clear why he would do this to his own property?

CHAPTER 18

The smell of dead charred animals, burnt wood and grass filled Josay's nostrils when she arrived in the mid-afternoon. She ran to her parents and brother David who were covered in soot and had red swollen eyes from the fight. They had tried to save as many animals as possible, and had succeeded in saving all but eighteen cows.

All-in-all they were lucky. The preponderance of the fire was limited to the large milking barn and some of the smaller sheds and structures. The fire also destroyed a good portion of the farm's fencing. It could all be rebuilt, but the family had no capital to mend it right now.

Josay had brought her four friends from the Poulet with her so she made the necessary introductions to her family. This was not the scene she had invisioned when she had invited them to come with her to help on the farm for a short time. They had lost their jobs, probably because they were her friends, and she had some ideas about how their expertise could help to make the farm a thriving enterprise instead of just a dairy farm. She was an entrepreneur at heart.

Somehow Donnel had once again found a way to twist the knife into her future and her spirits. She wondered just how a man could be so cruel and heartless. There was no doubt in anyone's mind that he was the one behind this tragedy. He was the only person with the motive, money or power to make it happen.

She hadn't even gotten over the despicable betrayal of Madame La Plume yet. She was hoping to find some rest and comfort at the farm with her family and loyal friends, but she found herself digging deep into her soul to deal with these adversities. She was determined to find a way to make this situation better. There was no time for self pity.

The little group gathered around Josay. They all held hands as Josay prayed, "Dear Lord, we thank you for the blessings you have bestowed on us this day, and seek the courage we will need to find our future. We are all safe, and most of our animals have survived this inferno. We will overcome this cruel deed, with your help, Lord. We also pray for the blackened soul who perpetrated this atrocity. May he repent and be redeemed in your eyes and never hurt anyone or anything again. Amen."

Everyone was amazed at her words. Some were thinking, *How in the world could this waif of a girl garner such strength at a time like this? And how could she be grateful*?

Josay spoke with reverence and power as she used the prayer to not only seek help and support from the Almighty, but to give her family and comrades the courage they would need to fight through this unfair set-back to their lives.

When she was through, David was the first to speak saying, "We must milk the cows and get the product to market."

At times of severe depression and tragedy, it's healthy to think only one minute at a time, not one hour, one week or one lifetime.

David had called them to action and it was just the right thing to say. Everyone began to clean up and find an immediate task to cover their sadness and remorse. Each one of the small group had been knocked to the ground with regularity in their lives and had found ways to get back up and face reality with hard work, commitment and without weakness. This was a resilient group of fighters and their beautiful young leader was a role model for not letting anything stop her from moving forward in her life. Josay was not the same shy, delicate and innocent young 18-year-old who had been unfairly cast out of her village and set on the road of life two years ago. She was a mature woman of substance who had proven her metal in the fires of misfortune.

In Paris, Madame La Plume met with Monsieur Voight to celebrate the official ownership of the Paradis Rue. All the paperwork had been signed and construction was already in motion again.

"We should target the well-to-do with this enterprise," said La Plume. "You know the fancy gentlemen looking for an evening away from the wife. We can do a higher level of programing. The dancing and entertainment must be of the very best quality. We should bring in the youngest and most talented hostesses to entertain our patrons. I know just how to organize this place to get the maximum return for our efforts."

"I know you do," responded Voight. "And I will set up the finest gambling facilities in all of Paris. This place will be able to get them drunk and laid. We will milk out every sou they bring in while still leaving them with the desire to return as soon as possible."

They laughed together and celebrated with a toast to themselves. After the toast, a dark expression came over Voight's face.

"You think we're really rid of that girl Josay? I have just learned that her dunce of a former lover, Donnel, burned her newly procured dairy farm last night. I suspect she will be seeking revenge. We should plan on her counterattack. It was really stupid for Donnel Regis to take such unnecessary action against her. You'd think robbing and raping her would have been enough for him. Come to think of it, I robbed and raped her too," he finished with a chuckle.

"Oh well, 'C'est la vie,' life moves on. I think her days of powerful friends and allies in Paris are over and she would be wise to pick up the pieces of her life and leave the aspirations of fame and fortune in Paris behind. If she returns, she may not be treated with such respect," he concluded as he laughed and toasted La Plume again.

Josay and all the others worked very hard for the next couple of weeks picking up the pieces of the shattered dairy business. She and Dr. Muse had taken the time to go into the village and file her deed and legal claim to the farm and surrounding pastures. The magistrate seemed happy to see Josay. She had known him to be a nice man in her childhood and he seemed genuinely gratified that she had become the owner of her family business.

While she was there she found out that after his father died, Donnel had lost most of his family's holdings due to his father's debts and his own gambling. He was now trying to sell off what remained in order to rejoin his regiment and live the military life he desired.

Gambling? I wonder of Voight and La Plume had anything to do with the loss of his property? she thought to herself. That would explain how they were in possession of the dairy and pastures.

She had mixed feelings about Donnel. He had been both her first love, and also one of the most despicable persons she had ever met. She knew that he was behind the fire and devastation at the farm. He had called her a whore and raped her. He had a contempt for her that she didn't completely understand. She could go to the authorities, but she had no real proof that he was behind the attack on her home, and absolutely no proof that he had raped her. She decided her efforts would be better spent by taking care of unfinished business in Paris.

She was still the 'face' of the Impressionist Exhibition and she knew the artists were depending on her to follow through. She finished signing the necessary documents with the magistrate, thanked him and left the office.

On the streets of the village, Josay saw one familiar face after another from her childhood; some that had been kind, and some that had been responsible for throwing her out of the small community. She used her best personal skills to demonstrate forgiveness with those that required it and friendly cheerful greetings for those that she knew as friends from before. The strategy seemed to work without exception. The forgiven were quick to apologize and the friends hugged and comforted her.

Everyone she met seemed to loathe Donnel, and yet Josay was able to keep her feelings about him to herself. Everyone offered to help her in whatever way they could with the dairy and all of them seemed to take Josay to their breast in friendship.

She graciously accepted some of the offers to help rebuild the farm. There was a buzz of activity over the next few days, and the dairy seemed to be rebuilding itself with the help of the neighbors in the village.

Dr. Muse was getting the books in order, and with Josay's suggestions, they were finding new venture possibilities for the dairy. Madame Foote was helping Josay's mother to organize the household in order to house and accommodate the group of four that was Josay's entourage. Chef Paul had been an apprentice in a cheese making factory before he had married, and was given a portion of the milk to make cheese and butter. He was thrilled about that and was very busy creating delicious products for market. Big George was helping with the cleanup and construction. Everyone did their best to secure a place in this new community of refuses (people who others may consider to be garbage).

She centered her thoughts on the future of the little community of the "Rue Family Farm Products" as it was now being called. After only a short time, it was being well integrated into the greater community. Josay felt things were going well enough for her to leave. She had many loose ends with her artist friends back in Paris.

She asked Dr. Muse to stay at the farm for now and help there, but to show her the latest facts and figures for the opening of the exhibition so that she could take care of business in Paris. She and Big George gathered a few clothes and were dropped off in town to board a carriage back to Paris. After what Voight and La Plume had done to Josay, George insisted on being by her side at all times.

She didn't yet know what she would do about La Plume and Voight. She had doubts that the authorities would help her, due to the fact that she willingly signed over the shares of the Paradis Rue and had no credible witness to the rape and assault who would agree to testify for her.

As she rode along toward Paris, Josay allowed herself to think about her pregnancy. She had almost forgotten Mr. Stewart and the deep seated grief she suffered when she found out that he was married. She didn't think she would complicate his life or hers by telling him it was his child. She believed she could face the future without him. She felt a deep sadness and emptiness in her heart and in her soul. Both men that she had loved had used and betrayed her. She asked herself, as the horse took rhythmic steps along the road, *What have I done to deserve these two vicious betrayals? I loved both Donnel and Matthew with my whole heart.* It was only a momentary indulgence of feeling sorry for herself and then she put it out of her mind.

In eight hours, Josay found herself at Lautrec's apartment in Paris. With Big George by her side, she knocked on his door. As expected, a red-eyed and smelly Toulouse opened the door.

"Mon Deus!" he exclaimed. "Everyone thought we'd never see you again. Come in. Come in. Would you like a glass of wine?" he said as he threw aside empty bottles and trash to make a way for Josay and George to enter.

"I came back to finish my job as a model and marketing agent for the exhibition. I trust it is moving forward?"

"Yes—and no. We have experienced some small bumps in the road, so to speak. There are more of us than we expected. Oh yes, and there are still squabbles about painting location. Everyone wants their work to be up front. We suspect that some visitors might not get past the first few steps in the hall, so we want to put our best foot forward. The problem with that is, of course, everyone thinks his or her 'foot' is the most beautiful."

Josay couldn't help but laugh. Henri was always so animated and his facial expressions were always amusing no matter what he was saying. He had a way of lifting her spirits.

"You are still held in high regard here. Having you on my posters and flyers has been an unqualified success. We are selling tickets."

"It seems that the news is as you say, good and bad. I think we need to have a meeting of our committee as soon as tomorrow to get back on track. Dr. Muse is not with me right now. He is at my farm helping us get things back in order after Donnel Regis hired some men to burn it down. "

"I knew that boy was evil and would be up to no good, especially when I saw him at the Follie Femme being led around by Madame La Plume about 2 weeks ago. He was drunk, gambling and had two prostitutes on his arm."

"What night was that exactly?" asked Josay.

"It was the night before you slept at the Poulet. That's why I wanted to paint those ugly pictures of him and La Plume the next day. I knew that something was wrong with that scene."

"You were right about that. It is obvious to me now that La Plume and Voight were exploiting Donnel to get his money and property, especially the Rue family farm and lands. They needed leverage to get the Paradis Rue from me and it worked. But they did it in a most cruel and degrading way."

"I am so sorry that this has happened to you, Mon Cheri."

"I don't want to discuss the details of that right now because I want to work on the exhibition. We need to meet to finalize the finances and fees that we will need to charge so that we can pay the last minute expenses. And, of course, we also need to pay off the loan we have with Blanc and Hover."

"Your generous contributions have gone a long way toward that end. We just need a few more francs to be solvent—I think," said Lautrec.

She turned to George, "Would you let all the members of the steering committee know that tomorrow we need to meet just outside the exhibition hall to resolve a few problems? It should be a short meeting."

"Of course, mon ami. You know I would do anything for you," George smiled and said sweetly.

She returned the smile and said, "Go to Renoir first and he will help you get the message out to the others. I will need a little time, so we will meet in the late afternoon—say around 5pm."

By the way, have you heard anything from La Plume, Henri?"

"Yes, she has come by to confirm and coordinate the exhibition opening with that of the Paradis Rue. The joint opening is still planned to go as previously scheduled. The cabaret will open the night of the 14th and the exhibition on the 15th. I already had contempt for La Plume and Voight, but without knowing about their larceny against you, we agreed to the original plan."

"Yes, that makes sense. I apologize for not telling you myself how they were able to steal the project from all of us. But I was very eager to get back to the farm. And I am glad that I did because of the fire there. But now we should move forward with our plans for the exhibition," said Josay. "I am looking forward to a wonderful success for all of you."

George rushed off as Josay excused herself to retreat to her small house to recover and figure out just the right approach for seeking help from Mr. Hover and Monsieur James Sommes.

She would confront Madame La Plume and Monsieur Voight tomorrow as well. She would take the fight to the enemy.

Just before she went to sleep, exhausted from her trip, she sent word to Mr. Hover to set up a meeting with him and James tomorrow at noon near the building site of the Paradis Rue.

CHAPTER 19

The next morning, Josay received word from Mr. Hover that he and James Sommes would meet her across from the Paradis Rue building site at a small outside café called "Café Enchanted."

George and Renoir were able to reach everyone but Camille Pissarro about the meeting that evening. He could not be located. He was likely somewhere in the countryside painting peasant scenes in "Plein air."

Just as Josay was about to leave for her first meeting, Monsieur Le Grande, the dairy vendor, came to Josay's door with a message from David.

"Bon jour, Mademoiselle Rue," said Le Grande. "Monsieur David wanted you to know that he has been able to buy lumber and building supplies from the estate of Donnel Regis on credit. Most of the old estate is being liquidated and much of what he needs to rebuild the barn and fence has easily been obtained.

"That is very good news, Monsieur Le Grande. Is there anything else?"

"It is rumored that Monsieur Regis is trying to sell off his estate before being charged with the desecration of your family farm and the attempted murder of your parents and brother. He wants to leave town as soon as he can, so he gave David, through his agent, an unbelievable good bargain and on a delayed payment schedule."

"So, am I to believe this 'bargain' to be out of the goodness of his heart?"

"I don't think so, Mademoiselle. I believe he did this **not** out of the goodness of his heart, but because of the threat of prosecution from the magistrate. You see, several men have confessed their roles in the assault to save their own skins. Monsieur Regis stated that he had nothing to do with the offense, but claims that because of his fondness for you and the long history he has had with your family, it was the 'Christian' thing to do."

Josay's temper flared, but again she controlled it and simply said, "How wonderful. Please tell my brother to accept this gift and to let Donnel leave with God only as his judge in this affair. There are many people that will depend on the success of this new reorganized dairy business and I think the disaster might just have been the spark that ignites a new future for us all."

Monsieur Le Grande bowed and kissed her hand and said, "You are a most gracious and forgiving lady, Mademoiselle. He assured Josay that he would carry her message back to David and her parents that very evening, and he left.

Josay put on her most fashionable pink dress and accessories. She wanted to give anyone she met that day the appearance that she was firmly in control no matter what road blocks or betrayals she might have suffered. She felt it important to keep up the appearance of being Josay Rue, the model and toast of Paris.

Even though the meeting site was only a short walk from her house, Josay decided to arrive at the "Café Enchanted" in a small elegant carriage, the kind of transportation befitting a fine lady. As she got out of the cab, Mr. Hover and Monsieur James Sommes were eager to offer her a hand.

"Mademoiselle Rue, it is so good to see you. You look magnificent," said Sommes.

As if by providence, Monsieur Voight was crossing the street when Josay exited the carriage. He felt his face drain.

"Oh, Monsieur Voight, I'm so glad I've run into you, perhaps we can meet in an hour or two here at the cafe to discuss your progress on the Paradis Rue? I still have strong feelings about your project even though I no longer have a financial interest. Of course there is the fact that I am currently still associated with it as the 'face' of the business. Please bring Madame La Plume, as well, if she's free. I have a few things to discuss with her too."

Big George who had been up front in the cab, stepped down, situated himself next to Josay, and smiled at Voight, showing a full compliment of teeth.

"Of course," responded Voight so taken by surprise that he was almost unable to speak. He hurried away barely missed being hit by a produce wagon on its way to the market.

"Now gentlemen perhaps we can find a quiet table to talk."

After taking their seats and several minutes of small talk, Josay said," I have a favor and business opportunity for the two of you. As you both know, I am backing the art exhibition scheduled to take place at the same time as the opening of the Paradis Rue here in Paris. You have both met a lot of the artists, and you, Mr. Hover, have been kind enough to give them a small loan to help them with their logistical and advertising needs. And, of course, your lovely wife, Elizabeth, is a member of our steering committee."

Mr. Hover said, "Yes, she has so enjoyed working on this project with you and the artists. She thinks it's a very worthwhile project to change things a bit in the world of Paris art—to modernize things a little."

"Yes, that's exactly what I am saying. Of course, it's difficult to modify any established way of doing things, especially in the realm of art. The traditional 'experts' who comprise the Annual Salon jury have a vested interest in keeping things the same. Some of that motivation for them is a financial one. They want to keep prices high for the kind of art that they own, so they only approve **that** kind of traditional art at their Annual Salon. A lot of the public depends on their leadership to tell them what kind of art to like and to buy. Their power is and has been immense for many decades.

My colleagues and I think that art should evoke a feeling in your soul when you gaze upon it. And artistic expression should not be stifled but encouraged. Therefore, I am hoping that you will both join me in supporting this brave new movement."

Both men asked how they could help.

"You are both men of good standing in the high society of Paris. I want you to tell your friends to give the Impressionist Exhibition a chance. Ask them to come and just look at the paintings with open minds— without prejudice. And of course, any personal donations for expenses will be very welcome and appreciated."

They both smiled and nodded in agreement.

"Now," she continued. "I have a business proposition for you both. I need an influx of cash for a dairy farm that I own. It's called Rue Family Dairy Products. We have over 70 dairy cows and we produce not only milk and butter, but fine cheeses and other products. You may think that this is a shaky bet, but you would be betting on me, and you know that I will do everything in my power to make it successful.

"Mr. Hover, you know that I have worked hard for the past two years to pay back the 5,000 francs that I borrowed from your establishment, and have repaid not only most of that amount, but also I have paid in full for my house. That should show you that I am a trustworthy borrower.

I am willing to give you two the sole distributorship of our products for one year, for a loan of 3,000 francs. That would be only 1,500 francs from each of you. We already have a capable man named Le Grande who can get the products from the farm to Paris. What do you say, gentlemen?"

Both men, captivated by the words coming out of such a beautiful mouth were speechless and impressed with the plain business tone of her voice.

Mr. Hover thought as she spoke, what a devastating combination of beauty and brains!

James Sommes, still in love with Josay, could mainly see the face of his heart. Josay was a wonder. Everything she touched was a success (if left to its future without subterfuge or intrigue). He had heard about how La Plume and Voight had stolen the Paradis Rue out from under her. He felt partially responsible for that because of his inaction to help her when she needed it.

Mr. Hover was first to come out of his daze and speak. "I would need to see the deeds and paperwork, but I think we could arrange a loan with the kind of collateral you possess. I would love to be in business with you again."

Monsieur Sommes, not to be outdone and eager to speak said, "I will buy the distributorship without collateral if you'll agree to have dinner with me tonight."

"Really? I'm overwhelmed. I would go to dinner with you anytime with or without business connections."

Josay was remembering her early and strong feelings for James Sommes before she met Matthew Stewart. James was young and handsome, a consummate gentleman and a true and honest friend. She didn't know why she had dismissed his advances and turned so quickly to Mr. Stewart?

Sometimes money and power can turn a girl's head. Mr. Stewart had all of that and more. He was very handsome, charming and sensual. But James Sommes, with his soft brown eyes and hair, his cultured and quiet spoken manner was clearly the kind of man she wanted for romance, as well as business.

James and his father, Le Marquis d' Sommes, operated a an estate in Marseilles, as well as an import and export business in Paris, dealing mostly with products from Algeria. They exported olives, wheat, citrus fruits and vegetables from their long-time family holdings in Algeria to other countries all over the world. They also exported specialty wines from France to world markets, including the United States. James, being only 23 years old was still learning the many facets of their enterprise, but he was a born businessman and was enjoying working closely with his father. He had attended the best schools in Europe and had finished his formal education only 2 years before he met Josay. Their mutual friends and business associates, Blanc and Hover, had introduced them that night and James was forever grateful for that connection.

He had fallen in love with her almost immediately. They were dancing their first dance together at the Ritz when he looked into her soft and kind green eyes. There was a sparkle in them that was mesmerizing. He couldn't look away. She was the most beautiful, exciting, mysterious, and intelligent woman he had ever met, and his heart melted that very evening. Sometimes she had said and done very puzzling things, but none of that mattered to him. For every moment in his life, since that magical night, he could think of nothing else but his wonderful Josay.

"It's settled then," said Sommes. I'll pick you up at your house at, say… 8:00 pm? I'll bring a bank draft for the entire 3,000 francs and have my counselor draw up the paperwork that entitles me to the Paris distributorship of Rue Family Diary Products for one year. By the way, if this business venture works, I'd like a gentleman's agreement that I can have the first right of refusal for the rights thereafter as well. I want to be associated with you for the long run as a business partner, friend and more."

"Yes, of course. This time we can make our project work and it will bring us together in many ways. I'm sure of it." She looked into his eyes and realized that he still loved her. She wished that she had never hurt him with her affaire with Matthew. She was so glad that he seemed to want to give her another chance.

"Well if Mr. Sommes insists on taking the entire investment for himself, I trust that you will use Hover and Blanc as your accountants and financial representatives?"

"Of course. I wouldn't think of any others to represent me," replied Josay as she kissed his cheek. "And, tell your lovely wife that I will see her tonight for our steering committee meeting at 5:00 pm just outside the exhibition location. And James, could you meet me there tonight? I'm not sure how long the meeting will last."

The three ate cakes and croissants before Josay excused herself to meet with Mr. Voight and Madame La Plume who were waiting across the street as Josay had requested. They walked over and seated themselves a few tables from the lingering Mr. Hover and Monsieur Sommes who watched from a distance. Big George stood a few feet away from the threesome.

"Mademoiselle Rue, it's good to see you. I trust that the little problem you had with your dairy business is going to be easily fixed? I never trusted Donnel Regis," opened Mr. Voight.

"Yes, and I am sure that Donnel Regis shouldn't have trusted you either, Monsieur Voight," Josay said with a knowing smirk.

"I see you are as lovely as ever Mademoiselle Rue," added La Plume. "I hope you can overlook the terrible misjudgements and missteps I have taken with our friendship. Can you ever forgive me?"

La Plume certainly had nerve. She is a brazen and fully evil person that, unlike a leopard, can change her spots at the drop of a sou. I wish I could have seen her face when Voight told her that Josay Rue wanted to see them both for a meeting across the street. Josay was a tigress in her own right as her anger tried to boil to the surface.

"Madame La Plume, I can never forgive you or Mr. Voight for the terrible things you've done to me, and I will never trust either of you again. I suspect these feelings are commonplace from anyone who has ever been associated with you. I feel pity for both of you because you must live your lives without true friendship, respect or love.

"I want to square our business entanglement before, I trust, I will never have to speak to either of you again. I want my name taken off of your property and I refuse to let you use my image or likeness in any way with your nightclub. This is a one-time offer to part without further conflict. Be assured that if you don't do this small thing, you will regret it. This isn't a threat, it's a true warning. I will not have my name associated with either of you from this day forward."

As she finished, Big George looked at the two of them with a smile of hatred that punctuated Josay's words. This kind of smile communicated messages to La Plume and Voight that they clearly understood.

Mr. Voight and Madame La Plume were speechless for a few seconds. When Mr. Voight gathered himself, he said, "I don't take well to threats or warnings. But I am sure that I don't want the credit for my successful business venture to go to some 'model' or 'celebrity' or whatever you might call yourself. I feel I have had my fill of you—although, some of my relations with you have been most pleasurable." He glared at her with an evil smile.

Josay, without thinking, and like she had done at the Poulet two years ago, leapt across the table in her beautiful pink dress and sank her fingernails into Voight's face, scratching him and causing his cheeks to bleed. At the same time, Big George put his arms around a struggling Voight and Josay got into his face and said, "You animal, I have given you the last warning you will ever get from me, smug bastard that you are. Take your whore partner out of my sight, and if you don't do what I ask, there will be consequences for you!"

By the time Josay was finished, Voight and La Plume were both encircled by Mr. Hover, Monsieur Sommes and Big George. George loosened his grip on Voight as he said with a whimper, "Did everyone see the way this vindictive bitch attacked me? She has a vendetta against me because I acquired her failed business. You better stay away from me."

He slinked across the street with La Plume holding his arm and directing his way.

I'm so sorry you had to see this, James. But you can't imagine what the two of them have done to me. I believe I'm developing a temper," she said as she straightened her outfit and seemed as well put together and beautiful as ever in an instant. "I hope we're still on for tonight?"

"Yes, of course, and you might as well know that your behavior today has made me ever more attracted to you. You are, without doubt, the most interesting person I've ever met. I want you and I to be associated with each other from now on, in business—and in life," said James.

The two embraced with mutual affection and smiled. She also bid farewell to William Hover as the cab arrived to take Josay and George the several blocks back to Josay's house to rest before the meeting at the exhibition location.

As she left, Josay called out to the two men, “You will never regret having me for a friend, either of you.”

CHAPTER 20

That evening, as the carriage rumbled down the cobblestone street through the streets of Paris, Josay wondered if her warning would be heeded by Voight and La Plume. If they didn't heed her threat, just what would she do? Could she go to the police? She wiped a little dirt off her sleeve and noticed a blot of blood on her elbow and wondered how it had gotten there. Just now she couldn't believe she had attacked Mr. Voight. She thought she might have killed him at that moment if she had not used great restraint. He certainly deserved the embarrassment and much, much more. She steeled herself with the notion that no matter what, no one else would abuse her again.

As the little carriage came to a stop near the exhibition location, she saw several of her friends sitting under a large oak tree at picnic tables enjoying wine, bread and cheese. What a welcome scene it painted in her mind as she got out of the coach. Within seconds, Renoir, Lautrec, Degas, and several of the women kissed her and lovingly embraced her.

"Come. Come and join us. We have missed you. What's the news about your farm? Are you alright? And what about your cabaret? How was that taken from you?" There were lots of questions.

With everyone listening, Josay gave an abbreviated summary of her last several weeks. Often the women gasped and the men shook their fist in the air as she told her tale. By the end, everyone was even more enamored with the courage and determination of this young vibrant beauty. As she came to the end of the story, she said, "Let me finish with the most important news I possess. I have secured enough money to open the doors to our exhibition."

"Oh my," said Renoir. "Where did you get the money? Don't you need whatever you can get to help your family rebuild the dairy?"

"I have enough to get the doors open and enough for improving the farm as well. I have also asked my friends who are well situated in the Paris elite to promote the exhibition among their friends. Between the posters, flyers and word of mouth, I think we will have enough publicity to attract real customers. We have to expect the Annual Paris Salon jury to push back, but I hope the newspapers will be on our side.

"As for me, I'll take a painting or two for my payment."

Lautrec laughed and said, "You don't require much payment since no one buys our paintings."

Everyone roared with belly laughs. Renoir added, "You certainly work for very little, but along with your choice of paintings at the exhibit, you have, and will always have our love and gratitude." He hugged her again.

"We have begun hanging our art in local bars and restaurants. You gave us the idea. And even if the Paradis Rue is gone and unavailable, maybe it will work-out this way."

Josay nodded. "That's wonderful! I do hope it does work."

"We just took the idea and ran with it. We have actually been able to drum up some interest in our work and the exhibition. Your pictures on our advertisement posters have gotten us some interest in the newspapers. Admittedly, the press and critics mostly condemn us and say our work is garbage and refuse. But any publicity at this point seems to attract interest. Who wouldn't want to see the Exhibition des Refuses?" added Renoir with a smile.

William and Elizabeth Hover arrived at that point and found that instead of a dry steering committee meeting, a celebration was erupting. The matters of whose painting would hang where would have to wait until another day.

The wine and fellowship and joy of the evening helped Josay forget her sordid afternoon with La Plume and Voight. As she was just on the edge of being a little too tipsy, she saw James Sommes walking across the plaza toward the small group. When he reached the gathering Josay couldn't help herself. She opened her arms to him and held him as she began to softly say, "I'm so sorry I left you. You are my rock, and I will never betray your friendship again. Can you ever forgive me?"

Nothing more was said about that. James held her face in both hands and kissed her softly. Josay was able to repress her deep secret about the pregnancy for the moment. It allowed her to revisit her love for James and enjoy her happy emotions for the night. As more and more friends and family of the artistic community arrived, they talked, drank wine, sang and danced. Happiness, a precious and sometimes rare commodity for this group, ruled the evening.

James called a carriage and offered to take Josay home. On the way back to her small house, James held her and made her feel the security she hadn't experienced in two years. He occasionally kissed her, but mostly just allowed her to snuggle close and relax. Josay was able to allow the feelings of love wash away her anxiety. When the small carriage got to her home, James asked her if she would see him again tomorrow. Josay responded that she would love to see him every day. He walked her up to her door, said good night and kissed her. She knew that she had to tell him about the baby sooner, rather than later, but not tonight. Tonight she wanted to enjoy the feeling of safety and happiness.

Inside the Follie Femme, Mr. Voight and Madame La Plume plotted their revenge on Josay.

"It's not over. No one treats me like that!" said Voight as he pounded his fist on the table. "I'll send out my boys to bring her here and we'll see if she is as brave as she was when that ape George had me pinned up. I'll call that club anything I like. I'm the owner now."

"Let's think about our next move," said La Plume. "You know we could just change the name of the club and let her go her way. What benefit does revenge do when we have won the war?"

Voight's face flushed and his nostrils flared when La Plume finished. He came to his feet and slapped La Plume across her face.

"You better watch what you say to me, you old ugly whore! Get out of my sight. I never want to see your face again!"

Mari pleaded with him, "But I love you Phillipe. We are supposed to run the Paradis Rue together. That's why I brought this whole plan to you."

He proceeded to take his anger out on La Plume with a harsh beating. Strike after strike with his fists, he pummeled her face and body. Her cries of pain attracted several of the workers. With a final kick into her side, Voight left her lying in the small office to be attended by the chorus girls.

"I'll get my revenge alright and I don't need any help from you."

La Plume was seriously injured. She could not get up. She felt a severe pain in her abdomen from the final kick administered by Voight.

As she whimpered, someone said, "We better get a doctor for this woman." That's when La Plume, still sprawled out on the floor, passed out.

The next day, one of the girls from the Follie Femme, knocked on Josay's door. "Mademoiselle Josay, I didn't know where else to go. I know you've had your differences with Madame La Plume recently, but she is very ill. Monsieur Voight beat her last night and she is laying in a small construction hut behind the Paradis Rue. I believe she will certainly die. Some of us called for the doctor, but Monsieur Voight refused to let him attend to her. He said there had been a mistake and no one at the Follie Femme was hurt. Madame could barely speak but the word she did say was, 'Josay.' Then two of the men carried her and dumped her into the construction hut."

Josay could not imagine why she felt anything but hatred for La Plume. After all, she had betrayed Josay twice in the most vile fashion. She was sure that if the circumstances were reversed, La Plume would let her die. But she wasn't La Plume.

"Alright, just give me a few minutes and I will come with you."

Josay found Big George and asked him to come along with them. She was certain that she might need someone to watch out for her. If Voight beat La Plume, a supposed ally, he would have no problem harming her if he could. Just as they were about to leave, Monsieur Sommes showed up and could not be persuaded to let Josay go without him.

When Josay, James and big George arrived, they found Madame La Plume still passed out in the small construction shed. Josay told George to get some water and James pulled out a brandy flask and poured a shot into Madame La Plume's mouth. She coughed and looked with terror into Josay's emerald green eyes.

"You're here. I'm so sorry for all I've done to you. I am a terrible and despicable person," she whispered as she passed out again.

When Big George got back with the water, they carried the unconscious La Plume to the carriage and took her directly to the local hospital. James knew the admitting nurse, having been to the hospital numerous times when his mother had been dying of a terrible cancer. Inside the hospital, La Plume revived and began to apologize over and over again in a fit of remorse.

Josay said, "Just close your eyes and sleep." The doctor administered something to ease the acute pain, and it did help her sleep.

"What are we going to do now?" Josay asked James.

"It's about time to let the authorities know about this devil Voight. I'll go to my childhood friend Chief Inspector Pierre Renet and tell him about this vicious assault, and the one he perpetrated on you. I'm sure he'll take action."

Josay had told James about how Voight had hit her and humiliated her in front of his minions, including Madame La Plume. But she didn't tell him about the rape part of the assault.

She didn't want James or anyone else to link her pregnancy to Phillipe Voight. She knew that Matthew Stuart was the father of her baby because she had shown all of the symptoms of pregnancy before the rape. It was important to her that James learn the whole truth of her pregnancy from her, and her alone, in private.

Josay said, "Let's keep it simple this time and only prosecute Voight for beating La Plume. It might muddle the water to mix my assault with this terrible beating. If we can get him convicted, I won't have to go through the humiliation of explaining why I didn't come to them with my complaint in a more timely manner."

"By the way, why didn't you?" asked Sommes.

"It's a long and complicated story, James. You'll just have to trust me for now and keep silent about that crime. I want to have time to explain the whole thing to you in private."

Big George and James left Josay beside the bed of her enemy, La Plume, and went to file a formal complaint about the beating with Inspector Renet. Josay was left to think about her secrets. She had many people to protect and defend. First and foremost, there was her family and the dairy which had already been attacked and burned once. She knew that Voight would have no qualms about finishing Donnel's work next time. Then there was the exhibition and all of the artist's hopes and dreams that could easily be damaged by a vengeful man like Voight. She must also keep her unborn child safe. Voight would seek to hurt it and her without a thought. She would be careful, but she would devise a plan that cleared the path for justice without putting anyone else in danger from Voight.

CHAPTER 21

At the dairy, David, a small group of Josay's friends, the farmworkers, and volunteering neighbors were making remarkable progress rebuilding the barn and fences while continuing to service and maintain their chain of distribution for the milk and dairy products.

David had the foresight and good sense to butcher all the cows that had been killed during the attack and distribute the meat to all those who helped with the cleanup and construction on the farm. It was a wonderful idea because it not only created good relationships among the community at large, but also fed most of the village for a weeks. This allowed them to spend a little of their time working on the Rue dairy as a repayment for the kindness. By working together, the subjugated group of tenant farmers and small businessmen became closer than they had ever been. They were all united against Donnel Regis.

The first batch of Chef Paul's cheese was an enormous success. He had been able to produce it in a very short time, and was already beginning to develop other recipes for more elegant cheeses that would require special storage and more time to produce. The specialty cheese would collectively be called, "Rue Family Fromage".

Parisians loved their cheese and ate it with almost every meal. Chef Paul had learned from the very best cheese makers in France. So this line of products had a real chance to clinch the success of the dairy for the future.

A large dairy business had been made possible by the invention of refrigeration which was invented in 1755, and the pasteurization process discovered in 1864 (only ten years or so earlier.) The building where their pasteurization took place on the farm had been destroyed by the fire along with their large refrigeration unit. These two things allowed the Rue dairy to distribute their milk and dairy products to Paris and other even more distant places without spoilage. They were the first items on the replacement list. Josay had sent money home immediately to secure these important tools.

All the finances for the dairy operation were being set up by Dr. Muse, David and Monsieur Rue. Dr. Muse was a master of business arrangements and before he became a drunk and lost his fortune, he was thought to be a financial genius. Now that he had sworn off alcohol, he was once again on top of contract development, taxation issues, permits, assets, liability calculations, and all manner of projections on supply costs, revenues and staffing. David was the operations manager and Josay's father was the general manager. Monsieur Rue had been in the dairy business his whole life and knew about all the logistics and maintenance that is required to run dairy farm. Mama was the kind-hearted patroness and 'face' of the dairy to the employees. She was a loving and nurturing person and well liked by all. Together, they made an excellent management team.

Josay had sent the extra money she had secured from James Sommes and a copy of the agreement to distribute the products to outlets in Paris. Dr. Muse was excited about the news and added it to the budget for the necessary expenditures.

Madame Foote knew how to implement plans as well. She stayed on top of all the practical work and standards for the staff. She had always valued cleanliness, even at the shabby Poulet. She made sure everything was scrubbed on a daily basis. She and Papa worked closely together and David found her to be an amazingly quick and diligent worker. She had grasped the workings of the dairy in only a few weeks. Along with the workers they had hired so far, she sometimes pitched in by milking the cows and cleaning the stables. She wasn't above any task at the dairy, but that was not her main function. She was very good with people and an expert at directing the workers and volunteers to do the necessary daily tasks. She had a cheerful and happy personality which made those around her enjoy even the most common work assignments. Having known abuse and poverty, Madame Foote had gratitude for being in a new business situation with people she genuinely cared about. She intended to make the most out of her good fortune and sincerely wanted to help the others to achieve their dreams, especially Josay.

It was this new found energetic business and commune environment that formed the basis of the positive dreams and hopes everyone had for the venture. The whole village wanted to be a part of this new found freedom, so long suppressed by the Regis family. With Donnel and his family finally gone and a fresh new spirit in the air, everyone looked optimistically toward the future.

Donnel had been able to sell the final few holdings of the former Regis monopoly to a group of investors from Paris. It included the old manner house and grounds, a few hundred acres of farmland and several old buildings in the village. Donnel cleared his gambling debts and the mortgage on the home with Monsieur Voight and had a small amount of money left over. He left the area, without saying goodbye to anyone, to rejoin his regiment. There was no fanfare, and certainly no one who knew him regretted his departure. He had become mean, arrogant and cruel since he left the village for the military academy and had alienated everyone who had called him a friend. He had squandered his wealth, his possessions and the love of Josay and everyone else. His jealousy and extreme sense of entitlement, along with rash and foolish actions had brought about his downfall. Now, it was only by Josay's forgiveness that he was able to escape prison for what he had done to her and her family. Of course, he blamed her for everything that had gone wrong in his life. He wished he had never met her, and had never loved her.

His parting thought was, *My life is ruined, and it's all because I thought I loved a peasant. If I had only done what my father demanded and married a highborn aristocrat's daughter, none of this would have happened to me. She and her whole family disgust me!*

When Josay came back for her first visit to the farm since the day after the fire, she found a smooth running and contented place. Everyone was given respect for their contributions and no one was treated as a second class citizen. Josay was hailed as a returning heroine when she stepped out of the carriage and surprised her parents and brother David. "Welcome home!" was the watch word of the day and a celebration was held that very afternoon with the entire village invited. There was dancing, singing and drinking. Everyone was merry and the air was light and smelled like cinnamon and roses. Josay was able to forget her problems in Paris and enjoy her homecoming.

The next morning included a tour and sampling of the cheese and other dairy products being produced at the new "Rue Family Dairy Products" farm. Josay loved the taste and smell of the wholesome milk products and the clean faces that showed up to work the farm. Madame Foote had everyone that worked the farm, most especially the ones that handled food, as clean as a whistle in their old, but starched, freshly washed and ironed clothes. Some of the wives of the dairy workers had been busy making work uniforms with the Rue Family Dairy Products emblem on the right pocket. For most of the workers, it was like belonging to a family. They wore their work suits with pride and felt their chests swell when they were given their coveralls with the new logo displayed prominently.

Everyone also ate together at the dairy. Everyday fresh bread was baked by Mrs. Rue, and all employees were offered a midday meal. As far as the villagers were concerned, the Rue dairy was the place to work and make a life for your family. The result was that the products they produced were amazing and quickly in demand in their area and all the way to Paris.

A few days later, Josay was to return to Paris for a final meeting with her artist friends before the scheduled opening of the Impressionist Exhibition which was now only days away. She felt very sick due to the pregnancy. Josay had not shared her situation with anyone at the farm but her brother and Madame Foote so far. Her mother and father seemed so concerned about her health, she felt it was time to tell them about the baby. So she told them in private and asked for their understanding and continued support for her decision to raise her child without his, or her, American father. They both readily agreed to help their daughter in whatever way she wished and thought she had made the right decision about Matthew Stewart. Her entire family pleaded with her to forgo her trip to Paris and stay in this new place that she loved and that loved her so deeply in return. She stalled one more day, but then left on the following morning feeling much better. Big George went with her.

Monsieur James Sommes met them at the carriage waystation. George excused himself to run some errands, and Josay and James went to her small house. He was ecstatic to see her and made a big fuss on the station platform with roses and hugs as if she were returning from an extended vacation. The two shared a few moments inside Josay's home with intimate kisses and soft words of love and desire.

Josay said, "I have missed you so much my love. I am quite sure I have fallen completely for you and I want to tell you something tonight after dinner when we have time to talk and be alone."

"Why not just tell me now," said James. "Is everything well with you? Do you need anything?" He could tell from the changed expression on Josay's face that there was an important topic to be uncovered."

Just as she was about to tell James the secret of her pregnancy, there was a loud knock on the door. "Welcome home," said Renoir and Lautrec. "We thought we might steal a few minutes to talk about our salon before you got too busy with this kind gentleman who seems to be dominating most of your time these days."

Both men had brought their easels and supplies hoping to render a few last sketches of Josay for new posters to be placed strategically around Paris for one last push to create interest in the Impressionist

Exhibition. Josay had become a symbol of youth and beauty and of change in Paris. Both artists sought to again capitalize on her image and celebrity.

"Can you at least let me wash my face and comb my hair before I pose for you?" she said with a goodhearted laugh.

"You two are always looking for a way to be alone with my girl," said James. "If you weren't so homely, Toulouse, and you so married, Auguste, I might be jealous."

Renoir and Lautrec sketched as James watched and occasionally looked around the room. While he was looking he accidentally noticed the letter from Matthew Stewart. "I see you and Matthew are still corresponding."

When his innocent statement fell on Josay's ears she became flushed and dropped the flowers she was holding in her pose. "Sorry," she said. "I'm feeling a little tired from the past few days. Can't you finish the rest from memory?"

"Of course," said Auguste, and the two artists began to pack up their easels and paints. "I'm sure you two have lots to say to each other without prying ears. We will be in touch within this week to further discuss the plan for the 'Grand Opening' of our salon. Until then, you have our love and thanks for all you've done for us."

The two men left, and Josay found herself standing in front of James unable to speak. She reached out and embraced him so tightly that he laughingly said, "I'm not going anywhere. You don't have to squeeze the breath out of me."

Big George knocked on the door at that moment. "I was able to get a few things for dinner and for the coming week. I hope I am not interrupting anything."

"Oh, no.... of course not George. Thank you for doing that for me."

The rest of the evening was spent with a quiet dinner. After eating James stayed for the first time with Josay in the little house until dawn. They didn't make love, but slept soundly, embraced in comfortable bliss. Big George was in the next room with very thin walls, so the explanation of her pregnancy was again put off until tomorrow.

After tea and cheese in the morning, he returned to the city center for meetings with his father and other businessmen. He was as optimistic and happy as he had ever been in his life.

CHAPTER 22

After James left, Josay took a bath and dressed herself in her green dress. She intended to visit Madame La Plume and finish, forever, her involvement with the evil woman. For some reason, despite all the harm La Plume had caused her in her life, she couldn't just walk away from her and leave her to her dismal and disgusting end. As she opened the door to leave, there stood Matthew Stewart about to knock. Josay almost fainted and fell back only barely able to catch herself from falling.

"What are you doing here?" she whispered.

On the dairy farm, David called a short stand-up meeting after breakfast with all the members of the community of workers.

"We are doing well but I've heard from Donnel Regis. He has contacted the local magistrate and claims that the sale of the farm and surrounding properties was conducted under duress. It seems that there was pressure exerted by a gangster named Voight to turn over the property in repayment for some trumped-up gambling debts. The magistrate says that the paperwork on the transactions between and among all parties looks valid, but he is obligated to investigate. Unbelievably, while he does his due diligence, our assets and cash are frozen. Our operating capital is not currently available."

"What? Are you serious? We don't believe for a second that the Rue family had anything to do with underhanded dealings. If anything, Donnel himself should have been prosecuted for arranging the 'night of terror.' He is a devil and we all know it," said one of the workers.

"Yes we all know that is true, but we are obligated to put a temporary hold on our growth and business development. I need to ask all of you if you would be willing to wait for your salaries. We will make sure that everyone is fed and properly cared for. After all, we are a farm and we can still conduct business as usual. We just can't do the expansion we hoped to do with the profits we have accumulated until the investigation is concluded. The magistrate has allowed us to continue working the dairy with the caveat that we must keep strict records of all of our dealings. Dr. Muse is doing that already. We can only hope that after this sham of an accusation is concluded, it will be the end of the curse of the Regis family's reign over this village and countryside."

Everyone was more than willing to cooperate and all trusted the leadership of the Rue family, Madame Foote and Dr. Muse.

"We would not have the hope of a successful future without you and your family. We trust you and pledge to stay with you without complaint," said another of the employees as all were nodding their approval.

The small group was breaking up when a rider approached the farm at a gallop. It was young Stephen, the county mail carrier.

"I have an important message for David Rue," he said excitedly as he delivered the sealed letter into David's hand.

It was from the local magistrate. David opened it slowly, and after taking a deep breath he read, "Donnel Regis has been killed in a knife fight in a brothel in northern France. The lawsuit has been summarily dropped. You are free to access your money. All the ownership rights to the farm and fields are firmly in the hands of the Rue family, without opposition at this time."

The news was met with a spontaneous elation. That day was celebrated for years to come as the beginning of freedom, and the end of oppression, for the entire region.

In Paris, Josay was conflicted. She still loved Matthew and was carrying his child. But she also loved James and knew him to be true and worthy of her love and faithfulness. She wanted to make a lasting and happy marriage with James. She didn't think she could ever trust Matthew again, no matter what he said to her.

"I'm more than surprised," she said as she blocked the door from his entry." Again she asked, "What are you doing here?"

"May I came in? he said as he took her hand to kiss. "I have to talk to you. I regret having to send you that letter, and I am so sorry I didn't tell you my true situation. But that situation has changed and I want to make things right with you. Please let me in."

Josay opened the door to her small house but blocked the full entry into the home so that Matthew was left standing in the entryway. She felt a rush of excitement at seeing Matthew in spite of his awful betrayal. She thought that asking him fully inside might surely be a mistake. *I must be strong,* she thought.

Matthew, realizing that he was to be given only a short amount of time, came straight to the point.

"I know that keeping my marriage secret from you was a mistake and that you must have been very hurt and disappointed that I would do something like that to you. I swear to you, it was never my intention to let our relationship go as far as it did. I admit that at the beginning, I was mostly sexually attracted to you. I had seen you in Renoir's painting and there was a strong urge to meet you in person. Then I met you in person and I was so smitten, I acted without reason or rationale. I just wanted to be around you, and yes, I wanted to make love to you. But as we were more involved and I got to know you, I lost my heart and came to realize that you would be the greatest love of my life. But the reality was that there couldn't be a real commitment unless I cleared the air with my wife and asked her for a divorce. My wife and I had not been happy for several years and a divorce should have been a relief for both of us. But she had received a letter detailing our affaire. I am not sure who wrote the letter or how they were able to find out where to send it, but she was very angry, hurt and humiliated. She was threatening to ruin me with the scandal and take my children away from me forever. So I gave up all my ties to France and to you and went home thinking that I would forget you, and that would be that."

Josay looked at his face and he certainly seemed sincere and truthful. Or, maybe it was just that the words she was hearing were what she had dreamed of in the past few months.

Matthew went on to say, "I have now been honest with my wife in America and it seems that she was of a mind to find someone else as well. In fact, with all of my travels and absences, she may well have already found a suitable replacement for me. I don't really know for sure. But her anger subsided, finally, and we have agreed to divorce. I didn't want you to know about all of these wranglings until they were concluded. It was not pleasant, after all. I suppose separations never really are. My wife got a really unfair amount of my money and formal custody of the children. I love my children, and fortunately I can still see them on a scheduled basis.

So, I made the trip back here because I thought it would certainly be worth a try to get you back and begin again, fresh and honest."

Josay did not respond. She was dumbfounded. She had put the thoughts of a life with Matthew completely out of her head and had allowed her heart to move on to the wonderful, sincere and honest James Sommes who had always been there for her. *Is it possible that I could love two men at once? She thought.*

She caught herself before speaking her innermost emotions and simply said, "I am in a relationship with James Sommes. I need to leave now to meet him."

She gently pushed Matthew out the door, and as she did, she said, "You hurt me very deeply. I still have feelings for you, but I don't think they could ever be as strong as they once were because of your lies and betrayal. What I do know is that I do love James very much. Please leave now and let me find a way to happiness without breaking open this hurtful old wound."

Matthew began to walk away but at the last moment turned around and said, "I am not giving up. I know I can show you how true my love and faithfulness can be. It seems that I'll have to fight for you, and I certainly will."

At that moment, Josay thought about calling Matthew back to tell him not to waste his time. Her love and future was now firmly committed to James. She didn't know why she failed to do this. Something kept her silent. Perhaps, it was the baby growing inside her. She would have to face telling both of them about the baby. But right now she was on her way to the hospital to visit Mari La Plume.

Madame La Plume was preparing herself mentally to see Josay at the hospital. She knew that she didn't deserve any considerations from Josay but also knew that deep inside her she felt extraordinary remorse for the way she had betrayed and hurt her only steadfast friend. Josay had never been anything but a faithful and true woman. Using the trust of others had been a technique in La Plume's arsenal of swindle. Just get the suckers to give you their trust and you could use them and get everything they possessed. It was a conman's basic tool. But this time it had backfired. She had twice brutalized Josay emotionally and physically and had been left with the consequences of her evil.

She, herself, had been discarded like garbage by the person who had conspired with her in her deceit and larceny against Josay. And Voight had finally destroyed her abusive heart by almost beating her to death. He had no love for her at all. He was merely pretending to care because of the promise of monetary gain. She had deluded herself into thinking that she could make him love her. Now she had nowhere to turn. She had no idea what she could say to Josay to make up for these wrongs?

As Josay entered the old and dingy hospital she saw the wretched dregs of the poor and ne'er-do-wells of the city of Paris, France. It could hardly be called a hospital. It was a series of large rooms with rows of cots and dirty beds . Their filthy occupants were visited by every kind of disease and injury.

The medical attendants looked tired, soiled and overwhelmed with the sheer number of patients to be treated. It was obvious that most of them lacked the basic skills required to comfort or treat their patients. There were only two doctors on duty. One of them was a disgraced drunkard that had routinely been declared guilty of every level of malpractice. The other was a young 22 year old intern who somehow found himself plagued with this assignment and was eager to get away from it as soon as he could find another position. In other words, this was a place where patients were condemned to die, if not from their ailment, then from being in the hospital.

As Josay walked through the rooms, she saw men, women and children in the most awful pain, and enduring unbelievable suffering. They were not only sick or badly hurt, but they were hungry, thirsty and crowded into conditions that would have been insufferable for healthy people.

Just before reaching the room where La Plume was warehoused, she passed by the worst place she had ever seen. It was the portion of the hospital called the lunatic asylum. She saw wretches, chained to the wall, naked and screaming at her as she passed. Most of them were barely skin and bones. Some were bound with belts to their beds. And some were not bound, but sat in awkward positions in stupors. They gazed into the air without emotion or life. These people were, it seemed to Josay, the living dead. It left a horrifying impression on her that she would revisit in nightmares forever after.

In the next wing, Josay saw La Plume bandaged, and clad in thread worn bedclothes. She was sitting in a straight backed chair near an open window. As La Plume gazed out the window, Josay tapped her on the shoulder.

"I'm here," said Josay.

Madame La Plume turned her bloodshot eyes and bruised face toward Josay and began to cry.

She sobbed and said, "I'm so sorry for my hateful behavior toward you. You were never anything but kind and honest with me. I have no excuse but I can say, without doubt, that after almost dying and having been face-to-face with my maker, I have heard an inner voice that has told me to beg for forgiveness and make my life mean something positive. Josay, believe me when I say that God actually talked to me. He showed me the endless darkness of hell. That experience and being around these lost souls condemned to suffer and die here in this place, I am changed, and you are the first wrong I intend to make right."

Josay had heard this from La Plume before and would not allow herself to so easily be fooled again. She continued to listen but did not respond.

"I know where all the bones Voight has buried are located. I know how he has robbed, cheated and abused almost everyone he has ever known. And, what's more important, I know exactly how he cheated you and your partners out of the Paradis Rue. I will go with you to the authorities, and I will testify to your assault and rape. I will tell them about the night club swindle. I also know about all of the other crimes he has committed against his employees, customers and everyone around him. He is an evil person, and I accepted that from him since that is the only thing that I have known up until I met you.

You see, I thought I was in love with him, and I wanted him to return my love because I was helping him with his evil deeds. But I was a fool to think that he would be capable of loving anyone but himself." She began to cry again.

Josay's forgiving heart was touched when La Plume finished her revelations. Josay said quietly, "I will try to forgive you. But you have tricked me before with your silky words. This time you must prove your loyalty by helping me stop this criminal forever. You must be a witness in court to right the many wrongs he has caused, not only to me and my partners, but others as well. We will go to the authorities when you are well enough. Until then, I'm going to have you moved from this terrible place back into my house and a clean bed."

La Plume began to sob again and said, "God's vengeance will be done to the evil that is Voight, but I will repent my many sins and I will keep faith with you, my precious Josay, for the rest of my life. I promise.

CHAPTER 23

After walking back through the crowded halls of the asylum and leaving the hospital, Josay felt her inner strength begin to surge. She knew in her heart that it was her responsibility to put Voight out of commission and to save others from his tyranny. La Plume was the key to this end, like it or not.

But before she could be brave enough to take on this monster, she knew she needed to find a way forward with Matthew, James and the baby. She sat on a bench opposite the Paradis Rue, once again under construction, and a few blocks from her little house. She had to tell both James and Matthew about the baby and accept the consequences, wherever they may lead. She sat there for what seemed like hours, just thinking.

At the exhibition hall there was great activity with the Impressionist Exhibition only days away. All the artists were making final adjustments on their paintings and deciding just how to hang them so as to make the greatest impression on the viewers. Edmond

Renoir, Auguste's brother, was the person who was doing most of the work hanging the paintings. Lautrec and Van Gogh were especially unhelpful, and drank absinthe, glass after glass. They were so intoxicated and smelly that Edmond and Monet took both of them by the neck and pitched them into a nearby fountain.

"Sober up," said Monet. "We will not have you ruin this exhibition and our chances to make a good impression on our patrons."

Lautrec and Van Gogh staggered away just as Josay was coming up the exhibition ramp. She watched as the two problem children of art were arm in arm walking toward the nearest bar. Wet and seemingly so revitalized by their dip into the cool pool, they sang drinking songs as they departed.

After greeting a few of the artists standing around to watch the Van Gogh/Lautrec show, Josay asked Auguste Renoir to step aside.

"I need your advice. I am in a very complicated and potentially dangerous situation."

She went on to describe the whole La Plume and Voight situation. After telling Renoir so much of her many secret conflicts and challenges, she almost even shared her most guarded problem, the pregnancy. But she caught herself. She felt she must tell Matthew and James before anyone else here in Paris.

Renoir was a good listener but wasn't used to having anyone come to him with their problems. He actually existed in his own orbit and although he was a good father and husband, he seldom solved any family problems. He left the management of his household to his dutiful wife. He was, therefore, surprised that Josay would confide in him and actually seek his advice and counsel.

His first response of, "Why are you telling me this?" surprised Josay.

"Because you are a trusted friend and I value your opinion. You have been like a father or older brother to me this past turbulent two years and you are the only family I have in Paris. But if you don't want to involve yourself in my problems, I will certainly understand. Forgive me, please. I have misjudged the boundaries of our friendship."

Renoir realized immediately as he looked into Josay's sad green eyes, that he had made an insensitive mistake. He did have a very deep and loving relationship with this petite girl and he did care about her problems.

His fatherly instincts took over and he said, "Of course you can tell me anything. But if I give you poor advice, you must know it was the best counsel I could give at the time."

Josay told her story in more detail, and Renoir was alternating between sad, touched and angry to the point of boiling.

How could anyone take advantage of this kind and caring young woman? he thought to himself.

When she finally finished telling him all but one of her deepest secrets, Renoir said, "Everything can be sorted out with the help of the many people that love you dearly. I will ask your inner circle of friends to come together and we will begin to reciprocate the kind of care and concern you have shown to all of us. We will deal with the Voight problem in a measured and well thought out way so that your personal future is secure."

"That is very kind of you. I need to take action quickly. I don't want this matter to interfere with the opening of the exhibition that we have worked so hard to bring to the public."

"I agree. Let's call James Sommes' friend, Chief Inspector Renet. You can decide what other friends and family and possible witnesses should be there to help in the explanation you want to give to the inspector. We can all get together at your house to produce a plan that will put Mr. Voight and his reign of terror to an end.

The time was set for two nights hence, and the two hugged as Josay felt a small part of the load she was carrying, lifted from her small shoulders. She would send a message immediately to David, Dr. Muse and Madame Foote. She hoped that they could arrange to come to Paris on this very short notice. She would also ask William Hover, James Sommes, Mr. Bleux and Mr. Stewart to be there. She hoped the star witness, Madame La Plume, would be feeling strong enough to tell her story by then.

The evening of the meeting with Inspector Renet, James and Matthew showed up at her door simultaneously, one hour before all the others. When she saw both of them together, she felt a cold chill run up her back. It was as if she had been discovered committing some awful crime. She asked them to stay just outside the little white house for a moment of private discussion before going inside for the meeting.

"Josay, James and I would like some resolution to this three person romance. Which one of us do you really want to be with?" said Matthew.

"Let me correct that statement," responded James, "He decided he needed to get involved in our love affaire. I see no need for him to interrupt the plans we have made for our life together. Unfortunately, he won't leave until you insist that he go, at once, and never return. Please tell him to go and leave us alone."

Both the men looked at Josay for a response and Josay could not speak for a long anxious moment.

"I can't talk about this with you right now. My family farm has been burned, and I am about to begin a very difficult criminal case involving Mr. Voight. It will take all my strength. I've also had a deep personal problem that you will find out about later. I am sorry, Matthew, but as I have told you before, I am with James. However, I do have something to discuss with both of you that may change the situation for all three of us." The men were puzzled by this statement.

There was silence until James spoke saying, "Of course, I will stand by you in this crisis. And while your commitment seems more tentative than I would like, I will continue to love you and help you to solve any problems necessary."

Matthew quickly added, "It wasn't the response I wanted either. But I think that maybe It did leave the door slightly open for me to get you back. I will try and make every effort to win your love again."

James lost his calm and sensitive demeanor and said, "I will wait for a firm decision, but it's hard to begin our relationship when this man shows up out of the blue and is able turn your head. You seem to be waivering in your commitment to me! I will give you the benefit of the doubt for a few days because of your situation, but I am deeply hurt by this ambiguity."

He looked straight at Matthew and said, "You keep away from me."

Then he confidently walked into the little house and took a seat at the table Josay had set up for the meeting.

Matthew said, "I know this is a terrible situation for you, Josay, but we can live through it and solve any problems necessary."

He was about to hug and console her as Renoir came to the door with several of the other painters. Matthew stepped aside, followed them and entered the room, seating himself at the opposite end of the table from James.

When everyone was situated and after introductions were made, it was Mr. Hover that took on the role of moderator and leader. He was about to let Josay speak when Lautrec appeared, straightened himself and sat on a tall stool so he could be at the same eye level as the other participants.

He was amazingly sober, or at least appeared to be, when he said, "Pardon me for being late."

He flashed a smile at Josay that communicated his desire to be included as a true, albeit frequently absent friend.

With Inspector Renet taking notes, Josay told the story of the larceny and degradation that she had endured because of Voight and La Plume. (She left out the rape itself.) She thanked everyone there and asked for their support in helping her bring Monsieur Voight to justice.

Then, it was Madame La Plume's turn to explain her part in the crimes.

"I have debased myself in countless ways trying to make my way forward in life. I have deceived and hoodwinked innocent people, turned my head to ignore sexual assaults, including the horrible assault endured by Josay, and I have lied and cheated almost every day of my miserable life. I have often paid for my life of crime with beatings, time in prison and the fact that I have no real friends or confidants. My childhood was very brutal but that affords me no excuse for the track I took in life. I chose the easy path of deceit and crime. The very worst offense of my hateful existence was the day I betrayed Josay for the second time, and allowed her to be used, cheated and cast aside like a piece of garbage. I paid a price for my betrayal with a beating from Voight which almost ended me, but it wasn't all I deserved. I intend to endeavor to clear away some of my evil doings by testifying here in front of the inspector about all the crimes against citizens, employees and patrons of the Femme Follie and the Paradis Rue. I have first hand knowledge of many of these crimes and I believe I can produce countless witnesses to corroborate every accusation. This will include the swindle perpetrated on these gentlemen and Josay which caused the Paradis Rue business to pass into the hands of Phillipe Voight. I humbly ask Josay, yet again, for her forgiveness. From this day forward, I swear to be an unwavering friend to her, even if it costs me my life."

No one spoke for a long second until Josay reached her hand across the table and said, "We will seek justice. I will offer a tentative but hopeful forgiveness to this woman."

Most everyone in the room reacted negatively when they heard this statement from Josay. Some were even verbally saying, "No!"

But Josay said, " If I can forgive, so can all of you. Surely she has harmed my body, spirit and soul more than anyone else here."

Everyone looked at each other for a long pause.

Mr. Hover said, "I'm sure all of us will try to forgive Madame La Plume as well, no matter how difficult it might be, in order to come together to rid humanity of this monster. But for now, let's continue to give the inspector all of the evidence and testimony he will need to make a quick arrest. Once he is able to put this creature in prison, he won't be free to harm anyone else."

Madame La Plume began to list details of other assaults, rapes and various other crimes that she knew about, including her own beating. She told about the blackmail of government officials to get a work stoppage for the Paradis Rue and the bribery of politicians to get the new law about cabaret ownership restrictions for females under thirty years of age. She also knew about the torture and murder of a few individuals but vowed that she was not a direct witness to those crimes.

As the meeting was breaking up, Matthew approached Madame La Plume and said, "You mentioned an assault on Josay, what kind of assault was it? Was it a sexual assault?"

Madame La Plume realized immediately that she may well have inadvertently shared a secret that Josay might not have had the time or courage to share with those most dear to her, especially Mr. Stewart who had only recently come back into her life. She knew how difficult it was for women to talk of rape with their loved ones and she had swung the door wide open without giving the person inside, time to prepare for the encounter.

La Plume replied to Matthew, "I think you better talk to Josay about the assault. It was brutal and it is among my greatest regrets that I didn't do anything to stop or mitigate the most severe punishment any woman can withstand."

"So you are saying that she was raped?"

"I'm saying that she needs to tell you all that she thinks needs to be said about that."

Matthew wanted to ask for more details but La Plume turned away and was embraced by Madame Foote. Then everyone in the room broke into spontaneous conversations.

Josay was comforted by David who said, "Why didn't you tell me about the assault? I'm your family. I would have immediately gone after this vile man! He was also probably involved in the burning of the farm with Donnel Regis, so I have reason enough to seek revenge even before knowing the fact that he abused my little sister."

Josay was unable to speak but allowed her head to bury into David's chest for immediate comfort, and to hide her undeserved shame.

Why had La Plume mentioned the sexual assault? She thought to herself. Josay was about to break under all the stress piled up on her small back and shoulders.

Inspector Renet finished the meeting by saying, "I believe we will have enough evidence to arrest Phillipe Voight very soon. I will work on preparing the indictment immediately," he said in parting.

He left to gather his police comrades to help him seek warrants for the arrests of the infamous and dangerous character and his thugs. He knew he must have everything submitted perfectly, because Voight was known to be smart and devious. He had somehow avoided prison up until this point in time, even though he was an obvious criminal. He also had people in high places that may try to help him because of blackmail threats against them.

After inspector Renet left, everyone in the room lingered to talk about the horror of Mr. Voight's crimes and the hurtful actions and cowardice demonstrated by La Plume. Renoir and Lautrec spoke in low terms about just how they intended to help this important young woman and to give her the support of the entire artistic community.

As the full moon rose over the little house in Montmartre, everyone departed except Josay, David and La Plume. All three, settled together on the overstuffed couch with David in the middle comforting each of the sobbing women in turn when a small knock on the door stopped their crying.

CHAPTER 24

David went to the door of Josay's little house and opened it to reveal several young women. One of them was bloody and was being supported by the others.

"Is Madame La Plume here?" said the oldest one, who like all the others was dressed in her brightly colored cancan costume from the Follie Femme.

"Yes, come in, please," said David as he lifted the badly injured girl and carried her to the bedroom. "What happened to her?"

"She was attacked and beaten for talking back to Monsieur Voight. She warned him that he shouldn't hurt the younger girls. Then his men held her while he swore at her, punched her and ripped her clothes off of her. He was about to rape her when a gentleman from the club knocked on the door. We took the chance to carry her out the back door, and the only thing we knew to do was to take her to Madame La Plume. Madame La Plume understands the struggles we go through and sometimes has sympathy and helps. She was attacked herself for standing up to Mr. Voight. Is she here? They told us at the hospital we would find her here."

"I'll find someone to attend to her wounds. It looks like it isn't a serious injury, although I'm sure she's scared and hurting. She will be safe here, as will all of you," David added.

Just then, another knock on the door revealed Matthew Stewart, James Sommes and Auguste Renoir.

"Oh no! Now we must go back for the midnight show or we will lose our jobs, or even worse. We could be next to be beaten and raped."

"You ladies will not go back to the Follie Femme tonight," said Matthew Stewart. "I guarantee you won't lose your jobs or one sou of salary. Just sit down until we can find a way to help you."

The small brunette to his right, held his arm and said, "What can you do? You don't know what Monsieur is capable of. He could kill us, or even one of you here tonight." Her voice was shaking in fear as she spoke.

"We will find Inspector Renet and we will have him arrested. Come gentlemen, we will get that scum put away tonight!" pledged Matthew.

Matthew, James, David and Renoir found the inspector at his home. He cautioned the men to go back to Josay's house and leave it up to him and the police. But they were all enraged with Voight and couldn't wait for Inspector Renet to gather the police officers and paperwork needed to enter the Follie Femme to arrest him. Instead, they all immediately piled into a hired carriage and headed toward the Follie Femme.

The four men arrived well before the inspector and the police. They walked straight through the central showroom and pushed aside the big man at the back office door. David knocked him to the ground and out cold with one swing. Inside the office, Voight sat at a big desk with several other mobsters. As the four men broke through the door, Voight pulled open the top drawer of his desk, retrieved a hand gun, and shot James Sommes in the stomach. David jumped across the desk before he could fire again and kicked him in the face with his boot. Voight scrambled to get up and three of the thugs grabbed David and began to punch and kick him. Matthew came to his rescue and hit two of the mobsters with a lamp, one with a right swing and the other as he swung back left. Both of the mobsters fell to the floor, but Voight lunged for the revolver. Before he could reach it, Renoir got the gun and aimed it directly at the head of Phillipe Voight.

"That's enough. Hands up," Renoir said with resolve.

Voight and his remaining henchman got to their feet and raised their arms. "What is this?" said Voight. "Who are you and why are you attacking us?"

"Let's just say we came to represent some showgirls," said Renoir.

Matthew, got to his feet and went to James. "You're wounded! Someone get the police and let's get him to the hospital!"

Just then Inspector Renet and seven police officers burst into the club and came straight to the back room. By now, almost all the patrons and employees had run out into the street screaming.

When Inspector Renet entered the back office he saw a wounded and badly bleeding James Sommes with Renoir holding a gun on five men. David and Matthew were attending to James' wounds.

"Arrest these men," said Renet pointing to Voight and the other four mobsters. "And get the one laying in front of the door in cuffs too."

"What the hell are you doing? This is my nightclub and these men came in, uninvited, and attacked me. You idiot! You should be arresting them, not me. I know my rights."

"Get him out of here," said Renet.

As the six men were being hauled away by the authorities, medical personnel arrived and began to attend to James.

"We have to get him to a hospital....NOW!" said the medic who seemed to be in charge.

"I'm going with him," said Matthew as they put James on a litter. Out the door they went at breakneck speed.

"You men should have waited for me. I'm afraid this is going to be a terrible mess for me to explain. It is at least an unnecessary complication in what was going to be an open and shut case," said Renet.

CHAPTER 25

When Josay heard that James had been shot at the Follie Femme, she and La Plume immediately left for the hospital. She told the show girls to relax and wait at the little white house until they returned.

In route, she passed several posters with her image advertising the coming of the Impressionist Exhibition set to begin in only a few days. Her mind was filled with a combination of concern for James and excitement at the prospect of the salon finally coming to realization. She questioned her own thoughts.

"*Why am I even thinking about anything but James? He is so true and faithful. He's kind and gentle; a perfect man really, and I love him very much. Why am I waivering at all? I know that James is the right man for me. Can my heart be so fickle? Am I a bad person? I still have love in my heart for Matthew despite his lying and unfaithfulness.*"

As these random thoughts dissipated, her mind went back to the horrible reality that James was shot by that despicable monster, Voight, and was in the hospital fighting for his life.

When she arrived at the hospital she immediately went to James and found Matthew, David and Renoir surrounding his bed. La Plume was shown to a chair as she was still in bandages herself.

"He has been asking for you," said Matthew with sincere concern.

When Josay saw James in the hospital bed, wounded and weak from his injuries, injuries that he had gotten because he had tried to help her, and other victims of a scoundrel that he would never have even known if not for her, she knew that she loved him deeply and completely. He had given all of himself for her. He was a kindred spirit who put helping others before his own safety. She knew that she would love him forever, despite any doubts that she may have had before.

The doctor came into the room as Josay took James' hand and said, "I am here, my Darling."

"Josay, I was afraid you wouldn't make it on time. I believe in one love…one love, forever. And my one love is you, my dearest Josay."

His voice was getting weaker and was now only a whisper. Josay told him to save his strength and rest and that all would be well.

He continued softly, "But in this life, I am sure that my time with you will be cut short. Come closer. It is very hard to speak. Please ask these other people to leave except for my father."

The Doctor told everyone to leave but cautioned Josay that she needed to be quick with her conversation.

"He has lost a lot of blood and we can't seem to stop the hemorrhaging," he concluded as he, too, left the room.

"Oh James, you can't leave me like this. I love you to the depths of my heart. I've been such a fool to let you think otherwise, for even a moment," she said as her warm tears dropped from her cheeks to his. She pulled him closer in a warm embrace, desperately wishing for some miracle to save him.

"Josay, I have no regrets. I want you to be happy. You are young and beautiful and I know you are going to be a wonderful wife and mother someday. But in case you don't marry, I want you to have everything I own. I have told my father that I want you to have my share of the Sommes estate....my inheritance."

He gazed toward his father and said, "Have the lawyers draw it up quickly before I sleep."

"We would have had a wonderful life together. I love you," he whispered. He coughed and closed his eyes.

The presence of intense pain left his face. It was over, and just like that, he was dead.

Josay could be heard throughout the hospital as she let loose a mournful wail, "James, don't leave me. No. No. No!"

As she burst into uncontrollable emotion, David, Matthew and the others came back into the room and pulled her away from James so the doctor could check his vital signs.

"I'm afraid he's gone," said the doctor with a sad but even tone to his voice.

James' father rushed to his son. He took him by the hand and said, "My boy. My kind and perfect boy." With tears running down his face, he held James to his breast. "What have they done to you? You are to blame." he said as he pointed his finger at Josay. "What did he ever do but be good to you and love you. But you could never return his love without doubts. You just couldn't love him back and honor his trust. You and your friends got him murdered! Get out! Everyone get out and let me grieve for my child. Please."

Josay continued to sob as both David and Matthew escorted her from the room and down the hallway. As they came to a bench in the waiting area, Inspector Renet approached them.

"I'm so sorry for your loss, he was a dear friend of mine as well. And even though we are all devastated by his loss, all of you will have to come down to the station to bear witness to the crimes alleged to have been committed by Monsieur Voight and his associates. I will be investigating all the crimes that surround the Follie Femme tonight, which includes the shooting of James. We also have a few more questions about the accusations that have been attested to tonight by Madame La Plume," said Renet.

Everyone nodded their heads and agreed to go directly to the police station.

"There are also numerous complaints lodged by other men and women that include assaults, rape and other murders. This will all take some time. For now, Mr. Voight and his henchmen are safely locked away. Naturally, Voight has obtained counsel and has a good chance of being set free within a few days, so we must be able to move the investigation along quickly."

Renet added with a stern voice, "Not waiting for me and my officers before you broke into the Follie Femme was a big mistake. It had the feel of a lynch mob. And I know that Monsieur Voight's lawyer will turn the script in that direction, expeditiously."

He paused for a moment, and then continued., "I will not arrest you now, because I know that you acted in the passion of the moment against an obvious criminal," he said to David, Matthew and Renoir. "But you should have waited for me."

Having given Josay a hug of support and concern, the inspector left.

They all went to the police station and spent hours answering questions by several different officers. It was daylight outside before they were allowed to leave.

Josay looked at her brother, Matthew, La Plume and Renoir and said, "I will call upon my deepest inner strength to help convict this animal. I know one person that will testify with firsthand knowledge of his violence....and that person is me."

La Plume said, "I will be a true friend this time. I know that I have many sins to account for with you, but know that I will sacrifice anything to help you get revenge and justice for yourself, your dear James, and all of the others.

"It will be hard to get the other girls and employees of the Follie Femme to testify because they are afraid of the influence, and far reach of a vengeful Voight. I will be true and begin immediately to gather whatever evidence we will need to have this man face the guillotine," said La Plume.

She imagined that she would be able to erase many of her sins againsts Josay with her testimony against Mr. Voight. She thought that she could begin to make amends and restart her own life on a truer path. She steeled her inner self for the days ahead, because she knew that there was a chance that she would be held accountable for some of the larceny.

Mari Belle LaPlume hugged the sobbing Josay as they made their way back to the little white house with David. The others went their separate ways.

Monsieur Sommes continued to mourn his son alone in the stark and dingy hospital room, not knowing what else to do. His entire hope for the future was lying dead on the bed in front of him.

A small group of painters who were assembled at Monet's home were abuzz with rumors and secondhand reports of Josay and Renoir's roles in a murder at the Follie Femme. They awaited Renoir's appearance and his account of events since this exhibition was so important to all of their careers and lives. They all held a dread about just the way these troubles would reflect on their exhibition. It was an event that all of them needed to move them from relative obscurity and irrelevance into the light of artistic success and financial security. Josay was the face of the exhibition and Renoir its principal artistic presence. They worried that the whole shaky foundation of their salon and their potential chance at professional redemption might collapse in a heap of bad press, innuendo and gossip?

Toulouse took an unexpected and atypical leadership role and banged a pallet knife on the table to bring the noisy group to quiet.

"We all know Josay and Auguste to be virtuous people. They have given us a chance to move our artistic lives forward by sacrificing their time and their energy and sometimes their money and careers. At a time like this, I for one, will not abandon them."

"Nor will we," agreed Pissaro with Van Gogh standing closely by his side. "We will support them as they have supported us."

As the group began to argue pros and cons of the dilemma, Renoir and David came into the room. David told the story of the afternoon's events in great detail, with amazing resolve, leaving out not one detail.

"We will need you to help us uncover evidence and provide support for all of our friends, especially my sister, Josay, and the Sommes family."

Renoir then added, "We will dedicate the salon to the memory of Monsieur James Sommes for all his contributions to our artistic community. Many of you did not know that he was a silent financial partner to this exhibition, as an anonymous benefactor. We owe him a great debt."

As the meeting broke up and turned into a work session for planning all the necessary details needed to open the exhibition, everyone pledged to do their best to help Josay and the Sommes family in any way they could and to make everyone they knew in Paris understand the ruthlessness and harm that Voight and his minions had done in Montmartre. The whole group joined hands and Renoir offered a fervent prayer to God for truth, justice, comfort and success over evil.

La Plume gathered most of the young women from the Follie Femme and other clubs in the Montmartre district. The group included dancers, waitresses, singers and other entertainers. They assembled at the nearly completed Paradis Rue. She then told them about the plans to open the cabaret under her management and that things would be different from then on. She assured them that they would be delt with fairly and equitably and they would not only be safe but would actually love working there.

At that moment in time, it wasn't clear just what would happen to this new night club, still called the Paradis Rue. Voight had, of course, obtained it with her help via fraud and extortion. And before he beat her almost to death, he had put her in charge of getting the operational problems solved for the opening. She decided she would do as she was asked, and get the Paradis Rue ready to open. It would not be for Voight's benefit, but for Josay and the other original owners. She thought that it might help witnesses come forward and be truthful if they were employed and treated well in the new establishment. The Follie Femme had closed for an extended time until Voight and his thugs were adjudicated, so they were out of her way.

She had secured a temporary loan from Matthew Stewart and Mr. Hover that very morning as well as some legal advice about just who might own the club when all the dust settled. She took the bull by the horns and had every detail of the Paradis Rue Grand Opening ready to coincide with the ribbon cutting for the Impressionist Exhibition which was set to happen on April 15, 1874. There was little time left.

La Plume was a master at managing a club and its many facets such as entertainment, food, drink, furnishings and all of the necessary functions such as bars, kitchens, stages and equipment. Even though a lot of planning had been done before now on these things, she felt the easiest and fastest thing to do was to move a lot of the furniture, and equipment from the Follie Femme to the Paradis Rue. She would have most of the employees simply assume their old positions in the new club. She felt sure they would work for very little on a bet that they would be permanently hired when the club opened and became a success.

After a full day of heavy activities, La Plume met with the artists and they all agreed that it would be best to have the opening of the Paradis Rue the night before the ribbon cutting of the Impressionist Exhibition. She would invite royalty and all the relevant business, theatrical, artistic, academic, literary and political community leaders to both openings, thereby creating an impromptu celebration of the Montmartre and the Parisian essense. She would also include many influential and relevant women to the openings in order to demonstrate that this club would mark a change in the safety standards for women in this type of environment.

This last detail was a strong suggestion made by Josay Rue who coordinated all of the invitation lists.

CHAPTER 26

While La Plume was organizing the opening of the Paradis Rue, she got strong help from the Rue dairy farm with food, and with key "temporary" employees. The project was facilitated by David and Josay's old friends, Monsieur La Grande, Dr. Muse, Chef Paul, and of course, Madame Foote.

Meanwhile, Josay worked to uncover evidence and testimony for Inspector Renet. She was researching paper trails to prove Voight's larceny and bribery. It was difficult work and required a good bit of charm to convince clerks to hand over documents to be inspected for possible warrants. These things should have been done by the police but since time was of the essence, Josay insisted on being of help. She was very adept at charming people to do things for her and she was able to procure several bits of evidence which caused warrants to be executed which uncovered even more evidence against Voight and his gang.

The entire landscape of Josay's future life was set to take shape in the next few days. The trial of Monsieur Voight, the opening of the Impressionist Exhibition, and most importantly, the decision to tell or not tell Matthew about his baby growing inside her. Josay was conflicted and sometimes not thinking like herself with the death of James so fresh in her memory.

She was determined to help Madame La Plume amass unimpeachable evidence against Voight. To that end, she walked to the Paradis Rue to find her to discuss what else could be done before the trial. She found La Plume working with her brother David.

La Plume said, "Oh, hello, mon ami. I am leaving in a few minutes to go to the police station. I will meet you there? No?"

"Yes. David and I will be on our way there presently, but we have a personal matter to discuss on the way," Josay said.

Josay and David strolled away from La Plume and David spoke to her in little more than a whisper, "Have you told Matthew that you are having his child yet?"

"No. Matthew doesn't know and I'm not sure if I want to tell him. When we made love, he was still married and left me to go home to his wife only days after our affaire. Since then, he and his wife have parted and he has come back to Paris to actively pursue our future together. But before James was killed, I was about to choose James and tell Matthew that I couldn't commit to him. Now that James is dead, I don't know what to do. What will happen to a baby who is born without a father?"

"First of all, your child will always have a family that loves him or her. I want you to come home to the dairy to live and raise your child. There is no need to feel ashamed or frightened. And secondly, you can take all the time you need to make the right decision. If you want to marry Matthew, it should be a commitment without pressure or feeling of desperation or emergency. Let's get through these next few days of the trial and then go home to think and decide on the best future path for you and your child."

Josay felt a large burden lifted from her shoulders. David was always her rock and he never waivered in his support of her. With David standing with her, she was ready to take on Voight and put him and his partners-in-crime away for good. As she walked, she steeled herself to prepare for the onslaught of hate, lies, shame and disgust that she knew would come. She said a silent prayer for strength and felt the power of a steadfast sense of right and honor inside her. She knew that God was on her side and that He would protect her and her child no matter what might happen.

When Josay and David got to the police station, they found Madame La Plume and ten young women assembled in a large room with Matthew Stewart, Mr. Hover, Monsieur Bleux and surprisingly Monsieur Sommes the elder.

At the sight of Josay, they all came together and Monsieur Sommes was the first to speak.

"I was hasty when I told you that you would never be forgiven for your part in James' death. In the last few hours, many of your friends and loved ones have set me straight. I ask your forgiveness. I know that James loved you and that you had no part in the evil that took him from both of us. I will be on your side, now and in the future."

As he finished, he broke down into tears and embraced Josay. "Together we will bury James and grieve together."

Josay hugged him as she might have done with her own father.

"We will get past the sharpness of this pain in time and I will love you and watch over you as he would have," said the grieving Marquis.

Everyone in the room was touched, but Chief Inspector Renet broke the tender moment with a stark announcement.

"Voight is claiming that you, Mr. Stewart, and your friends broke into his establishment and committed an assault on him and his innocent men. It is, of course, a thin defense but one the court must consider," said the inspector.

La Plume said, "I have brought these ten ladies here who have been abused by Monsieur Voight so that they might relate to you, Inspector Renet, what they have endured from him and his henchmen while working at the Follie Femme since it opened.

"Most of them, unfortunately, are reluctant to testify in court or in writing. They have been threatened by Voight's men to keep quiet or be killed or tortured. Certainly, however, you will have, at a minimum, the testimony of Mademoiselle Rue and myself. I will provide proof that Voight and his associates were involved in fraud, robbery, larceny, manslaughter, assault, sexual assault and even murder."

She took a long breath and continued, "Meanwhile, my associates and I will continue to prepare for the launch and 'Grand Opening' of the Paradis Rue. I will also ensure that the Follie Femme is closed, and the doors are barred; with your permission, of course, Inspector."

"You have it," said Renet. "It is clear that Marquis Le Sommes, Mr. Stewart and Mademoiselle and Monsieur Rue are the clear owners of the Paradis Rue based on the official document review and the testimony already taken from Madame La Plume who was an eye witness to the fraud and swindle."

As his short speech trailed off, everyone who had not already given their official written testimony, went to their respective corners to do so. La Plume had already given her testimony in writing so left the police station to return to planning and working on the opening of the Paradis Rue.

Unfortunately, none of the girls from the Follie Femme were willing to do a deposition at that time. They were afraid and wanted to be left out.

But before they left the police station, Josay challenged them by saying, "Please do not shrink from your duty as a human being. This monster must be stopped from abusing and killing others. I was raped, beaten and humiliated by Voight in front of La Plume and his disgusting men who are now in custody. I know that you have all seen and experienced these displays of violence, and even though you are afraid for your own personal safety, we must band together and get the justice that we all deserve. Please think about this and consider giving your statement, if not now, then later."

Everyone admired Josay's bravery and it was fortifying for all of the other injured women present, but they were still too frightened to go on the record against Voight.

Matthew Stewart and David winced when Josay admitted to everyone that she had been raped as well as assaulted physically. They both loved her and were deeply disturbed to hear what she had endured. They both embraced and comforted her after her brave speech.

David, Dr. Muse, Madame Foote and Chef Paul had brought several of the employees from the dairy to Paris, along with food and other cooking necessities for the opening of the Paradis Rue. After the business at the police station was concluded, Dr. Muse, Chef Paul and the other dairy employees retreated back to the farm to catch up on the work needed there. They would come back in time for the opening in a few days. Madame Foote decided to stay in Paris to help Madame La Plume, and David decided it best not to leave Josay's side right now. He was worried about the pressure she was feeling right now and felt he needed to fortify her in every way he could.

The next day, some of the painters and concession owners came to Josay's home to talk over the arrangements and the guest list for both the exhibition and opening dinner at the Paradis Rue. They also wanted to ask Josay to be one of many dignitaries at the ribbon cutting. They seemed very pleased with both the guest list and the fact that Josay agreed to actually cut the ribbon at the Impressionist Exhibition.

They were also excited to tell her that many of the artists agreed to hang paintings on the walls of the Paradis Rue for the official 'Grand Opening' and beyond.

"It is my hope that many of your paintings will be purchased the night we open the Paradis Rue and that people will be excited to see even more of your work at the exhibition the next day," said Josay.

"From your lips to God's ears, my dear. We will someday remember these days of hardship and artistic pain as markers for our souls. Perhaps it will make us better people and greater painters," said Renoir. (He was an optimistic philosopher at heart and loved to make such statements.)

The remainder of the evening was spent in going over ponderous logistics and last minute problem solving with the artists concerning the salon's opening. After several hours, David and Matthew insisted that Josay go to bed. She quietly cried herself to sleep, remembering the loss of James Sommes. Her heart felt empty. She was sure now that she had truly loved him above all others. She wished that she had made that clear to him before he died. Now it was too late.

CHAPTER 27

After two full days of witness statements and evidence gathering, Inspector Renet called for a preliminary inquest, to be followed by a formal indictment of Voight and his associates. But It wasn't, at all, a foregone conclusion that he would be formally charged with the murder of James Sommes. Since David and the others had broken into Voight's office without the police or proper documentation, it may be considered to be justifiable homicide. Nonetheless, Renet had steadfastly refused to charge and arrest David, Matthew and Auguste for trespass and assault as Voight was demanding.

There was also a good possibility that there were many more charges against Voight not yet even being considered. Voight was going to be tried and guillotined for his crimes, but he was evil enough to want to take innocents down with him. Voight had obviously bullied many underlings to lie for him and perjure themselves. It was a tricky predicament for Renet to navigate.

Josay was able to find a few minutes to visit the salon facilities. She watched as all of her artist comrades were busily working on their exhibits. Finally, the hard part of just who got which space in the building had been determined and Josay was amazed at how fast things were getting done now. She delighted in the many kinds and styles of the paintings, and sculptures that were being expertly arranged in the hall.

As she walked around the salon, she ran into Lautrec with another man she didn't know.

"Josay, come here," he said as he opened his arms to embrace her.

"May I introduce you to our friend, and Vincent's brother, Theo Van Gogh. He is an art dealer and has been quite helpful with the funding and endorsement of our salon to other dealers and collectors."

Josay smiled and offered her hand.

Theo reached out and kissed it and said, "Charmed."

"I have been following your many trials and tribulations here in Paris, and I wish you all the best with that evil Voight. Vincent has told me of his viciousness. I don't know how you have found time to be so involved in all the projects you have lent your name and image to here in Montmartre. You know, in fact, I have been selling many of the advertisement posters with your likeness in my gallery."

Josay smiled and said, "You are selling the advertisement posters?"

"Yes. I put one of you in a colorful dress done by Toulouse, here, up in the window of my office. Vincent had brought it to me as an advertisement for the Impressionist Exhibition. Before I knew it, someone came in and asked if they could purchase the poster. I sold it. But since then, I haven't been able to keep enough posters in stock to sell to everyone who asks to buy."

"How wonderful!" exclaimed Josay. "My friend Toulouse Lautrec is an amazingly exciting artist."

"I have, of course, given the money from the sales to help underpin the cost of the salon. In fact, you might notice that the posters that were developed by Lautrec have been disappearing from all the places they were hung throughout the city. I believe there might be a market for this kind of artistic expression. You have played a big role in the budding success of this creative form of art," said Theo.

Josay thanked him for his compliments and Lautrec said, " It's not just the Impressionist Exhibition posters that are being confiscated, it's the ones I did of you for the circus, ballet and the Beaumont. They have been disappearing as well. You may well have unknowingly created a business for me by being so beautiful."

Josay blushed at the compliment and hugged her friend.

Renoir, Degas, Monet and Cezanne were talking, and as Josay approached they stopped and greeted her.

"What do you think of the art and the exhibit?" asked Degas.

"I think it's wonderful and it will change the fortunes of all of you when you are given a fair chance for review by the public. Every painting is different. One shows nature as I have never seen it and another the emotional image of an innocent child about to perform her first ballet recital. Each artistic rendering is striking and each is unique to its creator."

"So you like it so far?" asked Monet.

"I love it! I have been fortunate to have been the subject of several of the paintings, and a sculpture or two. Each artist seems to see a different girl, and yet I know they are all me. It's the wonder of your kind of art. I really love the fact that it brings new ways of looking at people and the world."

"She understands our dreams and the aspirations for our art," said Renoir. "All we ever wanted was to have a fair chance to bring our visions to the world. Let's just hope that the critics give us a chance to do that without killing us with negativity in the newspaper. We have also found an ally in our midst with the staunch old Annual Paris Salon purists. Papa Corot has pledged his support and agreed to exhibit in our salon. With Jean-Baptiste-Camille Corot at our side no one can say we're not without artistic merit, and the old school will have been left with nothing to say without being ridiculous."

Josay's presence had attracted a small crowd that had listened to the spirited conversation. They spontaneously applauded and patted each other on the back. Josay was moved. Surely, she had played a small role in helping get this salon off the ground she thought. She knew in her heart that once it had taken off, like the new hot air balloons of the day, it would sweep across the sky never to be ignored again.

"I can't wait until we formally open the exhibit. You are all welcome to attend the opening of the Paradis Rue in celebration of the Impressionist Exhibition and the joy of the Parisian night scene. You will see examples of your art decorating the walls, wonderful entertainment and amazing food and drink."

Again, the now somewhat larger group of artists and workers applauded as Josay moved toward the door and excused herself.

Renoir walked after her and said, "We will be at your side with this Voight thing. Never fear, you are forever our sister."

Josay waved goodbye again and departed with a warm afterglow in her soul.

When Josay got to the Paradis Rue, she had never seen such a hectic scene. Madame Foote was supervising the table decorations, lighting, stage décor, while training the waiters and waitresses on their responsibilities in this new place. The bar set up was being handled by Big George, of all people. He took the responsibility very seriously, indeed.

Josay passed by him and he smiled and said, "Who knows bars better than me?"

He winked at Josay and smiled a heartwarming and very sober grin. He had completely given up alcohol. Josay was so proud of him for such a monumental accomplishment. She truly hoped that he could remain sober from now on, although it may be a bumpy road. She would be there to encourage him in any way she could. She was very fond of him and considered him as part of her family now.

Josay went into the kitchen and saw David supervising the delivery of more food, wine, and all manner of table clothes, napkins, table candles and large banners to be placed outside and inside the club announcing the opening of Paradis Rue and the Impressionist Exhibition.

In the center of the hectic kitchen preparations was Monsieur Paul. He was supervising all the chefs and sous chefs as they worked to revise old recipes for the grand opening. He wanted to reflect the originality, style and elegance of the new cabaret.

Chef Paul saw Josay and said, "Just look at the joy you have helped to create in this place. Every hors d'oeuvre, salad, entrée and dessert will be made with love and gratitude for another chance for professional pride. All of my fellow cooks, potato peelers, bakers and even dishwashers thank you for this second chance at happiness."

"Thank you, Chef. I am so pleased to see everyone so busy and content with their work. I know that everything you create for our guests will be delicious beyond imagination," replied Josay.

"Especially the cheeses, butter and milk from your farm, they are the best I've ever tasted, if I do say so myself," he added as he looked down with humility. Then he looked up and smiled.

"They will help to insure the highest quality for all our creations." He bowed and took Josay's hand and kissed it.

Josay went from the kitchen to backstage and dressing areas of the club. There she found all the actors, dancers, singers, makeup artists, stagehands and bouncers being rehearsed by Madame La Plume.

"Josay, my darling, what do you think? It's going to be the most special show Paris has ever seen. All the other clubs will go dark for our opening and have agreed to send their finest entertainers here to enhance our already amazing cast and crew on opening night."

"Madame La Plume, you have outdone yourself. That is amazing news. Just make sure that our security is in place and that all guests will be treated with every courtesy no matter what social station they occupy. You are surely trying your best to overcome your past transgressions and to earn my confidence and love."

"Of course, my dear. The Paradis Rue will mark the beginning of a safe as well as dynamic Paris night life, without the crime, and dirty dealings of the past. I don't know how you could ever forgive me for the terrible wrongs I have committed, but you can know that I have changed. I promise that I will honor my love for you and the world of entertainment from this day forward."

"I believe you. You are doing a wonderful job. I can see that you are working as hard an any human could work to get this project off to a successful beginning. I also think that you will find it personally rewarding when you see the fruits of your own labor."

Many of the show girls gathered around Josay and hugged and kissed her cheeks.

"You have helped us become the dancers and artists we dreamed of as little girls without the dark consequences of greedy and immoral men. We will dance with all of our talent at the opening and make the audience thrill to our kicks, turns and rhythm. Can you dance with us? We have a small role for you."

Josay blushed and declined.

"I have to insure that everything is ship shape and that all goes as well as we all want it to go. You are all wonderful. Enjoy yourselves and bring your gay spirit to everyone. Let's make this opening evidence of a revolutionary time that everyone will remember and talk about to their children's children."

Madame Foote then took Josay's arm and led her into the office where Dr. Muse was busily pouring over a large stack of papers.

"Josay, I don't know how we've been able to finance this opening. But we have enough money to finance the first night, and with a successful review or two, we can stay open for at least a couple of months at a minimum. Matthew Stewart has authorized Monsieur Hover to spend whatever it takes to prime the pump for this establishment. And, since Monsieur Voight and Monsieur Donnel Regis are completely out of the picture, Monsieur Sommes, Monsieur Stewart, you and your brother, David, are the primary owners of the Paradis Rue again."

"Thank you Dr. Muse, for all of the work you have put into this venture and to the dairy business. You are a true and faithful friend."

The Rue Family Dairy Products company owns a very small share of this venture, too, I'm happy to say. I believe we will all profit from this. It will enable your friends, which includes me, to work and live a very fortunate life. It is very exciting, I must say. For that, I thank you, my dear girl."

Josay touched his arm and was overcome with emotion. David entered the room and said, "Enough of this self-congratulations and heart-warming banter. We have work to do. Josay, you are scheduled to testify in the Voight case tomorrow. We must get you home to rest."

As Josay left the room, everyone watched her go and Madame La Plume said, "Don't you worry. I will be there to back you up. We will succeed in sending Phillipe and his men to hell where they belong."

CHAPTER 28

The next morning David, La Plume and Josay took a cab to the courthouse. As they moved along the busy streets, they saw many of the posters announcing the Impressionist Exhibition and the opening of the Paradis Rue.

"It's really going to happen," said Josay "I'm so excited." No sooner had she voiced those words when the carriage hit a pothole in the cobbled street. Josay felt a sharp pain in her abdomen.

"Oh!" she screamed. The pain happened again within a few seconds and she cried out again.

"Are you alright?" asked David, as La Plume took Josay's hand.

"Umm," Josay said as she bit her lip and grimaced. Fear for her precious child flashed through her mind as she felt the new life inside her move. She was now about five months into her pregnancy.

"I'm fine. These cobblestone streets are so rough and I took the jolt of that last one the wrong way," she said softly.

They arrived at the courthouse and entered to find the testimony against Voight had begun already. A very young girl with dark black hair was sobbing as she told of the beating Voight had given her for spilling a drink. Josay was surprised to see that one of the other girls was testifying. The girl was sobbing as she told in detail the horrible sexual assault he had administered as he and his fellow criminals laughed, joked and drank.

When she finished, the defense counsel asked her this question.

"Did you report this terrible crime at the time? And, if not, why not?"

The young girl explained that she was scared, alone in Paris and needed the job to keep her off the streets. Her voice broke several times as she told of the hardships she had experienced in her short but troubled life. Only now, with the support of Madame La Plume and the other women had she been confident enough to face Voight and the others.

The defense attorney said, "Are you sure they didn't tell you what to say?

"No, of course not," said the girl.

" Did you mistrust our police and this court?" he said.

He turned to face the room full of onlookers and then back to the judge.

He continued, "This is a witness that can't be trusted. She claims to have been assaulted and raped six months ago, but never complained and kept working at the Follie Femme for all that time. Surely you could have found a moment to sneak away and report such a colorful occurrence. But no. You only seemed to develop the courage to accuse my clients when Mari La Plume and the other women put you up to it. This amounts to little more than an unsubstantiated lie. This court knows that my clients can all vouch that the incident in question amounted to a loud reprimand and slap on the hand from Monsieur Voight. It has been exaggerated in the fantasy of this young woman and aided by this mass of hysterical women here assembled."

The young woman blurted out, "It happened just as I said! It's true. He raped and beat me!"

Then she stood up and wiped the tears from her eyes, looked straight at Voight and pointed her finger at him. Her anger had risen to overflowing as she screamed, "You did it. You did it all just as I have said. You're an animal, and I hate you!"

The judge said, "Order in this court," and banged his gavel several times before the courtroom calmed.

"Anything further?" he asked the defense counselor.

"No your honor", said the defense attorney.

"Then the witness is excused."

The young girl stood, straightened her wrinkled dress and composed her demeanor. As she stepped down from the witness chair, she looked straight at Voight and said, "I'm not afraid of you anymore. I'll gladly be on the front row to watch the guillotine drop on your neck to end you on this earth forever."

"We will take a ten-minute recess before we hear from the next witness. According to my agenda, Mademoiselle Rue is next to speak to the court."

"Right your honor," replied the prosecutor.

And with that, the judge banged his gavel again to signal the recess.

The prosecutor beckoned Josay, La Plume, David and several other supporters to come to the adjacent room for a quick strategy meeting.

He began by saying that Josay would be the next to testify and that he was saving Madame La Plume for later. He would use her only if he thought he needed her since she was, at best, a compromised witness. Several of the other girls had borne fragmented and unsubstantiated witness to atrocities committed by Voight and others in his gang of criminals. So far, the trial had been a classic case of 'he said—she said.' Voight had been able to produce witnesses that swore to his side of the stories. Josay's standing in the community qualified her to be the most important accusation leveled at Voight other than the James Sommes murder. That murder had several complications for the prosecution due to a plausible self-defense story being used by the defense. All the Sommes murder testimony had been rendered yesterday at a marathon ten-hour session wherein at least eighteen witnesses had testified that James, Matthew, David and Renior had barged into Voight's office, without warrant, and attacked him. Voight claimed that he was only defending himself and that the shooting was justified.

"I don't think the judge will convict Voight of the murder and I believe I will need to provide some convincing arguments just to get David, Matthew and Renior off without jail time for trespassing and assaulting Voight in his office."

Josay couldn't help but gasp when she heard this statement. *Surely this couldn't happen*, she thought.

The prosecutor continued, "That being said, Chief Inspector Renet has testified that he supported the raid and arrest of Voight because of the claims of injury and assault by the show girls who had made their way to Madame La Plume for help the night that James was murdered. He has also testified that he was on his way to Voight's office to arrest him and his gang, but it had taken a few minutes to assemble his men and paperwork. In the meantime, Matthew Stewart, James Sommes, David Rue and Auguste Renoir had arrived first, and were upset by the accusation of brutality they had heard from the young women. He also assured the court that these men were upstanding gentlemen and were unarmed at the time of the encounter, and that Voight had shot and murdered an unarmed socialite and businessman, who was only there to defend defenseless women. The judge seemed to be persuaded by that evidence but kept his leanings in the matter to himself," the prosecutor said as he paused to collect his thoughts.

"Mademoiselle Rue, are you aware that Madame La Plume's testimony might be jaded by the fact that she was present and did nothing to stop your assault or the assaults she witnessed that were perpetrated against no less than ten other women?" asked the prosecutor.

"Yes, I can see where that might be a problem. But she was scared of crossing him as well," replied Josay.

"The lack of judgment in the Sommes murder and La Plume's potentially compromised testimony in all the other rape and assault charges only magnifies the importance of your testimony. And finally, we need to leave no doubt that Voight is a villain. This judge may have been a visitor to the Follie Femme, and if so, he has benefitted in many ways from a relationship with Voight, as many judges have. We have no way of knowing if this is true or not true. If it's true, we could be in trouble. But we do have testimony in abundance, and the support of the police in this matter which carries a lot of weight. But you have the power to push a guilty verdict over the top," finished the prosecutor.

Josay felt another twinge in her abdomen and grimaced as she answered the challenge of the prosecutor. All present, read it as a non-verbal display of determination.

"I do have the strength to see good triumph over this despicable excuse for a man and his evil partners."

Josay was escorted back into the courtroom on the arm of her brother David and took her seat at the prosecutor's table. She noticed a waxed sealed note which was addressed to her, laying on the table. She opened it as the judge came into the room.

I know you are pregnant and I know that the father of the child is Voight. Furthermore, we know that you had several encounters with Voight and your pregnancy isn't the product of rape at all. I'm sure you don't want to insist that your baby is the product of a rape. Tone your voice down and the secret will be buried forever.

Josay looked around the courtroom expecting to see the glaring eyes of the person who sent this terrible untrue threat, but she found no such circumstantial visage. She felt a cold shiver run up her spine as the pain in her abdomen swelled in strength.

"All rise," said the bailiff.

"Let this court come to order. Next witness, Monsieur Prosecutor," said the judge.

"The prosecution calls Mademoiselle Josay Rue."

As the witness oath was being read, Josay's mind was racing. "*God, help me find the strength to bring this horrible man to justice.*"

"I will," agreed Josay.

"Can you tell the court in your own words what happened to you on December 15, 1873."

As Josay began to describe her vicious assault and rape, she found a determination that blinded her senses to the physical pain and emotional turbulence she felt inside. She did not waiver in her straightforward description of the heinous crimes committed upon her, and without emotion told the truth in a fashion that could not be impeached. The entire gallery, especially the judge, was transfixed on her every word. She spoke with the clarity of a seasoned debater persuading her audience to the side she represented. When she finished her account of the rape and beating, all present were without doubt that Voight and his men had been guilty of all the crimes for which they were accused. Even the defense filed only an obligatory objection pertaining to the fact that Josay, like the others, had taken her time to lodge these accusations.

When the judge called the defense team to question Josay, they said they did not have questions at present but held their right to question the witness at a later time.

"The witness is excused," said the judge. Josay was stepping down from the witness box when all of the anguish of testimony concentrated itself into such a rush of pain that she collapsed onto the courtroom floor. David and Matthew rushed to pick her up. They quickly took her out of the courtroom and to the adjacent hospital.

"What time is it?" Josay asked as she came back to consciousness in the hospital.

"It's six," responded a concerned David who looked at her from his seat drawn up next to her bed. You fainted after your testimony.

The trial is continuing, but took a recess to reconvene in two days on the 15th.

David worried about the defense's case. It was true that all of the victims had not acted upon their claims until Josay filed her case. This could provide an alternative "conspiracy theory." It was clearly true that the women who knew or worked for Mr. Voight, hated him, but without La Plume's testimony to corroborate Josay's account, there was room for reasonable doubt. It was possible that Voight could escape the charges. And further, It was a possibility that he, himself, could actually be charged with attacking Voight.

Josay asked to be taken home and David obliged.

CHAPTER 29

Josay was dressing with the help of Madame La Plume and Madame Foote. Her mind was on 1he note she had received in the courtroom.

Who could have sent that note, and why? Surely it couldn't have been Voight. He had been locked up along with all of his men. Did he have allies or accomplices who would benefit from this lie? That had to be the truth of it," she thought.

These questions lingered in the back of her mind along with the still dull but lingering pain she felt in her abdomen.

The night of the grand opening of the Paradis Rue had arrived with the trial still in session. The ribbon cutting for the Impressionist Exhibition would be held tomorrow. The past week had been a blur. The trial should be over, but it dragged on with the defense team presenting alternative theories of the events that had been presented by the prosecution's witnesses. They seemed to pull "alternate" facts out of thin air with the help of the false testimony of Voight's henchmen.

Josay didn't have time to think about that just now. The final hours of the trial would probably be tomorrow. However, since the defense rested with many lies left unanswered, the prosecutor decided he needed to call Madame La Plume to the stand no matter what the risk might be. Josay hoped her testimony would be the nail in Voight's coffin and would provide the final damning evidence needed for a guilty verdict.

Josay's dress and jewelry for opening night at the Paradis Rue had been supplied by several fashion houses eager to be associated with the most popular model and celebrity in Paris. The dress was a dark brownish-red paired with gold jewelry. The entire outfit was chosen to highlight Josay's reddish-blonde hair and fair complexion. A brilliant 7-carat diamond stone at the end of a string of smaller brightly glittering diamonds formed the centerpiece necklace. (It was, of course, on loan from the most exclusive jeweler in Paris.) Her overskirt and train was covered with red tinted silk roses that matched the flowers around the waist and dragged two or three feet behind her. The effects of the dress were magnificent, but it had been fitted two months ago, and tonight she was barely able to get into it. The corset that was necessary was very uncomfortable. She left it as loosely fastened as she could, but it exacerbated the pain in her abdomen.

David came into the room and sat by the window reading some papers.

"These notices confirm that the Follie Femme will go dark for the foreseeable future. We should have a smooth opening night," he said.

"David, thank you for taking care of everything while I have been so focused on the trial. I don't know what I would do without you. Can you ask everyone to leave for a few minutes? I need to speak to you alone."

"Sure, Sis."

After the room was cleared, she told David about the threatening note that she had received in court about her baby being Voight's.

"I don't know who it could be from. Only a very few people know that I am even pregnant. The baby's father doesn't even know."

"You and I will find out who sent that note and we will get to the bottom of this threat. We should tell Inspector Renet about this and we'll do it the right way. Don't worry, Sis, your baby will be safe and as respectable as any child born in France."

Those were the words Josay needed to hear at just the right moment. She was able to relax and finally feel happy about the opening tonight. It was something she had been looking forward to for almost two years. It was hard to imagine that it was really going to happen.

Lautrec and Van Gogh had been drinking absinthe and other spirits all day. Together they sat in the back of the sparkling, festive, fragrant main room of the Paradis Rue near the long ornate mahogany bar. Lautrec had on black tie and tails but looked like he had slept in them for several days and nights, and Van Gogh looked like a street peddler.

When Renoir and Degas saw them, they were enraged.

"What the hell are you doing? This is an important night for everyone we know and love."

Renoir got Monet and Pissarro to help lift them and carry them to the dressing rooms for a spit and polish. On the way, Renoir noticed one of his pastel nudes on the wall and thought to himself, *I need to rework that painting again, it's just not right.*

*R*enoir was never fully happy with anything he painted, which was the case with most artists. Even the great Leonardo da Vinci was thought to have tinkered with his renaissance masterpieces for years. (Non artists don't really understand this behavior.)

Josay saw La Plume talking to the waiters and waitresses at the entrance to the kitchen and joined them for a quick pep talk.

"Thank you for coming to work here on such short notice. I know you will find that this establishment operates in an entirely different fashion than that of the Follie Femme. We want your suggestions and we expect you to be happy in your work. You will help us create an atmosphere that makes our customers, men and women, want to return night after night," said Josay.

She ended with a warm smile, then went directly to the dressing rooms with La Plume in tow.

She entered the dressing rooms and was amazed to see all the color and splendor of the costumes, and the sight of so many musicians, dancers, singers and other acts. Everyone seemed excited in anticipation.

When they saw Josay walk into the room, there was a sudden quiet and attention given to her.

"Bonjour, mon amis," she started. "What a long and steep path we have all taken to arrive at this mountain top of our dreams. Show business takes a level of commitment and work that makes less dedicated people fall to the wayside. And talent, yes talent, is not equally spread out over us all. You are the most talented and dedicated of all the entertainers I have ever seen, and I pledge to you that you will be treated like the celebrities you are. Along with my artist friends and wonderful business partners, we expect this to be the first choice of places that entertainers will choose to work.

"Tonight is a special time for us all. It is the beginning of an era of making Paris truly worthy of the name, 'City of lights', because the light of your talents will outshine the 20,000 street lights lining the city streets! Someday, you will remember this night and will tell your children that you were here performing at the grand opening of the Paradis Rue."

Everyone screamed their emotions and broke into laughter and applause.

"We love you Josay," they all said, as they patted her and kissed her cheeks.

La Plume held her arms up and asked for quiet.

"I have long wanted to see this kind of place for our kind of people, and though I don't really deserve to be here, somehow God's forgiveness for my terrible sins has brought me to this time and place. I swear to you all, I will work for you with honesty and that I will never betray your trust again. Come to me everyone. As they all gathered together in a large circle, she said, "Vive le Paradis Rue and the the most wonderful city in the world, Paris."

At that, Josay left the backstage and went to her table. As she approached, she saw Matthew Stewart, Monsieur Sommes, William Hover with Elizabeth, a local magistrate, Inspector Renet, Auguste and Aline Renoir, Camille and Julie Pissarro, and her brother David all standing and waiting for her to join them at the centermost table.

Everyone held up a crystal glass filled with champagne and after handing a filled one to Josay, the magistrate said, "To the success of this magnificent establishment and may it long be a beacon of entertainment and fine cuisine here in Montmartre, the home of the artist; and to our beautiful Josay, the 'face' of Paris."

As the glasses clinked, everyone took their seat and the entire place was abuzz with the serving of the meal, laughter, high spirits and happiness. As the meal progressed and the drinking set the mood, La Plume came to the center stage and asked for attention.

"Everyone, please give me your attention. I have just a few announcements before we begin the most marvelous show you will have ever seen. This place, these people, and this great adventure in entertainment could not have taken place without the bold and wonderful backing of several people." La Plume then introduced everyone at the center table, then the various dignitaries, and other leaders behind the scenes to thunderous applause. She saved Josay for last.

"And, before the first dance on stage, the most important person in the room, a driving force behind not only this place but a wonderful exhibition set to open tomorrow, the Impressionist Exhibition, please welcome our beautiful and talented Josay Rue."

Everyone stood up to applaud. When Josay saw this, she was overwhelmed. Tears rolled down her face as David and Matthew held her on either side.

When the applause died down, La Plume motioned to the maestro, "Let the first notes be played in this very special house of entertainment. And immediately from each side of the stage came the beautiful and glorious cancan dancers to perform the boisterous theme of Paris and Montmartre. The crowd roared its approval and the Paradis Rue was christened.

Toward the end of the evening of what could only be called a complete success at every level, La Plume introduced Renoir and Josay again and invited them to the stage. Josay thanked everyone for their support and love and said that Paris not only is the center of the universe for entertainment, food and wine but also for fine art.

She said, "Tomorrow will mark the beginning of a period of artistic renaissance with the opening of the first Impressionist Exhibition. I am pleased to present to all of you my friend, Pierre -Auguste Renoir, one of the leaders of this new direction of creative artistic expression. He and his fellow artists are believers in having no boundaries for the artistic spirit; the hallmark of French culture.

Renoir first acknowledged the other artists in the audience and pointed out the examples of diverse and magnificent art that adorned the very walls of the Paradis Rue.

"Tomorrow you will be able to see color, form, expression and creativity in artistic endeavor unlike any yet seen in one place in the history of artistic exhibition. Our salon refuses no one, requires no rules of form or subject matter and above all allows you the viewer to be the judge each piece without academic or critical requirements. Come join Josay, my fellow artistic creators and myself for the beginning of a journey to freedom, so much the watchword of our beloved French passions. 'Liberty, Equality and Fraternity' in all things!" he shouted to the great loud roar of approval from the audience.

Josay asked David to take her home soon after Renoir's rousing speech. She knew the final decision of the trial, and the opening of the salon loomed on the morrow. She needed strength for what would certainly be another pivotal day in her life.

CHAPTER 30

Josay was awakened the next morning with a severe striking pain in her abdomen. She grimaced and sat up in her bed. She would need all her strength to get through this day. The magistrate had told David earlier in the morning that a ruling in the case would likely be delivered at 11 am this morning. Josay was in a state of constant worry that Voight would beat the charges and be returned to menace everyone as he had in the past, and that she might be called to testify again on new developments. Additionally, there was the lingering threat of the exposure of her pregnancy with untrue claims about it from Voight or some villain he had hired. (After all, someone had written and delivered the note.) Josay was, of course, the most worried about her pain and the threat of losing her child.

David knocked on the door of the little white house. He saw the pale and frightened face of Josay and was immediately concerned. "Are you well? What is the matter?"

"I continue to experience pain in my abdomen and I'm frightened about the decision of the court," she said with a shaky voice as she opened the bright green door wide for David to enter.

"I know, and what's worse, Madame La Plume is missing this morning. Someone saw her late last night being hurried away by two men. They were thought to be some of Voight's crew. No one has seen her since. I think she has been abducted so that she can't testify today."

Josay reminded David about the threatening note she had received in the courtroom and both felt a cold chill.

"Could these two things be connected?" asked Josay.

"All I know is that La Plume needs to testify about your rape before the final decision is rendered. She was the last witness, and possibly the most important to testify. But I can't for the life of me, understand how La Plume being missing and the note could be linked. It certainly worries me and makes me uneasy. Let's just get you to a doctor right now to see what's causing these terrible shooting pains."

Josay didn't argue and finished dressing in a loose fitting dress. She put on some makeup but her ashen face betrayed the fear and hurt she was feeling.

"Take your hands off me," said La Plume as she was slapped awake by two unshaven and rough looking men. She was tied to and sitting in a low-backed chair. She thought she recognized the smaller of the two as an errand boy for Voight. Her face was bleeding under her right eye which had swollen shut and her lip was busted wide open. Her clothes had been ripped and her right leg was swollen at the knee. They had worked her over pretty thoroughly from late last night until daybreak.

"Shut up you slut and sign the paper like I told you or you'll get more of what you got last night."

"I won't sign a paper that spreads some lie about Josay's testimony and pregnancy. I know that Voight is behind this and will use it to hurt Josay. I will never be a party to that."

Finally, the two men gave up and signed the letter for her since they were told that the defense counsel had to have it before 10 am this morning. The smaller one, a Spanish national, put on a stolen priest's collar and dark clothes, grabbed the document and left by the side door. As he was leaving, the taller one pulled out a knife and was about to strike La Plume when Dr. Muse, Big George and several other men burst in from the side door and tackled him from the back. The man fell over a chair only grazing the right arm of La Plume. Big George, an experienced bouncer, easily got him into a head lock and with one twist the fight was over.

"I hope you didn't kill him George," said Dr. Muse. "We might need him to help tell the story about this kidnapping in court . At any rate, this man will do some time in the bastille, or lose his head for his role in this brutality. I am just happy that we have foiled Voight's efforts to keep you from testifying this morning, Madame La Plume. Are you alright?"

Outside the weather had turned bad as big thunder clouds spread across Paris. It began to rain just as the small man, dressed as a priest, hurried to deliver the letter to Voight's counselor. He feared that the paper was getting damp and would be ruined. There was nothing to do except grab an umbrella from a tiny bent over old woman. He then ran as fast as he could to reach the courthouse, leaving the old woman crying in the rain, and wondering what kind of priest would do that.

Dr. Muse untied La Plume and she sat up in the now very dark room with water dripping down from the ceiling.

"Yes, I am alright. But how did you know to come here?" asked La Plume.

"It was really just an accident. We were sent here to the Follie Femme to find some extra chairs and tables to take back to the Paradis Rue for tonight's dinner and show. The word is out everywhere that the Paradis Rue is the place to be and we expect an overflow audience for the foreseeable future. I figured we could squeeze a few more tables in the back and sides so we came here to the storage house behind the club thinking we might find some. When we arrived young, Jean, here, told us he had seen you through a cracked window being tied up and hit late last night. He didn't go to the police because he is afraid of Mr. Voight and his men. It was a real stroke of luck that he told us about it."

Madame La Plume straighten herself and urged the small troop to get her to the courthouse as quickly as possible. Off into the rain they ran.

When Josay arrived at the office of the doctor she found him out on a call. It had begun to rain very hard. Josay shivered on the front porch of the office that had a small overhang just enough to keep most of the rain off of her head.

"We can't wait for the doctor. I must get to the courthouse within the next 45 minutes. The pain is bearable if I am still. No matter, we must go now."

David found it difficult to hail a cab as it always is when it's raining, so he stepped in front of one. It stopped just before running him over. After he explained the urgent circumstances, he asked the passenger if they would let he and Josay share the cab. The young woman in the cab took one look, recognized Josay and immediately agreed to slide over and let the two of them settle on the black pleated and rolled leather seat.

Inside the courtroom the prosecutor sat on the left side of the room at the large table pouring over papers and notes. Occasionally he looked up at his opposition who was seated to his right at another large table with the witness box in the center dividing the two sides. The raised bench of the judge was in the center and front of the room.

The judge had, at one time, been associated with the Follie Femme and a certain amount of government corruption. He was a remnant of the kind of dogmatic, self-centered group that terrorized the city under the rule of Robespierre one hundred years before.

But fortunately for Josay and for justice, he had rather recently found God and was converted to being a true Christian man. No longer being a Christian hypocrite, his conscience had changed his behavior both in and out of the courtroom. He had rightfully earned the robes and bright red cap of the highest order of the courts, and along with a jury of six men, he would decide the guilt or innocence of the accused and would determine a sentence. According to the rules of litigation, the judge had the right to veto any finding of the jury. The judge held maximum sway over the entire procedure.

Obviously, this man had deep dark secrets and was being watched by others in the government for his past mistakes. He was a man with many regrets and was desperately trying to earn back his own self-respect and the love of his wife and grown children. Josay had certainly been fortunate to draw this man, because he was no longer susceptible to blackmail or bribes.

The prosecutor noticed a slightly wet young priest come into the room and deliver a letter to the defense counsel. He was seated behind their table and was in intense conversation with the defense counselor and Monsieur Voight. Any evidence making such a sudden and unexpected appearance at this stage of the proceedings rightly worried the prosecutor. Not only that, but Josay and La Plume were absent and the judge could come in and begin at any moment. He looked around the gallery and saw a large group of young ladies in the back of the room. Some of them had been in the courtroom when Josay had testified and he had seen them teary-eyed. He also noticed a few well-dressed men. Among them were Marquis Le Sommes, Mr. Hover and Matthew Stewart. All of them were serious and engrossed in conversation near the front few rows behind his table.

Just as the bailiff was pronouncing, "All rise. The court of Judge Jean Paul Fruge is now in session," Josay came in the back door and walked down the aisle with David. There was an astonished look on the faces of all those who were seated around the defense table.

Judge Fruge banged his gavel on the table and demanded, "Order! The room will come to order."

The defense counsel asked to approach the bench. He and the prosecutor came to the front of the room for a muted conversation with the judge.

"I would like to introduce some new testimony and a new witness. I know that Madame La Plume was to be called next, but she is absent." said the defense counselor.

"This evidence has just come to my attention and it has a strong bearing on my case."

"Who is that new witness? This is highly irregular. I should have been notified and had time to depose this witness before his testimony is entered into the court record," argued the prosecutor.

"I'll allow the request, but I don't like last minute changes. This new evidence had better be very important and relevant to this case. You may proceed, Counsel," the judge said to the defense.

The two men parted and walked back to their respective tables and the defense called the rather short hispanic to the stand.

The young Spaniard shuffled up to the slightly raised witness stand and swore to tell the truth.

"We are in need of a translator, your honor, so I have provided one for the court," said the defense counselor with a sly smile.

A heavy set woman joined the witness in the witness stand, and the attorney asked, "What is your name and where are you from?"

In Spanish, the Priest told the court his name was Frederico D' Santos from Madrid.

"Can you tell the court what brings you here this morning?"

"I was asked to witness the writing of a letter to the court written by Madame Mari Belle La Plume early this morning. I met her when she intrupted me while I was at the Chapel St. Claire for morning prayers. She approached me in a rushed fashion and said she needed to clarify her testimony in this court before she left Paris."

"And you saw Madame La Plume write this letter yourself in the Chapel St. Claire and in the presence of God almighty?"

"I did."

"Is this the letter you saw Madame La Plume write and sign this very morning?" said the judge as he held the letter up for all to see.

"Yes, Monsieur. It may be a little damaged by the rain. I was told to rush it over and it rained on me before I could buy an umbrella."

"What, if anything did La Plume say as she was writing this important letter?"

"She told me she expected to be in a great deal of trouble when this letter was delivered because she had not told the truth in her written testimony. She said that she feared her incarceration for perjury. She was quite shaken and carried a small, very worn looking carpet bag with her. And although she wore a wonderfully adorned evening dress and looked very fine, her face was showing that she was stressed and panicked.

"I agreed to bring the letter directly to you and she left with two other women in a small cart in the direction of the Paris city limits."

"Again, is this the letter La Plume had you deliver and has anyone other than you seen the letter or read its contents?" asked the defense attorney.

"No, Monsieur."

"Then let's read this important letter," said the defense counselor as he took the wet letter from its envelop and began to read it.

Let me first say how much I regret having to write this letter. I was certain I could leave my past behind and have a new life here in Paris but it was not to be. As you know, I testified that Mr. Voight raped and beat Josay and several other young dancers and waitresses over a period of eight months that I worked for him. And, that he had also assaulted me numerous times. It was not true. I never saw Mr. Voight rape anyone. And although I have seen him cuff a woman or two in the office who deserved it for having solicited sex, or cheated patrons of the Follie Femme, I realize that it was necessary. It's difficult to manage these show people and lower class servants without some discipline. I thought I would get promoted for all my efforts and when Mr. Voight chose another younger, prettier woman to manage his place, I saw my opportunity to get rid of him by bringing these false accusations to Inspector Renet. But now I know that I was wrong and would soon be caught and trapped in my lies. I am therefore, moving on as I have done so many times before.MonsieurVoight is innocent.

Madame Mari Belle La Plume

There was an audible gasp in the court room. Everyone looked at each other and the prosecutor shouted, "I object."

"I cannot disallow this evidence brought to us by a servant of God. Let it be entered and considered as evidence in this trial," said the judge.

CHAPTER 31

La Plume, Dr. Muse and Big George raced across town in the rain. They feared that La Plume would not arrive in time to complete her testimony. As they dodged carts, horses, muddy puddles and strong wind gusts that almost knocked them over, they slowly made their way to the courthouse.

Inside the courtroom, the defense attorney was finished and said, "Your witness."

Josay screamed out, "These are lies!" as the defense attorney read the La Plume letter.

She couldn't compose her anger any longer.

"Order! Order! Quiet!," said the judge.

Josay's lawyer approached D' Santos and said, "Are you aware you that can be thrown in jail for most of the rest of your young life for perjury? And, I suspect that it would not go easy for you in jail if you are a priest, and even harder if you are only posing as a priest."

"I swear by the Holy Virgin Mother that what I have said is the truth, so help me God," replied the faux priest as he crossed himself.

“So you said that Madame La Plume had on an evening dress. Could you describe what it looked like in more detail?”

The prosecutor waited patiently as D’ Santos accurately described La Plume and the dress she had been wearing last night at the opening of the Paradis Rue.

Clearly this man, whoever he was, had at least seen La Plume, thought the prosecutor.

“Where is your parish and why are you here?”

“I do not currently have a parish of my own. I was assigned to be present on Spanish ships carrying trade goods to many parts of the world and was let off only a few days ago. My ship continued on to Africa. As a traveling priest, I am allowed some rest as I wait for another ship to come into port to take me on my next assignment.”

“So, no one can vouch for you or your backstory. How convenient.”

“I suppose I have no further questions at the time,” said the prosecutor.

The defense attorney promptly stood up and said, “I move for dismissal of all charges against my client. Without La Plume’s testimony, there are no corroborating witnesses that have testified about the alleged rape of Josay Rue. Not a single employee of the Follie Femme heard or saw this seemingly violent and loud assault. In fact, several of Mr. Voight’s associates have testified that no such attack ever happened. They say instead that it was an elaborate plan to eliminate the competition in the nightclub business of Montmartre, and it worked. My client was jailed and Mademoiselle Rue has now opened her new club, not only without competition from my client’s very successful Follie Femme, but with his employees, acts, dancers, equipment and patrons.”

He paused and looked at Voight.

"Additionally, La Plume is the only witness to the other supposed rapes and assaults suggested to have been committed. The court has seen all the other young women prosper from their accusations by taking better jobs that they were, no doubt, promised at the Paradis Rue. It's seems like they might have been motivated to move up a level or two by falsely accusing my client. And I believe it is true that Mr. Voight may well have cuffed employees around from time to time, but never did he severely beat or rape anyone. Other witnesses have supported Mr. Voight against these accusations as well.

"And, finally, it has been clearly established that Mr. Voight acted in self-defense when David Rue, Matthew Stewart, Auguste Renoir and James Sommes stormed into his office. He was afraid for his life and is allowed to defend himself. Something he must be ready for in his line of work. And I might add, it is a tragedy that Monsieur Sommes was mortally wounded. Our sympathies go out to his family and friends.

"So Your Honor, I demand that the charges be dropped for lack of evidence."

"I object," said the prosecutor.

"We need a recess to review this new evidence."

Before the judge could rule, Madame La Plume, Dr. Muse, and Big George raced into the room. George was gripping an unknown man by the back of his collar.

Everyone in the gallery watched La Plume and Dr. Muse run to Josay.

"Where have you been and what has happened to you," asked Josay.

"I was kidnapped last night by two men. One sitting at the defense table dressed as a priest and the other being held in the back by Big George. They beat me and tried to force me to sign a false document, but I refused. When I refused they beat me some more and finally signed it for me. Then the little one dressed as a priest, took the document and left. The other one slapped me again and was about to stab me and kill me when Big George and Dr. Muse showed up and overpowered him."

Everyone in the courtroom heard La Plume's exclamation and the young priest jumped up to escape but was held in place by the bailiff.

"Arrest that so-called priest and the man currently being subdued by the big fellow in the back, and the court will be in recess," said Judge Fruge, as he loudly banged his gavel.

After a recess of two hours, the prosecutor called a meeting in the hallway composed of Josay, La Plume, David, and Dr. Muse.

"In light of Madame La Plume's appearance in court this morning, I have convinced several of the girls and young men from the Follie Femme to formally testify about the rapes and assaults they experienced and observed. They are not afraid now and are more willing than ever to substantiate the testimony you and La Plume have rendered at this trial. Two dishwashers and a bartender saw your rape and beating and are now willing to come forward. I think we have enough to send, not only Voight to the guillotine, but most of his men."

The prosecutor ended by saying, "This nightmare is finally over for you Mademoiselle Rue."

Josay held Madame La Plume and said, "I knew that you would not betray me again. Thank you for saving everyone today," she said as she collapsed.

David scooped her up and took her out of the courthouse and directly to the doctor.

Madame La Plume turned her thoughts to Josay's pregnancy. She had heard that Voight was planning to claim that Josay was pregnant with his child to destroy her reputation and complicate her life if he lost the case. That's what the note meant. She would stop it somehow. But first, she must talk to Matthew Stewart and Monsieur Sommes.

Josay laid on the soft clean bed in the doctor's office and felt better. Maybe the pain was being caused, at least in part, by the stress of the trial. It seemed like a fait accompli that Voight and his men would be convicted and never hurt her or anyone else. She felt a great sense of relief and safety with David by her side. The quiet time was not to last, however, because La Plume came into the room and announced that she had brought Matthew Stewart and the Marquis Le Sommes with her.

La Plume whispered to her softly, "Josay, we have all guessed that you are pregnant. These two gentlemen wanted to talk to you about that and maybe you need a few minutes with Matthew and Monsieur Sommes to clear up any misunderstandings that they might have?"

"Yes, I would like to speak to each of them separately."

Josay had been rehearsing what she would say to each of them and she now felt the courage and ability to follow through with her plan.

She asked to speak to Matthew Stewart first, while the others waited in the hallway.

"My dearest Josay. Are you well? Are you pregnant? Am I the father? I want very much to marry you and raise this child you carry. I know we can patch up any differences we may have had in the past and I will dedicate the rest of my life to making you happy."

Josay looked away and out the window to see the clouds parting and the sun beginning to shine in the clearest blue sky she had ever seen. It was like all of her troubles had been swept away and her path was now clear and straight.

Josay lied and told Matthew that it was not his child. She loved Matthew, but not enough to let him into her heart again which was filled with the memory of James Sommes. Besides, she wanted him to go back to America and raise the two children she knew he cherished. She hoped that perhaps he would reconcile with his newly divorced wife. She knew she could never be happy realizing that she had been partly responsible for breaking up a family, even though she did not know that he was married when they were romantic. She did not like lying to him about something so important, but she felt that it was the right thing to do.

She had already confessed to her priest that she had sinned and had sexual relations with two men, Donnel Regis and Matthew Stewart while she was not married, under God. She was sure she had received forgiveness from God for this and she hoped with everything in her being that God would also forgive her for the lie that she just told to Matthew Stewart about his child.

"I'm sorry, but if you care for me, you will leave today and go back to your family. I want you to be happy and I hope we can be friends, but I can never marry you. I will raise this child myself and will never tell anyone about the father. Just know that the baby is not yours and that you will always hold a special place in my heart and life."

Matthew processed what he heard and said, "I will do as you ask. I will have Mr. Hover make all the business arrangements for me to offload my shares of the Paradis Rue business that you had returned to me. I know it will be a big success, but I feel we need a clean break. I do miss my children and I will return to them. It seems that you have made up your mind about this, so I will cause you no further grief."

"These are my sincere wishes," Josay said as a small twitch in womb called her attention to the fact that the child's real father would never be in its life. But she was certain that this was the best way forward for all three of them.

Matthew bent over and kissed Josay for one last time and with sadness, he left the room.

No sooner had he left than Monsieur Sommes the elder was ushered into the small white room.

"My darling girl, Is the baby my grandchild?

"I will tell you, and only you, the true identity of the baby's father for reasons that I will try to make clear right now. The baby's father is Matthew Stewart. I have told him that he is not the father because I want to raise my child myself. I don't want Matthew to abandon his children in America which he most surely would do. When Matthew and I had our affaire, I did not know that he was married with two children or it would never have happened.

After Matthew left to go back to America. I realized that I had made a terrible mistake to abandon James and his affections. He and I got closer over time and were very much in love and planning our life together. Then Matthew came back to Paris to tell me he had divorced his wife and wanted me to marry him. I knew that my baby was his so I had planned to sit both he and James down to tell them about the baby. I was hoping that James could forgive me for being pregnant with another man's baby, but before that could happen, James was taken from us both in that most horrible way. Now my heart and my life has an empty hole that no one else can fill but my dearest James.

I only tell you this because I know that you need to know the truth. I know how much you wanted the baby to be James' and if it were true, I would be the happiest of women. But this child is not his, and I love his memory too much to lie about it, especially to you."

"Dear Josay. Of course I would love it if the baby was my son's. But the fact that it is not does not change the fact that I pledged to James that I would always love you as my own daughter. And I will love your child, even if it is not James'. I intend to leave his inheritance to you upon my passing as he wished. I am so sorry for the irrational and severe initial pain that I suffered which caused me to falsely blame you for his death. I know that he died trying to right a horrible wrong because that is who James was, kind, gentle and compassionate. I intend to fulfill all of his wishes, and by the way, they are my heart's delight as well."

"Let's not think about inheritance right now. We will have time to cross that bridge in the far distant future. For now, I only need your solemn promise that you will never reveal that Matthew is the true father of my child."

"You have my word."

He kissed her forehead, left her bedside and the doctor came back into the room. He called for his nurse.

After about ten minutes the doctor invited David and La Plume back into the room.

"She is stable now. But I fear this will be a difficult pregnancy. I estimate that she is about 21 weeks into her term, and she will need to carry the baby at least 15 or 16 weeks longer to insure a healthy chance for the baby and the mother. She must be confined to bed rest and a stress free environment. Is that possible? I know she is in the midst of a trial, opening a new night club and hosting an art exhibit."

"We will make sure she leaves as soon as possible to return to our dairy farm outside Paris for quiet and rest," replied David.

"I will gladly go after helping my artist friends open their exhibit this afternoon. All I need to do is cut the ribbon at 6pm and I promise I will go home and rest. In fact, I look forward to returning home more than you could know," said Josay.

Everyone left the room and Josay was able to get a three-hour nap.

CHAPTER 32

After her nap, Josay had another visitor. It was the judge who was accompanied by the prosecutor.

"Mademoiselle Rue, I'm sorry to bother you but I thought you might want to hear from my lips that Voight and three of his men have been convicted and sentenced to death by the guillotine. The other seven members of his gang received very long prison sentences. After La Plume's testimony, the prosecutor called one witness after another, after another to testify about horrible crimes committed by Mr. Voight, including rapes, assaults and even several murders. When the defense attorney finished the cross examination of only a few witnesses, he seemed to give up and it took the jury only minutes to convict all accused. I rendered the sentences with due haste and the trial is over. I might only add that I feel great remorse that you had to endure all the hurt and pain that can come to women when they try to demand justice. Maybe the world will change someday, but at least this time, justice was served," said Judge Fruge.

"May I kiss you?" asked Josay.

"It would certainly be my pleasure," said the old man as he bent over and received a soft kiss on his cheek and a warm tearful embrace.

"Bonsoir," he said.

And before they left, the prosecutor also received a grateful kiss and warm hug.

David had helped Josay return to her own bed after the good news from the court officials. Josay looked around the small bedroom in her little white house and really noticed the wallpaper for the first time. It was pastel blue with flowers and breaking light between the petals.

H*ow lovely,* she thought. *Now I must get ready for the opening of the Impressionist Exhibition, I can get dressed and just about make it there on time.*

David sat in the oversized coach waiting for Josay to emerge from her room with Madame La Plume, Mr. and Mrs. Hover, Monsieur Sommes and Madame Foote. When Josay came out of the house, she noticed the flowers in her small garden blooming and laden with the scent of early spring. As she was helped into the coach, she was reminded of her small room at the farm where she could see the fields of blooming flowers and smell the warm hot bread her mother had made.

David said, "Are you ready to finish this most eventful of days?"

"I am," she said.

At the entrance of the Impressionist Exhibition, a nervous group of artists watched the still muddy road that ran up to the salon location. Renoir and Lautrec were especially nervous that Josay wouldn't be able to join them and they really needed her at the ribbon cutting. She was the "face" of the exhibition and almost everyone that was there was only there to see her face. The few art critics and newspaper reporters looked as if they had been brought to this venue under false pretenses and continually yelled questions at the small group of huddled painters and their wives.

There were several posters by Lautrec that featured Josay and a very large Renoir poster over the entrance with Josay and ten to fifteen impressionist artists sitting around a lake house eating, drinking wine and laughing in the summer sun. It was a take-off on one of the paintings that Renoir was exhibiting inside that he called, "A summer party at the boathouse." All of the beautifully colored pastels mingled with the sunlight and shade of a summer's day, inviting the viewer to enter.

Degas was the first to see Josay's carriage slowly moving down the entrance road over muddy water filled puddles and bumps. "I see her coming now!" exclaimed a relieved Degas and everyone looked to catch a view to insure that it was really her. Inside the carriage Josay took several deep and refreshing breaths and noticed that the pain in her abdomen had subsided.

Out the window, Josay saw a hundred or so people. It was a Montmartre mix of the elegantly dressed and the common folk with their sleeves rolled up and with some wearing aprons as if they had taken a short break from work to see what was happening.

Everyone assembled to form a receiving line for the little group in the carriage. Van Gogh dressed in his finest britches and smock, shoved his way to the front to be the first to greet the arriving party. He offered his hand to Josay and bent at the waist in a formal bow that somehow looked awkward and elegant at the same time. Josay's eyes met his and she winked at the usually sorrowful soul, who seemed extremely alert and excited today.

Degas then offered his arm and ushered Josay to the small podium in front of the large Renoir poster at the entrance to the exhibit.

When Josay and all of her party were on the stage, an elegant man who Josay had come to know quite well while working with him on the steering committee, welcomed the small crowd. He introduced himself as Gustave Caillebotte. He was, behind the scenes, the principle benefactor for this salon. He kept many of his fellow artists afloat by buying their paintings. He was also an aristocrat like Degas but with a much bigger heart.

"I am honored to welcome all of you to the first ever Impressionist Exhibition. This exhibit represents the soul of French art, the spirit of brotherhood we all experience in each other, and the creation and expression of emotion, beauty and, yes, truth. Our artistic leader, Auguste Renoir and his nature loving comrade Monet have challenged each of us to our best and truest efforts. Look around you and see that we don't look alike, don't think alike and have never been considered to be in the forefront of an artistic renaissance. But each of us has been denied the ability to show our art because of the bureaucratic rules that govern the Annual Paris Salon. We don't conform to the so-called rules of artistic expression, in subject, style or technique. A few of our artists like Degas and Renoir, and even a few others, have exhibited in the Salon but have opened their minds and hearts to change and growth. We could never have opened this show without many, many people.

But in the interest of common and equal brotherhood, I will only say 'merci' to all. I will let the art be the principle speaker and recipient of all our love and gratitude. Welcome to our exhibit."

Renoir and every artist and patron on the small stage, and off, held hands and after a short prayer of thanks to God, the ribbon was cut by Josay Rue.

Josay felt a swell of pride and admiration for this group of long suffering geniuses and many warm real tears covered her face as she saw true friends gathered around her. Some of these friendships, she knew would last for the rest of her days. Madame La Plume, Madame Foote, and all the others could be seen teary-eyed too. This day was the milestone for so many people and a time to be forever remembered as a day in which lives were truly changed. As Josay turned to enter the exhibit, Renoir stopped her and pulled her aside.

"Josay we simple artists can only and best express ourselves with and through our art. We have little to no money and debts owed to you we cannot pay. Nonetheless, these three paintings we hope will show our true love for you and our hope for an everlasting and true friendship. As she turned she saw two paintings and one poster. The first painting was one of the three original paintings done that fateful day in her home village. It was the Pissarro that showed the innocent simple beauty who was the 17-year-old Josay. (The Renoir from that fateful day had been bought by Matthew Stewart. He had returned it to her through Monsieur Bleux when he left to return home to the USA the first time. The Gauguin that caused the trouble and led to her two year adventure in Paris was returned to her by Madame La Plume. It was now in the possession of the court as evidence, but would be returned soon.) The poster was a Lautrec that advertised the opening of the Paradis Rue and the Impressionist Exhibition, side by side, on the same poster. It showed a bright vibrant Josay adorned with her finest Paris coiffure wearing a beautiful blue gown with clear green eyes, rosy cheeks and strawberry hair that was her anthem. The third painting was anonymous. It showed a young girl in a starched pinafore, praying as the day dawned. The light in the painting caused Josay to blink, and her heart to skip a beat. It was magnificent. It was her unrefined, unbroken heart. She was still an innocent child of God and an Eve before original sin. Josay was so touched, more tears rolled down her cheeks.

David took her by the waist and led her into the exhibit as Dr. Muse collected the paintings and took them to the carriage.

Josay wondered through the maze of paintings exhibited in the fading light of the impending sunset. She saw freshly painted vibrant paintings by Monet, Renoir, Cezanne, Pissarro, Sisley, Degas, Whistler, Cassatt, Morisot, Cezanne, Caillebotte, Van Gogh and many more. It was an hour trip through color, emotion and soul that could not ever be matched in the world of art.

The exhibit hall had been the studio of a photographer who had generously loaned it to the painters for the salon, so there were lots of large windows to let in natural light. Tonight the combination of the beautiful sunset, the candlelight and the gas lamps illuminated the paintings giving them a golden glow. This phenomena added a sense of magic to the overall experience. For Josay, it was like heaven on earth. She felt all of the hurt leave and her youth and optimism return. She felt like she did the morning she went to meet her young lover Donnel. And although she was now an experienced woman who knew the sometimes cruel ways of the world, she still possessed the passion and unsuppressed optimism that there is innate good within everyone.

While the last rays of the sun created a rosy-yellow-orange and purple glow amid now distant storm clouds, Renoir said, "I wish I had my easel and canvas for this is a magical display of our sun and its dominion. I know I will never see this sight again and I will treasure that I have seen it with all of you."

Josay smiled and felt the exhaustion of the day hit her all at once.

"It has been a miracle day for me, but I must rest now. Can you please excuse me? Will you rejoice for me tonight with the opening of what, I have no doubt, will be a world changing event in the yet to be written history of art?"

"Of course," said Degas. "But please, join me for a last toast."

Van Gogh and Pissarro gave each member of the small touring party a glass of champagne. Then Renoir exclaimed, "Let us drink to our patron and little sister, Josay, for her belief in our cause and her undeterred drive to help us achieve the thing we had only dreamed about before. God bless, Josay Rue!"

Josay woke the next morning to find that David had packed all of her clothes and belongings for the trip back to the farm. She was clearheaded and was handed a copy of the newspaper. She saw the accounts of the opening of the Paradis Rue, and the trial of Monsieur Voight and his cronies. She had to search the pages to find the local reviews of the Impressionist Exhibition.

She only glanced at the headlines that set forth the absolute guilt of Voight and his death sentence. Josay was ready to have the thoughts of the evil world of Voight forever banished from her mind. She focused instead on the small review of the salon located deeply buried in the back of the paper. The headlines read, "THE IMPRESSIONS OF A NEW GROUP OF ARTISTS." Inside the article was an explanation that the label "Impressionist" had been given to the collective group of painters for what the author called their "unfinished" paintings. He said they were trying to capture the impressions of light in the natural world without actually finishing their paintings. The article rated the exhibition as amateuristic and without the necessary guidelines of classical formatting. It blasted the predominate subject matter of country people and simple landscapes as "common." Josay was sure that this review would actually please her artist friends because she knew they wanted, above all, to express the world as it is, second by second, with real drama and simple majesty. They felt no need for classic Greek poses or dancing cherubs. Reality exposed far greater splendor and timelessness.

She was elated about the rave reviews for the Paradis Rue. They predicted that the cancan as it was danced at the Paradis Rue would become the signature dance of Paris nightlife. They praised the passion and creativity of the combination of revolutionary art, amazing food, drink and advant-guarde entertainment. They also mentioned the smiles and kindness of the wait staff who seemed to love what they were doing.

Before she could finish the short articles, Renoir and Lautrec entered the room and confirmed her understanding of the great tribute the single column written about their salon had paid them. Everyone in the house laughed and a happy moment was experienced unlike any other. It was like the feeling one gets when they have completed a marathon or after having finished marital vows with the love of one's life. Real joy in accomplishment is not often so succinctly experienced.

David told everyone that they must depart for the farm to allow Josay to follow the doctor's orders for bed rest, quiet and relaxation. Everyone conceded that they wished Josay could stay to go to the Paradis Rue for a true celebration that tonight. But they yielded and agreed that there would be many times in the years to come to share the moment in recollection and in spirit. It was time for Josay to temporarily leave Paris.

As the country carriage and baggage cart rolled up to the front of the little white house in Montmartre, Josay felt the cool morning breeze on her cheeks. The smell was one of roses and the clean air of a just-past rain. Josay waved to the group of friends she had made in past two years and left the city along the same road she had come. Josay knew she would be happy. She had been a success in every aspect of her life and she had done it without compromise. She knew in her heart that the road home would be straight and clear for the rest of her life. For her, it was the true road to paradise.